MURDER IN THE
MILL-RACE

MURDER IN THE MILL-RACE

with an introduction by Martin Edwards

E.C.R. LORAC

Poisoned Pen
PRESS

Published by Poisoned Pen Press, an imprint of Sourcebooks, in association with
the British Library
P.O. Box 4410, Naperville, Illinois 60567-4410
(630) 961-3900
sourcebooks.com

Originally published in 1952 by Collins, London.

Library of Congress Cataloging-in-Publication Data

Names: Lorac, E. C. R., author. | Edwards, Martin, author.
  Title: Murder in the mill-race / E.C.R. Lorac ; with an introduction by
  Martin Edwards.
Description: First U. S. Edition. | Naperville, Illinois : Sourcebooks,
  Inc., 2019. | "Originally published in 1952 by Collins, London"--Title
  page verso.
Identifiers: LCCN 2019022890 | (trade paperback)
Subjects: LCSH: Murder--Investigation--Fiction. | GSAFD: Mystery fiction.
Classification: LCC PR6035.I9 M87 2019 | DDC 823/.914--dc23
LC record available at https://lccn.loc.gov/2019022890

Printed and bound in the United States of America.
SB 10 9 8 7 6 5 4 3 2 1

Introduction

Murder in the Mill-Race (known as *Speak Justly for the Dead* in the U.S.) was first published in 1952. Like many of E.C.R. Lorac's post-war novels, it is notable for a well-evoked setting in rural England—this time on Exmoor in Devon. Dr Raymond Ferens and his wife Anne relocate from a mining town in Staffordshire to Milham in the Moor. The move is prompted by Ferens' poor health, together with a yearning for a different kind of life: he is still affected by two years spent as a Japanese prisoner of war, as well as by pressure of work in a busy urban G.P.'s practice. At Milham, an elderly doctor's impending retirement offers the prospect of a geographically far-flung but sparsely populated practice which should not prove unduly taxing, and will enable the Ferens to "live the dream".

This notion evidently appealed to the author, who had grown up in London, but always had a soft spot for Devon, where she spent many holidays. After the Second World War, she too had escaped to the country, moving to Lunesdale in the north west of England, which became an attractive setting for several of her mysteries. One suspects that Anne Ferens is speaking for her creator when she tells her husband: "I'm not being selfless in saying I want to live in the country. I'm sick to death of cities and soot and slums and factories and occupational diseases." She tells him to "watch the emergence of a countrywoman. I shall be debating fat stock prices before the year's out, and prodding pigs at the market."

So the young married couple set off for their destination, a village on a hill-top lying close to both the moor and the sky. On the surface life there seems idyllic. As an estate manager called John Sanderson tells Anne: "Throughout the centuries, Milham in the Moor has been cut off from towns and society and affairs. Here it has…flourished because it has made itself into an integrated whole, in which everybody was interdependent… 'Never make trouble in the village' is an unspoken law, but it's a binding law. You may know about your neighbours' sins and shortcomings, but you must never name them aloud. It'd make trouble, and small societies want to avoid trouble."

Another local, an old fellow by the name of Brown, also holds forth on the nature of life in such a community: "You try reforming a village and see how popular you are. Villages are all alike, made up of human beings who love and lie, who're unselfish one minute and self-seeking the next, who're faithful one day and fornicators the next. Human nature's a mixed bag." Raymond Ferens takes a similar view, and again one suspects that he is speaking for Lorac: "Whenever you get a group of people living together…you find the mixed characteristics of humanity—envy, hatred, malice and all uncharitableness mingled with neighbourliness and unselfishness and honest-to-God goodness."

Sanderson also talks about a formidable woman called

Sister Monica, who is in charge of a children's home known as Gramarye. She is regarded by some villagers as saintly, yet Sanderson takes a very different view: "she's dangerous, in the same way that a virus or blood poisoning can be dangerous... She is one of those people who can not only lie plausibly and with conviction, but she can tell a lie to your face without batting an eyelid, knowing that you know it's a lie." Most menacingly of all, Sister Monica "knows everything about everybody".

Anne takes an instinctive dislike to Sister Monica, whom she describes as "plain wicked", and soon learns that the old woman is making trouble for her. Seasoned readers of detective fiction will not, therefore, be entirely surprised when Sister Monica meets an untimely end, drowned in the mill-race. It's another case for Chief Inspector Macdonald, who needs to overcome the villagers' hostility towards inquisitive outsiders in order to make sense of the mystery of her murder.

The pen-name E.C.R. Lorac concealed the identity of Carol Rivett, or more precisely Edith Caroline Rivett (1894–1958). She was not regarded as one of the Queens of Crime who flourished during the "Golden Age of murder" between the world wars, but nevertheless she enjoyed a career as a detective novelist over a span of more than a quarter of a century. The pleasantly persistent Macdonald first appeared in *The Murder on the Burrows* (1931) and solved crimes in all the books which came out under the Lorac name until the posthumously published *Death of a Lady Killer* (1959). As Carol Carnac, the author also created a second long-running series cop called Julian Rivers.

Sister Monica is far from the only character in the Lorac books whose saintliness is more apparent than real; it's evident that Carol Rivett had a deep distaste for supposedly spiritual hypocrites. One can only speculate as to whether this was inspired by personal dealings with someone of that type in real life; people in Lunesdale, where she lived in her later years, have recalled that several characters in her books were thinly veiled portrayals of people in the area.

Writing about Lorac on my blog, "Do You Write under Your Own Name?" in September 2009, I referred to her as "a writer forgotten today by the general reading public". Thanks to the British Library's Crime Classics, her work is enjoying a renaissance. This novel is another example of her capable storytelling, and illustrates why the revival of interest in her novels is well deserved.

—Martin Edwards
www.martinedwardsbooks.com

CHAPTER I

1

Milham Prior is a place-name familiar to motorists who take the shortest route from Taunton to Barnsford, on the north Devon coast. It is seldom anything more than a place-name, coupled to a visualisation of a rather tall church tower, and a long hill which you can rush in top gear if you have been able to take advantage of the down slope on the other side of the cross roads. It is a good stretch of main road, wide and well engineered, and by the time holiday-makers reach it from the east, they are aware that the Devon coast is not far away, and that they will soon see—and smell—the wide river estuary at Barnsford, where shining sands indicate the delights in store a few miles farther on.

Milham Prior has but little to attract the holiday-making hordes, neither—to do it justice—does it want to attract them. The Milham folk are not at all sorry that their High Street is at right angles to the new main road and not part of it. Milham is a prosperous, self-respecting market town, which caters for the country folk who live in the huge scattered moorland parishes of Milham Prior and Milham in the Moor. Conscious of a long history—it is one of the oldest Parliamentary constituencies—of a reputation for sound and shrewd dealing, Milham Prior is satisfied with its plain stone High Street, its old-fashioned Georgian Inn, and its ancient church (whose interior restoration is only regretted by busybodies from away).

Anne Ferens, sitting in the dining-room of the George Hotel in Milham, looked around her with amused and interested eyes, though most people would have found the room neither amusing nor interesting. It was rather dark, its long windows discreetly curtained and screened: its furniture was heavy mahogany of mid-Victorian date, and its tables had a full complement of enormous cruets. Anne smiled at her husband. "I like it," she said. "It's restful. Completely conforming to type without the least element of the incongruous."

"That's because you can't see yourself sitting in it, angel. You look a complete anachronism. The meal, as you say, conformed to type, including the cabbage. The beer's good—also true to type." Raymond Ferens studied his wife with eyes that were at once affectionate and worried. "Milham in the Moor… It's a sin and a shame to take you there, Anne. When I think of all those antiques and funnies, not a soul of your own age to amuse you, miles of moorland and Milham Prior for your shopping town. Seeing you now, against this musty background, I'm appalled to think what sort of life I'm taking you to."

Anne laughed. "How little you really know about me, Ray. We've been married for four years, and you still don't realise that I'm the most adaptable creature on earth. Chameleons also ran. You'd better leave off thinking of me as a sophisticated

wench who is snappy at cocktail parties, and watch the emergence of a countrywoman. I shall be debating fat stock prices
before the year's out, and prodding pigs at the market."

"I've no doubt you will," he said. "You can pick up anybody's jargon in two-twos—I should know—but how can you
be happy away from all the things you value?—intelligent and
amusing friends, and the sort of life you have made your own."

"My good idiot, must I inform you again that I've put all my
money on one value?" she retorted. "I can be happy anywhere
provided I've got you. If you'd packed up on me the rest would
have been Dead Sea fruit. And do get it into your thick head
that I'm not being selfless in saying I want to live in the country.
I'm sick to death of cities and soot and slums and factories and
occupational diseases. Sick of them." She drummed on the table
with clenched fists. "Come off it, do," she pleaded. "I took you at
your word when I married you. Take me at mine, now. Give me
another glass of sherry and let's drink our own healths—good
health and long lives—and no more arguments."

2

Raymond Ferens was a doctor. Born in 1915, he had qualified
in 1939, joined the R.A.M.C., been posted out in the Far East,
been taken prisoner by the Japanese and survived the experience. After a few months' rest, he had taken a partnership
in a practice in the industrial midlands and had worked in a
Staffordshire mining town. It had been a strenuous practice
involving interminable surgeries, a lot of night work and a
minimum of free time. In such leisure as he could wrest from
the exigencies of occupational diseases, Ferens had tried to
continue the specialist work which had fascinated him when
he first qualified—the study of asthma and kindred nervous

disorders. He went up to London, when he could make the opportunity, to consult with the physicians at his old medical school, and on one of these visits he had met Anne Clements. They had fallen in love and got married without any dilly-dallying. They had been very happy, but excessive work had undermined Ferens' constitution, already weakened by two years of a Japanese prison camp. He had been ill, on and off, for a year, before Anne persuaded him to take the advice of his colleagues. "Get right out of this and take a country practice," they said. "You'll then have a useful life of normal duration. Go on as you're going now and you'll have had it in a twelve-month."

Both Anne and Raymond had favoured the west country, and when they heard of the approaching retirement of an elderly doctor at Milham in the Moor, Anne fairly bullied her husband into investigating possibilities there. The practice covered an enormous sparsely populated area on Exmoor: apart from the driving involved, it was not a heavy job, and the moor fascinated Raymond Ferens. The fact that a good house was offered him was an additional inducement. Anne paid a whirlwind visit to view the house, and after that for-malities were concluded with record promptitude, so that by Lady Day, Anne and Raymond had seen their furniture into the pantechnicon, packed themselves into their own car, and had set out to Milham Prior, to spend a night at the George there, since their goods would not be delivered until the following morning.

3

When Raymond Ferens had started enquiries about taking over the practice at Milham in the Moor, one of his first questions had been about a house to live in. Old Dr. Brown, who had been in practice there for over thirty years, did not want to give up his own house, but informed Ferens that the Dower House belonging to the lord of the manor would be available. Ferens decided to go and have a look at it, and he had driven to Milham by himself, telling Anne that he wasn't going to let her in on it until he had decided if he wanted to take the job on: she could then have her say, a final yes or no, taking house, locality and amenities into consideration and weighing the pros and cons for herself.

Ferens drove to Milham one bitter day in January, when the industrial towns of the Midlands were wretched with sleet drifting down from a drear grey sky and smoke mingling with the sleet in a grimy pall. He drove by Gloucester and Bristol, and once clear of Bristol the snow and sleet had disappeared, the country looked rich and green and Raymond Ferens found his spirits rising. Milham Prior was clear of snow, but a keen wind was blowing: beyond Milham Prior the road rose steadily to the moor, and though the sky was clear the country became whiter and whiter with crisp dry snow. When he had his first glimpse of Milham in the Moor, Ferens thought, "Why, it's like a French hill town." The village was built well and truly, on the top of a hill. Its tall church tower stood out in silhouette against the clear saffron of the western sky, and snow-covered cottage roofs were piled up against the church as though they, too, were aspiring heavenwards. It was a lovely sight, but Ferens found himself thinking "Ten miles from anywhere and nothing but the moor beyond, all the way to the sea."

He had stayed the night with Dr. Brown and been thankful that there was no question of taking over the old man's house. It was a dark, cold, dreary house, shut in with overgrown shrubberies and tall conifers, auraucarias, Irish yews and cedars pressing almost up to the windows. Brown seemed a very old man to Ferens, and rather a snuffly, grubby old man, but he was clear-headed and businesslike enough. He produced large-scale maps and gave details of the scattered steadings and hamlets and their inhabitants, and eventually spoke of the Dower House. It belonged to Sir James Ridding, who lived at the Manor House. "They've been trying to let the Dower House for some time," said Dr. Brown, "but what with folks not wanting to come to anywhere as remote as this, and the Riddings being fussy about who they let it to, well, it's still on their hands. I think you'll be able to make them see reason. The fact is, Sir James and his lady don't want to be without a doctor in the village. Anyway, you'll see. It's a good house—a beautiful and historic house."

Raymond had been surprised when he saw the Dower House. Dr. Brown took him there next morning, and in the bright pale sunshine the stone house looked enchanting. It was obviously late Tudor and early Jacobean in period, with lovely mullioned windows, a fine stone flagged roof and handsome chimney stacks. It stood within the walls which surrounded the Manor House and demesne, but was shut off by clipped yew hedges, and had pleasant open lawns around it. After one glance at it, Raymond promptly asked, "What's the snag? Don't tell me they can't let a house like that unless it's pretty grim in some particular."

"There's nothing the matter with the house. It's dry and weather-worthy, modernised as to plumbing, got a good water supply and electricity from the Mill plant," said Dr. Brown. "The trouble's been that Lady Ridding has wanted to let it furnished, and people won't take it on."

"Furnished? That's no good to me," said Ferens promptly. "That means a fancy price and no security of tenure."

"I know, I know," said old Brown testily, "but you talk to her ladyship. She's not such a fool as she looks, and Sir James is tired of paying rates on a house no one wants to live in."

They met Lady Ridding walking her dogs in the drive of the Manor. Raymond enjoyed telling his wife about it when he got home. "They're a blooming anachronism, keeping up traditional style on inherited capital, I suppose," he said. "Lady R. is about sixty-five, stout and having the sort of presence which went out with Edward and Alexandra. She was a beauty once, that's obvious: in fact she's still beautiful; silver hair, blue eyes and a complexion which owes nothing to a box, and she has a manner which compels admiration: as a technique it's perfect."

With grace and dignity, Lady Ridding welcomed Dr. Ferens charmingly. "My husband has heard of you from his London consultant," she smiled, "and we do hope you will decide to come here. Dr. Brown has worked so hard, and I do sympathise with him wanting to get out of harness. Now you'd like to see the Dower House. I'm sure your wife will approve of it, it really is a lovely house in its own way."

Dr. Brown excused himself and Raymond Ferens was left alone with what he called 'the old-time lovely'. He glanced round as they stood in the wide sweep of drive before the Manor House and said: "It's a notable group of buildings, all on a plateau as it were."

"Yes, it looks very beautiful from the moor," said Lady Ridding. "The Manor, Dower House, and Church are all within our walls and Gramarye seems to lean against us, does it not—you can see the roofs just beyond the Church. They're all the same period, built between 1590 and 1650."

"Gramarye?" echoed Ferens. "Oh, yes, that's the children's home, isn't it? Brown was telling me about it. An unusual feature in a remote village."

"Gramarye is unique," said Lady Ridding. "It is a very ancient foundation, and generations of Riddings have been proud to be its benefactors. We love having the children there, and Sister Monica, who is the Warden, is a genius with children. But you want to see the Dower House. I'm so glad it's such a beautiful sunny morning, you will see how much sun the house gets."

Raymond Ferens followed the lady of the manor through the Dower House, his keen modern mind disregarding everything but essentials. How much of this building would be acceptable, practical, and enjoyable for Anne and himself to live in and work in? Lady Ridding's practised showmanship, her knowledge of panelling and masonry, her expertise on furniture, carpets and china, was a matter of indifference to him, though he replied with adequate courtesy and intelligence when she paused in her commentary. Ferens was counting rooms, judging space, making adaptations in his own mind, all the time he was listening to the lady's informed prattle. Eventually he said:

"Thank you very much indeed for taking so much trouble, Lady Ridding. I think I have grasped the essentials. I'd like a few hours to consider it, and then I will write to you, and you can consider my offer at your leisure. Before I make a decision my wife will have to see the house, of course. She will have the job of running it."

"Of course," said Lady Ridding, with her sweetest smile. "I'm sure she'll like it, and do tell her that she can get domestic help in the village and that we can supply so many things from the gardens and home farm. Indeed, we're nearly self-supporting here."

When Raymond Ferens rejoined Dr. Brown in the latter's dank dark dining-room, Ferens said: "Am I right in supposing that beneath the cloak of graciousness, Lady Ridding has an eye to the main chance, as it were?"

Dr. Brown gave a derisive snort. "She is a very shrewd woman and an exceedingly capable one," he replied. "It's true that both she and her husband are wealthy, apart from the estate, but it's Lady Ridding's ability which makes the home farm a paying proposition, and the gardens and greenhouses yield a good return. I believe they've developed a good market, supplying greenhouse produce to the luxury hotels on the north coast, and it's Lady Ridding who supplied the business head."

"Well, if she thinks that I and my wife are going to pay a high rent for the privilege of being glorified caretakers in charge of her *objets d'art* in the Dower House, she's very much mistaken," said Ferens. "She wants it both ways and so far as I'm concerned she can't have it."

"Tell her so," replied Brown. "She won't respect you any the less when she realises you've got a head for business, and I tell you straight she doesn't want to have to rely on the Milham Prior doctors when she and her family are laid up. They've got plenty to do in the Milham Prior practice, and Lady R. was once told she could come to their surgery when she wanted advice on minor ailments." The old man chuckled. "She didn't like that one," he said.

4

Raymond enjoyed telling his wife about his investigation into the moorland practice. "The village is only a small part of the job," he said. "The outlying farm houses are scattered all over the moor. There are a few hamlets, clusters of cottages around some farm houses, and there's one mining village where tin mining goes on on a small scale, out on the moor. It's incredibly primitive so far as housing goes, but they look a fine healthy lot of toughs. In addition, there are a few minor gentry around, mostly elderly folks. I think it'll be quite an experience. The moor provides a few deficiency diseases— enough to make it interesting."

"And the Dower House?" asked Anne.

Raymond laughed. "It's a lovely house, Anne, but much too big for us. However, I think I've arrived at a formula, if you really want to go there. The house is furnished, just as the last Dowager left it, and Lady Ridding wants to keep everything in it, ready for herself if Sir James pops off. Her idea was that you and I could provide heating, cleaning and skilled caretaking, and pay a good rent while we're doing it. Moreover, there are no safeguards for ensuring continuous tenancy in a furnished house. She could have turned us out more or less at will. No sort of proposition."

Anne nodded. "I agree. So what?"

"Well, after a careful inspection, I realised the ground floor was quite large enough for you and me. There's a butler's pantry and servery off the dining-room which will make a very natty kitchen for you; a morning-room which will make a good study for me, a drawing-room, and two other rooms for bedrooms, and a slip room for a bathroom. I proposed to Lady R. that I would pay her £150 a year for the house, though I only proposed to occupy the ground floor, and convert out-buildings for a surgery. I would let her the upper floor and the old kitchens at a peppercorn rent for her to store her antiques in, she to have access by the back doors and service stairway to reach her property. There's a central heating plant in the cellars which her minions can stoke, and we pay pro rata for the fuel."

"Well, you've got a nerve. She'll never agree to that," said Anne.

"She has agreed, in principle," replied Raymond. "She's enough sense to see that it's a reasonable proposition. She gets the rent, is relieved of the rates, and has the larger part of the house for her belongings. The adaptations are comparatively inexpensive and the moving of her furniture not a large job. So there you are. Go and have a look at it and see if you like it."

"Well, you do surprise me," said Anne. "She must have been profoundly impressed by you to agree to such a radical alteration in her ideas of what's fitting."

"I'm rather amused with her," said Raymond. "On the surface she's all graces, graciousness and *noblesse oblige.* I suspect that she is derived from robber barons of the industrial revolution and a latent sense of profit-making is emerging in these hard times. Incidentally, you'll have to keep your eyes open when dealing with her. She expects to supply us with milk, eggs, and birds from the home farm, and there were murmurs about cream, and butter if we're pressed. Fruit and vegetables come from the Manor gardens, now being run as a market garden. Doubtless game, salmon, and trout are marketed also."

"Cr…ripes," said Anne. "Does she think we're plutocrats?"

"I gave her no grounds for such an opinion. My own bet is that she knows to a penny what the practice is worth, and she's hoping for a rake-off. The whole show's a comic turn, Anne: the feudal system wedded to modern business methods."

"Who else is there in the village?"

"A few dozen inhabitants, the men mostly employed on the land and the estate—there's a lot of valuable woodland: there's a stream with a big fall which provides electricity and there's a saw mill. There's a decent Inn, run by an ex-butler, a smithy, one or two village shops and of course the vicar and his wife. In addition a few odd birds of the gentry class, mostly elderly, and the Warden of Gramarye, the children's home. Sister Monica: she's wonderful, everyone says so."

"What's the matter with her?" asked Anne promptly.

"Well, I've only just seen her, and the home's not my department. Old Brown is keeping it on to give him a spot of interest in life. As for Sister Monica, she has the rapt with-drawn look of the religious fanatic, and I never fancied that breed. However, she and her set-up won't be my pigeon any-way." He broke off, and Anne put in:

"It all sounds a bit odd, not the typical village at all."

Raymond laughed. "How right you are, my wench. It's damned odd—that's why it's interesting. You see, the village hugs its remoteness. It's out there on the hill-top with its back to the moor, cut off from the commonplaces of cinemas and chain stores and railways and tourists. There's ten miles of road between Milham in the Moor and the world as we know it, and it cherishes its own ways, its own feuds and loyalties and way of life. And somehow it's damned interesting. But it's up to you to say yes or no. I'll drive you there next week-end, and you can make the decision."

"I think I've made it already," she replied. "We said we should like something out of the way. Milham in the Moor appears to be it."

"Think carefully, angel. It's a long way out of the way."

"With its back to the moor and the sea beyond that," said Anne. "This is where we learn to cultivate our individual gardens and turn our backs on mass production."

CHAPTER II

1

One look at the Dower House had been enough for Anne. She knew a beautiful house when she saw one, and her heart rejoiced at the big sunny rooms, nobly proportioned and enriched with panelling and carven stone. She agreed with Raymond that the ground floor would suit them admirably and be easy to run: that the enormous old kitchens and the service stairs could be shut off and left to the owners as storage space, and that the garden was of manageable size. Anne had only had a few hours to inspect, measure and memorise her new home. Lady Ridding had shown both tact and common-sense in spending only a few minutes with her tenant-to-be, and had then sent in the bailiff to discuss the necessary adaptations, and he had proved to be reasonable and helpful. That had been in January. Now, on Lady Day, Raymond drove his wife from Milham Prior so that she could be at the Dower House when their goods arrived. It was a lovely morning: March winds scudded white clouds across the blue sky, and tossed the daffodils in poetic fashion: the sun shone on golden willow palm and budding greenery; away and beyond, the moorland made a tranquil background, fold upon fold of grey and brown and mauve like a far-off rampart against the sky.

Raymond had lost his qualm of the previous day: the sight of Anne's face when he opened the front door of the Dower House was enough. Bare and clean, barred with sunshine and shadow from the mullioned windows, the rooms looked serene and welcoming and lovely. Anne went from white-panelled drawing-room to dark-panelled study, from honey-coloured bedroom to leaf brown of dining-room: inspected the Aga and the new stainless steel sink which had been installed in the old servery, the cupboard space in the one time butler's pantry, and she whooped with joy over tiling and porcelain in the new bathroom.

"Ray, it's marvellous! Everything's been done quite perfectly. I'll never scoff at the aristocracy again. The noblesse have jolly well obliged this time."

"It looks pretty good to me," he said. "Nothing makeshift or shoddy about."

"I'm going to love this house so much, I shall never want to go away anywhere," said Anne. "It'll be a full-time job and a dream of delight simultaneously. Ray, come and sit on the window seat in the sunshine and tell me a bit more about people in the village. It'll help such a lot if I can get them placed and learn their names before I meet them. I'm awful at names."

"Right: let's start with the hierarchy. Sir James and Lady R. You won't forget them. I suppose the parson and his lady come next in the book of precedence: the Rev. Eversley and Mrs. Kingsley: he is thin and she is fat and I swear she bullies him. They're both elderly, conservative to their marrow bones, and my guess is they'll take a very poor view of anything in the way of progress or reform. Mrs. K. will certainly leave cards on you, so put out the salver. Other card leavers will be Col. and Mrs. Staveley of Monk's Milham—two more old dodderers—and Miss Braithwaite of Coombedene. You may like her: old Brown says she talks like a Bolshie, which means she isn't hidebound. So much for local gentry."

"Give me a line on the village."

"I don't know too much about it myself, angel. The most important bodies I've heard of are Mrs. Yeo, who runs the Post Office, the village shop, W.I., M.U., and all the other worthy efforts. You'd better make friends with her, she's a power in the village. The innkeeper is Simon Barracombe. He was once a butler and he looks it: too much hand washing and kowtowing for an innkeeper, but his wife takes in visitors, which may be useful if we want to ask folks to see us. You saw the bailiff—Sanderson. He struck me as a sound chap. If you want information, he'd probably be the best person to ask. Villages all have their private politics, and there's generally some scandal or schism or what have you, and it's often useful if you're given a word off the record by someone who isn't involved."

"Yes, I think you're right there," said Anne. "I shall have to watch my step: newcomers are suspect in villages. Is that someone at the front door, Ray?"

"I didn't hear anybody."

Anne jumped up and ran across the room. The drawing-room, where they sat, faced south, as did the front door which stood wide open to the sunshine. Glancing through the open door of the drawing-room, Anne had been aware of a shadow in the wide entrance hall beyond. When she reached the hall she had to choke back an exclamation of astonishment. In the doorway, silhouetted against the sunlight, stood a figure so tall and dark and unexpected that Anne had a sudden qualm of discomfort, a sense that she was facing something unreal and utterly unlike anything she had ever known.

2

"Miss Torrington, is it not? May I introduce my wife?"

Raymond's easy voice behind her brought Anne back to the realities of a sunny day in a new and lovely home, and she realised who this tall woman must be—the wonderful Sister Monica of Gramarye. She was certainly a very tall woman, but her garb accentuated her height: she was dressed in the long dark cloak and veil which hospital nurses had worn as uniform in the early nineteen hundreds: the dark silk veil was drawn smoothly over silver hair, parted in the centre, and below the wings of intensely white hair her eyes were unexpectedly black. Into Anne's mind flashed the thought: "She's simply fantastic…unbelievable…" even as she pulled herself together and held out her hand.

"I do apologise for troubling you," said the visitor. "I thought the house was still empty and you would not be arriving until later in the day. I just brought a little bunch of flowers to welcome you. The children picked them for you, and they are from all of us at Gramarye. Rosemary, give the flowers to Mrs. Ferens, dear."

From behind the dark cloak emerged a very small fair child. Without a word or a smile she held up a posy of flowers to Anne, and the latter gave a cry of pleasure.

"Oh, but they're lovely! What a kind thought—and I adore wild daffodils. Look, Raymond, aren't they just adorable?"

The posy was indeed a thing of delight, tiny wild daffodils, dog violets, primroses and wind-flowers put together with much skill and surrounded with a delightful paper frill. "It's the prettiest bouquet I've ever had, Rosemary. Thank you *very* much, Miss Torrington. Nothing could have given me more pleasure."

"I'm so happy that you like them. I'm always called Sister Monica, if you don't mind, Mrs. Ferens. Now I'm not going to stay. I just wanted to wish you happiness in your new home. Say good-bye, Rosemary. Perhaps Mrs. Ferens will come and see us all some day later on."

"I should love to," said Anne, and bent to kiss the small pale child, but Rosemary drew back, her eyes startled, and hid behind the long dark skirts of the nurse.

"Forgive her, she's very shy," said Sister Monica. "She'll soon get over it. I'm so glad you've got such a lovely day for your first day in Milham. Good-bye."

She had a deep soft voice, and she smiled benignly at Anne—but the smile was only on her lips, not in her eyes. Anne waved to her as she went, repeating words of thanks, and then followed Raymond back into the drawing-room, closing the door after her this time.

"Cripes!" she exclaimed. "What a woman! She gives me the horrors. Why on earth didn't you warn me what she was like?"

"I thought I did, angel. I told you I didn't like her. The pseudo-religious female always gets my hackles up."

"I can't bear the look of her. That dreadful old-fashioned uniform is just an affectation, and it's enough to give any small child the jitters," said Anne. "I'm certain she's bogus, Ray."

"Look here, Anne, don't be too censorious about the female. I admit she's a shattering apparition, but you've got to remember she's been running Gramarye for thirty years, to the admiration and satisfaction of all concerned. Not only that, she's worked for the church, she's been emergency nurse and midwife in the village, and during the war she did all the Red Cross collections and other cadgings. Flag days and the lord knows what else. I admit I'm thankful I haven't got to have any professional dealings with her—old Brown's still M.O. at Gramarye—but I think we've both got to watch our step with Sister Monica, and be very careful not to criticise her to anyone else."

"Oh, I see that: I'm not a fool, Ray: but I've never seen anybody I disliked so much at first glance. I saw her shadow right across the doorway."

"You can't blame a woman of that size for casting a shadow, angel, and it was very amiable of her to bring the flowers. They're very pretty flowers."

"They're lovely, but Ray, don't you realise she was listening to us talking? She must have heard our voices, and she didn't ring the bell or knock or call to us."

"Yes. Quite characteristic, I expect. She's a dominating type behind that smarmy manner, and she's been sovereign in her small domain for a very long time. I can well believe she's a snooper who kids herself it's her duty to snoop. Well, that's enough about that. We're agreed we don't like her, but bear in mind that she's the cat's whiskers here. Listen, Anne. That's the van. This is where we get busy."

3

Anne Ferens was much too busy for the remainder of that morning to think any more about Sister Monica. Being a methodical woman and a bit of a genius at home-making, Anne had thought out the position of all her belongings beforehand, and she was kept busy running round after the vanmen, seeing that everything was placed where she wanted it placed. At intervals she paused to sing songs of praise to herself because she and Raymond had furnished with old pieces and not modern ones. It had been a toss-up when they started as to whether to invest in modern 'functional' style, or to collect old furniture, and Anne's decision had been made partly because she had inherited a few beautiful old pieces from her parents, partly because she found modern furniture boring and lacking in character. When everything was in place, Anne had to admit that the big rooms looked a bit empty, but it was a very pleasant emptiness. The floors were all of beautiful wood, and if carpets and rugs were rather like islands on the parquet or oak boards, it didn't seem to matter, and spaciousness was dear to Anne's heart.

At lunch time, Raymond took her out to have a meal at the Milham Arms, and they fed in style on very excellent salmon caught in Sir James's waters. They were waited on most ceremoniously by the ex-butler, Simon Barracombe, who was almost pontifical in his slow solemnity, and the meal was rounded off by that rarest of pleasures in an English inn, first-class coffee. After the meal, Anne went and stood outside the inn while Raymond paid the bill, and she studied the village street with delight. She stood on a plateau; there was a little open square in front of her backed by the lovely stonework of Church, Manor and Dower House. To right and left the street ran steeply down hill between cottages which were mostly thatched and colour washed, built straight on to the street, but each cottage had a strip of flower bed below its front windows, where aubrietia and arabis and saxifrage made vivid carpets and cushions of mauve and white and yellow and pink around the daffodils and narcissi. To Anne, who had been inured for four years to the drab sootiness of an industrial town, the vivid colouring of flower beds, cottages and thatches was as exciting as music or poetry, and she stared with delight, her eyes gay with happiness, so that the villagers who passed smiled back at her.

When her husband joined her, they stood for a while, while Raymond pointed out the places he knew: "Post Office to your right, the pink cottage: smithy farther down the hill, also on your right: Sanderson's house is the white one, and the Mill is at the bottom of the hill, near the bridge. The vicarage is behind the church and Gramarye just below that. There's also a garage and another small shop and the village Institute. That's about the lot, except the Infant school. The older children are taken to Milham Prior, much to the fury of their parents."

As they strolled back across the little square, Anne said: "That was a very good lunch, Ray. Did it cost the earth?"

Raymond screwed up his face. "Well, for a village inn, it was a bit steep, but, as you said, it was a very good lunch, and a very good sherry and the best coffee I've had in years, apart from yours."

"He's a wicked old man, that Simon the Cellarer. I felt it in my bones," said Anne. "Thank you very much for my good lunch, but we won't do that again."

Raymond Ferens laughed as they strolled in through the wrought iron gates of the Dower House. "I've always thought of you as a kindly, charitable sort of woman, Anne, very tolerant of the backslidings of poor humanity. You've only met four people in this village: our noble landlord, whom you confidently expect to overcharge us for all produce supplied: poor old Brown, whom you described as a bad old man at the first glance: Simon Barracombe, whom you say is wicked, and Sister Monica, who according to you is bogus."

"Oh, she's plain wicked. I know she is," said Anne. "And it looks such a virtuous village, Ray: could anything be more innocent looking?" She paused and looked back at the sunny coloured cottages, and her husband laughed.

"Human nature's never innocent, angel. Whenever you get a group of people living together, whether in town or village, you find the mixed characteristics of humanity— envy, hatred, malice, and all uncharitableness mingled with neighbourliness and unselfishness and honest-to-God good- ness. This place is beautiful: Stourton was hideous, but if a social statistician could get busy in both, he'd find the same percentages of human virtues and human failings. But I like humanity, and even its sins are sometimes endearing."

"Yes. You're perfectly right," said Anne soberly, but he laughed.

"No one is ever perfectly right, my wench, neither you, nor I, nor anybody else. And remember this: the country *looks* innocent and towns often look the reverse, but human nature is the same whether in town or country—it's a mixture of good and bad. The only people who really get my goat are the ones who kid themselves they're a hundred per cent good. Now do you want me to do any heaving or shoving or manhandling this afternoon, or can I go and get the bits and pieces fixed in my surgery?"

"You go along to your surgery, Ray, or go and talk shop with that snuffy old mass of iniquity in his surgery. I know you're panting to get started on a nice pneumonia or obstructed twins. All manhandling's done: I'm going to make beds and get rid of the mess. Tea at five and don't be late. And I won't criticise anybody else or say anybody's wicked."

"Leave the aspersions to the village," he laughed. "They've had a good look at you, and they'll all have a few words to say on the subject of Jezebel, bless them."

4

It was just as Anne had produced broom and dustpan that the old-fashioned bell jangled at the front door, and Anne found a strangely assorted group awaiting her: Lady Ridding stood in the porch, a picture of gracious benevolence and dignity: behind her was a buxom village woman, and in the drive an aged man standing by a wheelbarrow, with a tow-haired boy beside him.

"Welcome to the Dower House, Mrs. Ferens, and may you and your husband be very happy here," smiled the great lady. "Now I haven't come to interrupt you: I know how busy you must be, but I've brought Mrs. Beer to introduce her, and if you would like someone to help, she will stay now. She's a great standby with polishing these old wooden floors. Thomas has brought you some flowers from the greenhouses as our moving-in gift. The arum lilies look so beautiful in this house, and he'll collect the pots again when the flowers are over. And young Dick will bring your milk and cream and take any orders for vegetables. Now I won't stay. I know you're busy—and do send for Sanderson at once if you want anything done in the house."

Anne tumbled out a breathless "Thank you...thank you *very* much, Lady Ridding," as she looked at the noble pots of arums and primulas, and the older lady smiled back:

"Not at all. It's a great pleasure—and how nice to have someone so young and pretty for a neighbour! I'm delighted to have you here, my dear."

She sailed away like a galleon in full rig, her ample coat billowing out in the wind, and Mrs. Beer greeted Anne serenely.

"Good-afternoon, ma'am. Her ladyship's like that, rather sudden but so good-hearted. Now if you're not wanting me, I'll just go straight home, but I've got some time free if so be you'd like me to sweep and polish."

"I should like it very much, Mrs. Beer, so do come in," said Anne, and the buxom body turned to old Thomas.

"Now do you ask Mrs. Ferens if she'd like them pots stood in the porch meanwhiles and how much milk she wants this evening, and don't you step inside in them mucky boots, young Dick."

Mrs. Beer turned out to be the sort of body whom overworked housewives pray for but seldom attain. She set to work clearing up the debris the vanmen had left and was polishing the floors in two-twos, while Anne got the beds made and tidied up the bedroom, realising how much easier it was to work in big rooms rather than in small ones. It was nearly four o'clock when she went into a drawing-room already shining and tidy with the pots of arum lilies standing on the wide window sills. Mrs. Beer was just putting the posy from Gramarye on the mantel shelf, and she said to Anne: "I see you've had Sister Monica here, ma'am. I'd know her little bunches of flowers anywhere; she's clever the way she arranges them."

"I think they're beautiful," said Anne. "I expect you've known Sister Monica a long time, Mrs. Beer."

"Indeed I have, ma'am. I mind her when she first came, thirty years ago that be, and her cap and veil just the same as she wears to-day, never altered one bit she hasn't except her white hair. Maybe she do look odd and old-fashioned to people from away, but we're so used to her we never notice. I had my niece to stay with me at Christmas, she's a Plymouth girl, and she was proper startled when she saw Sister. But there, she's a wonderful woman. Old Dr. Brown, he do think the world of her, and so do Vicar and Lady Ridding." Mrs. Beer looked around the room and then said: "And now, ma'am, if you'd like me to light Aga, I'm used to they. Two they've got at the Manor, and I know them's little ways."

"Then you know more than I do," laughed Anne. "I've got everything to learn about them."

"They're easy if so be you treat them proper," said Mrs. Beer. "Wonders, I call them."

"Like Sister Monica," said Anne.

Mrs. Beer stared at her a moment and then said: "I'd rather have Aga—but there, Sister's worked here a powerful long time and she has her little ways too, maybe."

Anne's final visitor that day was John Sanderson, the estate manager. He was a tall, quiet fellow of about forty and both the Ferenses liked him and judged him to be trustworthy and kindly.

"I just came in to see if there was anything you wanted done, Mrs. Ferens. There are often odd jobs to be attended to in these old houses and we've got a couple of old chaps who're very handy at small repairs."

"That's very kind of you," said Anne. "In fact everybody has been so good I can't be grateful enough. Everything you have done is quite beautiful and I'm simply delighted with it all. The only thing I've noticed is that one of the drawing-room windows won't open. I think it's stuck."

"We'll soon see to that. I meant to have sent in a man to look at them. The woodwork's very old and they do tend to shrink and swell." He went across the drawing-room to examine the window and Anne saw him glance at the posy on the mantelpiece.

"Sister Monica brought me those flowers," said Anne, and he nodded.

"So I see. Her speciality."

"She looks a character," said Anne innocently.

"Yes. I think she is a character," he replied. "You can't live in this village without knowing that." He paused, and then added: "Sister Monica either likes you or doesn't, and I'm one of the people she doesn't like. I'll send in a man to put these windows to rights, Mrs. Ferens. Sure there's nothing else?"

"Nothing, thank you very much," said Anne, "not in the house, anyway."

He turned and looked at her, his eyes intelligent and amused. "If you want to know anything more about Sister Monica—"

"—you can only say she's a wonder," laughed Anne.

"You never said a truer word," he replied. "Good-bye, and I hope you'll find everything works. If not, just let me know."

5

Raymond came in at five o'clock to find tea ready and his wife in a pretty frock, sitting like a lady in the big drawing-room. "Well, angel, I hand it to you for energy. You've got straight in just about record time."

"It was easy," said Anne. "Everyone's been falling over themselves to be kind and helpful. Lady Ridding brought a treasure of a woman to help clean up, to say nothing of the flowers: don't those arums give us an air of chaste superiority? This is a wonderful village."

He cocked an eyebrow at the word, his lean, pale face

crinkled in a grin. "D'you know, I think we'll delete that word from our vocabulary, Anne."

"As we deleted the word culture after its redefinition by an eminent poet," murmured Anne. "For the same reason, Ray?— because it implies too much and is understood too little?"

"Let us not be controversial," he said, sitting down luxuriously in a chair which offered comfort and yet avoided engulfing him. "If we are not careful, the word 'wonderful' will become a gag."

"How right you are," she laughed. "Have you been collecting evidence about the person the word is applied to locally? I don't believe I'm far wrong, Ray. She's a menace, only nobody dares say so out loud."

"According to my informant, being old Brown, she's the noblest creature the Almighty ever made," said Raymond. "Judging by more indirect evidence, she's the focus point of most of the village bickerings. The fact is they've all been here too long, Anne—doctor and parson, landlord and warden, postman and postmistress. Venner, down at the mill, hit the nail on the head. 'Time we had some fresh blood,' he said. You must go and see the mill, Anne. It's amazing the power they get from that fall."

"All in good time, sir. To begin with I'm going to have my work cut out. A. Not to be managed by our noble landlady: she'll be ordering my dinner if I don't look out. B. Not to be hypnotised by Sister Monica. She's mistress of the evil eye. C. Not to be bullied by old Thomas, the gardener. He wants to have control over our garden. Now come and see the Aga. It's functioning. So is the central heating. It's really rather… impressive," she ended, after a rhetorical pause.

"I am duly impressed," replied Ray. "It's a grand day's work you've done, angel. How do you feel about it all?"

"It's lovely," said Anne, "but we shall have to work hard to avoid using that newly banned word. How were the pneu-monias?"

"They weren't. But Sir James has rather a nice asthma. That's the real reason why we're here."

"How useful of him," said Anne.

CHAPTER III

1

Anne Ferens was a friendly soul, and she was soon on good terms with her neighbours, both villagers and 'quality'; she found the former much more attractive than the latter. "The quality are always grumbling while the village folk are always cheerful," she said to her husband, and Raymond replied:

"Perfectly reasonable. The villagers are better off than they've ever been before and the gentry are worse off. Some of them, like our Lady Ridding, are adaptable enough to develop a business sense, but most of them, like the poor old Staveleys, just sit and moan over the injustices and hardships of 'England—now.' Incidentally, 'England—now'—is doing us pretty well. You're getting to be a nut-brown maid. You're looking prettier every day, Anne."

"Thank you for those kind words. May I say in my turn that you're looking much less like something grown in a cellar, Ray. I shall admire your manly beauty if you continue the good work."

The villagers of Milham in the Moor were by nature conservative and tended to be suspicious of newcomers. When they first saw Anne Ferens, they were almost startled by her vividness and vitality. She was a gypsy type in colouring: black hair, smoothly parted and plaited into a big bun low down on her neck, dark eyes and amusingly tilted dark eyebrows, a brown skin and lips that were red even without her habitual cherry lipstick. Her eyes were bright and expressive, her cheeks dimpled and her lips curved easily to a wide smile and she loved bright colours, scarlet and orange and yellow, emerald green and cerise; no colour was too bright for Anne to wear. If the villagers were a bit startled at first by both the modernity and the vividness of the new doctor's young wife, they soon got to enjoy the look of her, as well as her gaiety and spontaneous interest in everything.

It was a few weeks after the Ferenses had settled into the Dower House that Anne received a note from Sister Monica, conveying a courteous old-fashioned invitation 'to take tea' at Gramarye. Anne tossed the note across to Raymond at breakfast time: "I suppose I've got to go sometime, so I might as well go and get it over. I shall jolly well keep my eyes open while I'm there."

"I shouldn't, angel," he replied. "Treat it as you would treat any other not very welcome social occasion. Be polite and dignified—you're very good at both—and come away as soon as you can, having uttered nothing but courteous platitudes."

Anne sat and thought. Then she said: "I don't believe that woman's fit to be trusted with the care of little children, Ray."

"Anne, let's get this clear," he replied. "Gramarye is not our business. The home has a qualified medical man in charge: it is regularly inspected by the committee of management and it is known to the county authorities, who see fit to send homeless or maladjusted children there. It's nothing to do with you or with me." He paused, and then went on: "I think we've got to be very careful, Anne. Sister Monica has held a position of trust here for thirty years. I have said I don't like her. I think she has all the bad qualities of an ageing, dominating and narrow-minded woman, but she is woven into the very fabric of the life of this village and she has a lot of influence here. If I thought that the situation was such as to warrant interference from me, I would interfere and devil take the consequences, but I don't think such interference is indicated."

"Would you feel the same if a child you were fond of was there, Ray?"

"I don't know, and I'm not going to debate a hypothetical case. To the best of my knowledge and belief those small kids at Gramarye are well housed, well fed, and well clothed. Their health is supervised by Brown and their general welfare supervised by a committee of whom Lady Ridding is chairman. Don't go tilting at windmills, Anne."

Anne suddenly grinned. "All right, but do just tell me this. What do you mean by windmills?"

"You know, my child. We both believe that Sister Monica has the defects of her qualities—a very useful phrase. I think she's deceitful, and she deceives herself as well as other people. I'm prepared to believe she's a liar, a fomenter of trouble, a sneak and a hypocrite. I also believe she's a very competent nurse and an excellent manager. May I have some more coffee?"

"Do. It's good coffee, isn't it? All right, Ray. I will refrain from observing anything."

"Oh, no, you won't," he said, "but kindly remember this. If you have any grounds for complaint, you can lay them before the Committee. Not before me. It's not my pigeon."

2

After Anne Ferens had been to tea at Gramarye, she went for a walk in the park. The land to the south of the church and the Manor House fell steeply to the river. Beyond the river valley it rose again in a magnificent rolling chequer board of farm land—'landscape plotted and pieced: fold, fallow and plough'—until the cultivated fields faded out into the greater sweep of the high moorland. Anne never tired of the wooded loveliness of the park and of the vast prospect seen from the Milham hillside. She walked to-day because she wanted to order her turbulent thoughts before she talked to her husband; generally a reasonable person, she admitted to herself that she was being unreasonable on the subject of Gramarye, and she made a deliberate effort to think things over.

She had been given tea in the parlour, a small room whose furnishings and garnishings seemed a hybrid of Victorianism and a nunnery; it had white 'satin striped' wallpaper on which hung religious colour prints of a sentimental variety: much laundered cretonne covers and curtains were palely hygienic rather than decorative and the linoleum on the floor was polished to a perilous degree. Sister Monica, in navy blue alpaca and a white veil, seemed to brood over a low tea table which held a really beautiful Rockingham tea set, (a 'silver jubilee' gift to herself from Lady Ridding on the twenty-fifth anniversary of her wardenship, she explained). Sitting thus, dispensing excellent China tea and wafer-like bread and butter, she had kept up a murmur of polite platitudes and had agreed obsequiously with all Anne's cheerful common-places. Later they had seen the children at tea; twelve infants between the ages of three and five sat in dreadful decorum at a long low table, presided over by an elderly woman in nurse's uniform. When Sister Monica entered, all the children stood up in silence, and Anne had a sense of horror. How did you make infants of that age stand in silence? Sister Monica murmured their names: then a small girl recited a verse of poetry—"I once had a beautiful doll, dears..." and finally they sang a verse of a hymn, which made Anne want to scream, so automatic were the thin shrill tuneless little voices. Then Anne had been conducted round the house and shown the white dormitories and whiter bathrooms, the play room, the kitchens, the chapel room. It was all very well equipped, faultlessly tidy, and clean to the point of the aseptic. The staff consisted of 'Nurse,' who had presided at the children's tea, a dour-faced cook and three uniformed maids aged about sixteen who looked at Anne with owlish suspicious eyes.

"Don't the children ever make a noise?" she asked and Sister Monica replied:

"Indeed, yes. It's right that little children should be noisy, but we teach them to be quiet at meals. It's so much better for their health. It's wonderful to see how the little newcomers get into our ways. Never any trouble after the first day or two. I have a great belief in the healing influences of quiet and cleanliness and orderliness. Ours is such a simple, gentle routine and they respond to it wonderfully."

Walking down the steep path which led to the mill, Anne thought, "That's the most dreadful place I ever was in. They're not children at all, they're little automatons. It's enough to make potential criminals of all of them...and that awful hymn." When she reached river level, she went and stood on the little wooden bridge which crossed the mill stream and watched the play of light and shadow in the deep clear water as it swirled by to rejoin the main stream. She was aware of a deep perturbation in her mind, as though she had been having a strenuous argument in which she had been worsted. She loathed Sister Monica, but she was aware of the woman's strength of character; somehow, all through that inane conversation over the tea table, there had emerged that feeling of struggling with something like an eel, something which eluded your grasp and defeated you because you couldn't come to grips with it. A footstep on the far side of the bridge made her look up quickly and she saw John Sanderson, the bailiff: Anne and her husband both liked Sanderson, and Raymond had taken to asking him to their house for a drink occasionally.

"Why, Mrs. Ferens, you're looking worried," he said. "I don't think it's a good idea to stand on this bridge and meditate. It's rather a melancholy spot."

"Why?" she asked. "I was thinking how fascinating the water is, so clear and deep and swirling. I came here to cheer myself up. I've just been to tea at Gramarye."

"Oh dear," he said, and Anne caught his quick glance round.

"Are you afraid somebody's listening in?" she said. "Walk up through the park with me and come in for a drink. I feel I need one."

"Thanks very much," he replied, and they left the bridge and turned uphill.

"I think that children's home is simply ghastly," she said. "It gave me the horrors: such little children—and they're all frightened. Have you ever been there?"

"Yes, quite often," he replied. "It's my business to survey the fabric and order decorations and repairs. I hate the place. To me it has the authentic flavour of a Victorian orphanage, in which fear was the dominant factor."

"But can't the Committee members see what we see?" asked Anne.

"No. For one thing they don't want to: for another they're all old: Lady R., Colonel and Mrs. Staveley, Dr. Brown, the vicar and Mrs. Kingsley, and old Mr. and Mrs. Burlap from Coombe. The fact is that all these worthies are overjoyed to perceive what they call discipline in the home: they don't like modern ideas or modern children and they do like charity children to seem like charity children."

"I'm certain there's something fundamentally wrong there," said Anne. "Even the little maids looked as though they were bullied."

"They probably are—for their souls' good. That's what they're there for. They are girls who have gone wrong in one way or another, and Sister Monica is responsible for their moral welfare. Shall we change the subject until we get inside the house? Some of the estate men use this path, and if walls have ears, the same is true of trees and thickets."

"As you will. I'll pick that one up again later," said Anne. "Meantime, what books have you been reading lately?"

"Travel books. I always do. Someday I'm going to exciting places, by sea for preference. A nice leisurely tramp steamer which expects to be at sea for a couple of years and stops at every port from Gib. to Sydney."

3

"Your very good health, sir," said Anne, raising her glass to Sanderson with an air half gallant, half mirthful, and wholly charming. "And now will you tell me why you're frightened of Sister Monica?"

"I'm not frightened of her," he replied. "I'm aware that she's dangerous, in the same way that a virus or blood poisoning can be dangerous. I take steps to avoid trouble from them.

You see, I like my job here. There aren't many good jobs going in estate management, and this is an interesting job. Sister Monica nearly got me sacked some months after I came here. If I gave her the opportunity, she'd try it again."

"How?"

"By telling lies about me with a grain of truth in them. She is one of those people who can not only lie plausibly and with conviction, but she can tell a lie to your face without batting an eyelid, knowing that you know it's a lie, and it's very hard to bowl her out."

"But doesn't Lady Ridding realise that?"

"She won't let herself realise it. Sister Monica is very useful to her. Lady Ridding wants maid servants at the Manor, and Sister Monica can always produce some village youngster whom she has 'influenced'—hypnotised is a better word—and trained in the ways of genteel service. It's a wonderful gift, and Lady R. profits by it."

"I think it's awful," said Anne.

Sanderson put his glass down and leant forward. "Look here, Mrs. Ferens. Don't let this thing worry you. Those children aren't ill-treated, they're only dominated. At the age of five they go on to other homes connected with schools. They soon forget the Warden of Gramarye. And in the nature of things, Sister Monica can't go on very much longer. She's over sixty now. When she retires Gramarye will be closed."

"I'm delighted to hear it, but I can't bear to think of her going on in that unctuous way. It's terribly bad for small children to be terrorised as those poor scraps are being. Besides, if she's a liar, somebody ought to bowl her out."

"Nobody's ever managed to do it. There are plenty of people who have tried, and it's they who have suffered. I tell you she would take your character away more easily than you could take hers. She has all the powers that be in this place on her side. Give her a wide berth and ignore her. She'll die one day, in God's good time."

"That's one way of looking at it," said Anne. "Do tell me, why did she take a dislike to you?"

"Because I criticised her adversely. I thought she was—well, a tyrant and a bad influence in some respects. It was pointed out to me that I had no evidence and my opinion had not been invited. Oh, it was a sickening story. Don't let's talk about it."

"All right. I won't, but do tell me this. Is there nobody in the village who dislikes her?"

"Plenty of them, but they won't say so. This village has its own peculiar character, you know. You'll realise that when you've lived here a bit longer. At first one sees only its charm, everybody fitting together pleasantly, according to their station in life—but there's more to it than that." He broke off, laughing a little. "I'm getting prosy. I don't want to bore you."

"You're not boring me," said Anne. "I want to get this village in focus, and you can help me. Please go on."

"Well, you've always got to remember its remoteness and its antiquity. Throughout the centuries, Milham in the Moor has been cut off from towns and society and affairs. Here it has been, on its hill-top at the edge of the moor, and it has flourished because it made itself into an integrated whole, in which everybody was interdependent. A small group of people living in such conditions are conscious of their interdependence. 'Never make trouble in the village' is an unspoken law, but it's a binding law. You may know about your neighbours' sins and shortcomings, but you must never name them aloud. It'd make trouble, and small societies want to avoid trouble."

Anne nodded. "I think I follow. And applying what you

say to the subject of Sister Monica, nobody will attack her because she'd hit back. And then there would be hell to pay."

"There would, indeed. She knows everything about everybody, and quite a lot of people in this village don't wish their affairs to be made public. Villages, as you may know, are not really more virtuous than towns. They only look more virtuous, and are more successful in coating the past with lime wash, as they do their cottages. What's underneath is nobody's business."

"That's a very good exposition," said Raymond's voice at the door. "Are you teaching Anne a bit about villages, Sanderson? She's never lived in one before." He came into the room and sat down happily in his favourite chair, while Anne fetched him a glass of sherry. "How nice all this is," he murmured. "I'm enjoying our village. Apropos of what you said just now, Sanderson, people in villages don't want their transgressions to be publicised. That's true: but it's also true that everybody knows where everybody else has erred, only it's a convention that it's never mentioned in public. That's the very essence of village life—never noise it abroad."

He turned to Anne. "And how about the tea party, angel?"

"A most elegant tea party," she replied. "China tea in Rockingham cups and pre-war b. and b., cut like wafers and arranged on lace doyleys. I saw all over the house and it's the cleanest house ever. I saw the children at tea. One of them recited a little po'me, and they sang a verse of a hymn. All very high-minded. It roused the worst in me, but Mr. Sanderson has given me a good talking-to, and I'm going to emulate village conventions. Say what you like, but say it within doors and let not your right hand know what your left hand doeth."

4

"Wicked, my dear? Of course she's wicked," replied Miss Emmeline Braithwaite.

Anne Ferens was returning a call—the country still practised formal manners, she found—and she was sitting in the white-panelled drawing-room of Miss Braithwaite's house. China tea again, good smoky Lap San Suchong, but the cups were Royal Worcester this time, and savoury sandwiches replaced thin bread and butter.

"Do help yourself. I always eat a good tea," said Emmeline Braithwaite. She was seventy-ish, Anne guessed, very robust, very weather-beaten, brindled hair and an equine profile, but she had a delightful voice and said exactly what she meant.

"We're all wicked in some ways," went on old Emmeline. "I've been a mass of iniquity in my time, but that woman combines all the worst sorts of wickedness. I'd disregard her cant and humbug, but I can't stomach the way she hypnotises those wretched infants. Like a stoat and a rabbit. Most unpleasant. Of course they kicked me out of the Committee. Very polite and all that, but a quite definite kick. I had a magnificent row with Etheldreda Ridding over it. Her name really is Etheldreda, by the way. We both said the most unpardonable things to each other, strictly in camera."

"Why did they kick you out of the Committee?" asked Anne.

"Because I told the truth, and it's an embarrassing habit. I said—and I maintain it—that some women get a kink as they age. Sister Monica's kink is domination. She's got to dominate something, so it's the wretched orphans and those Borstal-faced maids. I think she was a competent, rather possessive creature originally. Very clever. Make no mistake about that.

She's had undisputed authority in her small realm for don-key's years, and she's become almost a megalomaniac. It's so long since anybody has criticised her effectively, or interfered with her in any way that she feels she's above criticism. And that's a very dangerous state of mind for a woman who is in control of young things."

"It's an extraordinary situation," said Anne. "*You* feel she's dangerous and a bit mad. I'm sure she is. John Sanderson feels the same—"

"Oh, John Sanderson—he knows all about it. He's a very nice fellow," said Emmeline. "I've always liked him. He had the courage to say what he thought at the time, and nearly got sacked for his pains."

"But what happened?" asked Anne. "He didn't tell me, and I didn't like to ask."

"It was a wretched story," said Emmeline. "One of those miserable little maids at Gramarye drowned herself in the mill-race. It was all very distressing. The girl—her name was Nancy—was a very naughty girl. She'd been put on proba-tion for stealing and she had a bad home. She was sent here because Sister Monica is said to be so good at dealing with difficult girls. She couldn't deal with Nancy, and the girl got into trouble in the usual way. She wouldn't tell who it was got her in the family way and so far as I could make out Sister Monica gave her a hell of a time—prayings and fastings and locking her in her room of nights. The result was that the girl broke out of her room and drowned herself. It was John Sanderson who found her body."

Anne gave an exclamation. "Oh dear—how dreadful. So that was why he didn't like seeing me brooding on that little bridge over the mill-race."

"He certainly wouldn't have liked it," said Emmeline

brusquely. "Finding that girl's body gave him a shock. He'd been overseeing some work at Gramarye, and he knew that Nancy had been locked in her room. He stated that in his evidence at the inquest and was reproved by the coroner. The upshot was that Sister Monica confided to several people that she couldn't believe that it was he who had seduced the girl. That is her method. She suggests slanders by denying them. It's a subtle method."

"But don't the village people realise what she's like?" asked Anne. "There are some very shrewd, sensible people in the village. Mrs. Yeo, for instance."

"Yes, Mrs. Yeo. She's Post Mistress. Without going into details, I don't think it would be worth Mrs. Yeo's while to make trouble for Sister Monica. You see, the woman has wormed her way into everybody's confidence. She has always been willing to help with nursing the sick. Sometimes the district nurse is away for hours, out at midwifery cases on the moor, and Sister Monica volunteers to help with the aged, dying or the chronics. It's marvellous how people chat to a sympathetic listener after a laying-out or a crisis in sickness. I'm not being macabre. I'm simply telling you how it happened. It's been a slow and insidious process. She got herself trusted, she learned everybody's secrets, and her own character had become steadily more dominating. The plain fact is that everybody's afraid of her. Etheldreda's afraid of her. Butter and cream, perhaps. But I'm being waspish. Have some more tea."

Anne began to laugh. "Apart from being frightful, it's so utterly preposterous," she said.

"Utterly," agreed Emmeline Braithwaite. "I wish I could explain to you how overjoyed I was when you and your husband came here to live. Two vigorous, intelligent, normal young people, absolutely fresh and untouched by all the ins and outs of this queer village. I love the place. I've spent my life here. Too many of us have done the same. The vicar's been here for twenty-five years, Dr. Brown for over thirty years: the village people never change. You and your husband and John Sanderson are the only people from the outside world who have come here for about a quarter of a century."

"About Dr. Brown," said Anne suddenly. "I know he's old now, but he was a good doctor once, wasn't he? Why didn't he see what Sister Monica was growing like?"

Emmeline Braithwaite did not reply for a moment or two. Then she said: "Did you know that his wife went out of her mind, poor soul. She had to be taken to a mental home."

Anne stared back at the older woman's face: it was a square, weather-beaten honest face, and an intelligent one, too.

"But what's that got to do with Sister Monica?"

Miss Braithwaite sighed. "I think he got to rely on her. He said she was a tower of strength, and I think it was true that Sister could manage the poor demented creature better than anybody else before she was put in a home. I was terribly sorry for Dr. Brown. I wanted to say to him 'Don't rely on Sister too much. I don't really believe she's trustworthy.' But how could I? Anyway, after his wife's death, the doctor said he couldn't be grateful enough to Sister, and since then, of course, he's always upheld her through thick and thin. For instance, when she was turned sixty, one or two people suggested she should retire—I was one of them. Brown wouldn't hear of it. When there was something approaching a scandal in the village over charitable collections which were never audited, Brown steered a way through the suspicions which gathered round Sister Monica—she has always organised all the collections. When Brown gave up his practice, he retained his work at

Gramarye. There it is. It's better you should know, because if you're going to try conclusions with Sister—and I believe you are—you'd better realise how tough a proposition you're up against."

"It certainly is tough," said Anne slowly. "I'm a doctor's wife, you see."

"Yes. Freemasonry is nothing compared to the determination with which doctor upholds doctor. Don't wreck your married life over Sister Monica."

"No. I shan't do that, but I shall watch out."

"Do, my dear. And one last word. You may be interested to know that if you walk up through the park with John Sanderson and ask him into your own house when your husband is out, Sister Monica is quite sure there's nothing wrong in that."

"Well, I'm damned!" said Anne.

CHAPTER IV

1

It was early in the morning of Midsummer Day that Anne Ferens heard her front-door bell jangling away. She had been awake for some time, delighting in the sunshine and the bird song, and debating in her own mind whether she would go to church to honour St. John Baptist (as a Christian should) and the summer solstice (as a pagan should). Anne wasn't quite certain which element was predominant in her mind on that divine morning, but she certainly woke up quoting "Bliss was it in that dawn to be alive."

It was half-past six when the bell rang, and she said, "Oh bother!" because Raymond hadn't got to bed until after two, for he had been out to a confinement at Long Barrow, away up on the moor. Nevertheless, he woke up when the bell rang, and was out of bed before Anne was.

"Bad luck, but it's a heavenly morning," she said to him, as he snatched his dressing-gown and went out of the bedroom muttering, "I bet it's that Chandler girl...she just can't count."

He was back within a minute, all the comfortable sleepiness gone from his face, and he snatched at his shirt and trousers without a word.

"What is it, Ray? Can I do anything?"

"No, and nobody else either, I imagine. It's Sister Monica. She's drowned in the mill-race. Young Rigg found her and came pounding up here."

Anne gave a gasp, and Raymond said: "Yes, here's trouble…" as he flung his clothes on.

"Shall I come?" she asked.

"Lord, no. Stay here and get breakfast. I shan't be long. It's the police they want, not me—but one's got to do the usual."

He snatched his coat and hurried out of the house, across the garden, through the gate in the yew hedge and across the dewy lawns of the Manor, taking the short cut to the steep path down through the park. All around him thrushes and blackbirds were calling from the tree tops, and chaffinches and bullfinches poured out their clear liquid song: the air was fragrant with the sweetness of midsummer, fragrance of pinks and roses in the garden, hay and meadow flowers in the park. Fat white lambs rushed to mother ewes as Ferens made his way down the steep path, the world vivid and vibrant with life and sunshine.

Raymond Ferens found a sombre group standing by the mill stream. Venner, the big rubicund miller, was there, and Jack Hedges, the cowman from Moore's Farm. Wilson, in charge of the generating engine, and Bob Doone from the saw mill, were there. They stood round the long dark-cloaked body which lay beside the bank, with wild roses stretching out delicate sprays of palest pink, gold centred, above the pallid face and dead white hair.

"A bad business, doctor. Nought we could do," said Venner.

Ferens knelt down beside the dead woman: one touch was enough to tell him she had been dead for hours.

"We'm telephoned to sergeant at Milham Prior," said Venner. "He'll be along soon. Hours ago it be since her was drowned, be'n't it?"

Ferens nodded as he busied himself over his examination. "Yes. Several hours. Do you know where the body was found?"

"By them piles, doctor. Her was swept down by the stream and her cloak caught in them bolts and the weeds twisted all around she. I helped get her out, and a tidy weight her was."

"She'm been wandering at nights, months past, she has," said Wilson. "Reckon her mind went, poor soul. Brooded over that young maid, maybe. Same place 'twas. I mind that well."

"Wandering at nights?" asked Ferens sharply.

"'Tis true enough, doctor," said Venner. "Us have seen her. Down through the park she'd come. My wife, she saw her once in the moonlight and fair scared she was. Looked all strange with that white hair and the dark cloak."

"Iss…" Jack Hedges gave the sibilant affirmative which still sounded strange to Raymond Ferens' ears, accustomed to Midland voices. "Us have seen her, too, like a fay, fair moonstruck. Us marked that. Fearful, 'twas."

"I reckon 'twas brooding like. Her threw herself in, poor soul," said Venner, and the others made mournful sounds of agreement.

"We'd better wait until the sergeant comes before we move her," said Ferens, "but we shall have to decide where to take her body. There will have to be a post-mortem. I don't think it's desirable to take her to Gramarye, with all those small children there."

"You'm right there, doctor," said Venner. "All they tiny tots don't want no more fearsome things. I'm meaning childer should be kept clear of corpses and all," he added hastily. "But Dr. Brown, he'll be along any minute. My wife went to tell he. A shock, 'twill be, poor old gentleman. He thought the world of Sister. He'll best decide where to take her. Knows everything here, Dr. Brown does."

Ferens nodded. He had got up from his place by the body, removing his useless thermometer. The body was stark cold, the temperature of the swirling water which came down from the moor. The woman had drowned—no doubt about that— and the rest could wait.

"You're quite right," he said to Venner. "Dr. Brown shall decide. I sent Rigg on to the Manor. Lady Ridding will tell them at Gramarye. Ah, here is Dr. Brown."

The sound of Brown's ancient car was known all over the village, and its brakes squeaked vilely as he pulled up on the road beyond the Mill House. He came slowly towards the bridge and leant heavily on the hand rail as he crossed the stream. He was pallid and looked worn and weary, but not without dignity, and he walked steadily up to the body and stood looking down at the clay-coloured face and sodden white hair. Venner spoke, very gently.

"We'm sorry, doctor. Her had worked here a powerful long time."

"Yes… Too long. She wouldn't give in," said the old man. "I've been worried about her. I should have made her give up—but it was her life."

"She knew she was failing like, and chose to finish it," said Venner. "Poor soul—but she do look peaceful now. Where shall we take her, doctor?"

"We were waiting for the sergeant from Milham Prior," said Ferens, his voice quiet and normal, "but it'd be as well to decide where to take her. There's a stretcher in the Red Cross cupboard at the Institute, I believe."

"Yes. We got it in 1939," said Brown, as though he were glad to turn to ordinary trivial things. "You can bring her to my house, Venner. That'll be best. The examination…should be simple." He glanced at Ferens and the latter replied:

"Yes. She was drowned."

A klaxon horn shrilled importantly somewhere up the hilly main street of the village, and some cows bawled as though in protest. Hedges suddenly jumped.

"That'll be sergeant," he said. "I know that dratted horn of his. Maybe I'd better go and see to my cows. Milking's got to be done, no matter what."

"Aye, Jack. You've got to milk the cows, no matter what," echoed old Brown. "Life goes on, thank God, no matter which of us passes out. You go and get on with your milking and I hope that hustling policeman hasn't knocked your cows sideways. What does he want to blow his horn at the cows for?"

2

"Never was good coffee more enjoyed," said Raymond Ferens. "Lord, I wanted that." He passed his cup across to Anne to be refilled and pushed his plate aside, having polished off the eggs and bacon. "It's going to be a peck of trouble, Anne. She was drowned all right, but I'm afraid she didn't jump into the mill stream herself. She was shoved in—after somebody had batted her over the head with the inevitable blunt instrument. At least, that's my diagnosis."

Anne sighed. "You mean her head was damaged while she was still alive?"

"Undoubtedly."

"Couldn't she have hit her head on one of the piles as she jumped?"

"The back of her head? If the coroner and jury are willing to believe that, nobody will be better pleased than myself. But I don't think they will. Wherever she went in, whether from the bank or the bridge, she'd have gone slap into deep water and she would have sunk. Her body would have been carried towards the piles by the current, but she couldn't have hit the back of her head on them."

Anne sat silent, her face troubled, and Raymond went on: "Sergeant Peel was on to it like knife. He must have driven about fifty miles an hour to get here from Milham Prior in the time he did. His attitude was one of expectancy. 'I expected this' was written all over his face."

"But why?" cried Anne. "What did he know about Sister Monica?"

"I don't know what he knew, angel, but it appears that he was never satisfied they'd got to the truth in the last drowning case here—the wretched Nancy Bilton. The verdict was suicide while of unsound mind, and there was no evidence against it. The girl had sworn she'd kill herself and there it was. But there was a lot of talk about it here afterwards." Raymond held out his cigarette case to Anne. "We might as well talk it over now, Anne. It's better that you should know what's been said, and what's being said now. We've only been here three months, but it's surprising how much gossip comes a doctor's way in three months. It's some of the old chronics who do most of the talking—it's all that life has left to them, the power to chatter. After the verdict had been given on Nancy Bilton, more than a few folks surmised that the reason she was found drowned was that Sister Monica pushed her into the mill pool."

"You don't believe that, do you, Ray?"

Raymond sat and looked at his wife with very thoughtful eyes. "I don't know, Anne. I've always refused to discuss Sister Monica with you. We both took a dislike to her, and I was very anxious to avoid being unfair by judging the woman at first glance. Then I made up my mind to avoid taking sides in local feuds. I expect I heard very much what you heard, because I noticed that you left the subject of Gramarye severely alone after our first few weeks here."

"Yes. I did," said Anne. "Tell me this: gossip which somebody else has told you isn't evidence, is it? If this sergeant comes round asking questions, I've only got to tell him what I know at first-hand, haven't I?"

"Yes. That's right. Now to get back to the Nancy Bilton rumours. Venner and Wilson and Bob Doone all state that Sister Monica had been wandering at night, around the park and across the bridge and into the lower end of the village, and this is apparently no recent habit. She has been known to do it for years at infrequent intervals, but latterly has done it much more often. Now it was agreed that Nancy Bilton was a night bird. If Nancy spied on Sister Monica, I wouldn't put it beyond Sister M. to have shoved Nancy in the mill stream, because it does seem to me that Sister Monica was something less than sane."

"You say 'if Nancy spied on Sister Monica,'" said Anne slowly. "It might have been the other way about. Sister Monica may have spied on Nancy. Do you remember the first thing you said to me about Sister Monica—that you sensed the religious fanatic in her? Isn't it true that religious mania, like any other mania, can make a sort of megalomaniac of anybody? They can no longer see themselves in focus, or realise their own shortcomings—only other people's."

"That's true enough; they see themselves as 'chosen vessels,' above criticism. This was particularly true of Sister M. She had developed a mania for taking people's characters away. But what were you thinking about when you said that perhaps it was Sister Monica who spied on Nancy?"

"I was wondering if Nancy went for her and tried to shove her in the stream, without realising that Sister M. was much bigger and stronger than herself—and it happened that way. She was a very powerfully built woman, Ray, and she had enormous hands. They gave me the horrors."

"Yes. I noticed her hands, too. But all this doesn't get us any nearer to who shoved Sister Monica in the mill-race."

"Did they ever find out who was the man Nancy had been going with?"

"No. She never told anybody, and when the police enquired in the village, the answer was 'I don't know.' Nobody knew, which meant that nobody would tell. This village has a very strong defence mechanism of the 'I don't know' variety. They're nearly all related or connected by marriage, and they present an unbroken front to outside interference. That's why they resent the fact that the village children are sent to school at Milham Prior now. Children chatter, one to another."

"Do you think the village rumours got to Milham Prior that way?"

"Yes. I think Sergeant Peel got wind of what was being said in secret conclave in this village—to wit, that Sister Monica pushed Nancy in the mill stream. Incidentally, he doesn't believe it, but he holds there's no smoke without fire."

"And so what?"

"Peel's own belief is that there's a killer in the village, responsible for both deaths. Whether he's right or wrong, it means a full dress police investigation. He'll go on asking questions until somebody cracks."

"How grim," said Anne. She paused a moment, and then said: "Well, thank heaven I don't know anything about anything: and in the meantime, ought I to offer to go and help at Gramarye?"

"I'd much rather you didn't, but I suppose we ought to offer to help," said Raymond. "I'll ring up Lady Ridding and find out how things are. My own opinion is that it would be much better to have all those tinies dispersed to other homes. They're bound to hear some of the gossip and they'd be better out of it."

"Oh, do try to get that done, Ray. It'd be so much better. That aged nurse and the old cook will be fairly spreading themselves over death and disaster, and the brats of maids will be gossiping like ghouls. It's bound to happen. They've all been battened down and kept under, and now the tyrant's hand is removed they'll go haywire."

"I think that's probably perfectly true," said Raymond.

3

Sergeant Peel was a competent and zealous police officer, but he tended to develop a bee in his bonnet over Milham in the Moor. In actual fact, the village defeated him. It was a law-abiding village, and the constable who occasionally patrolled it had no complaints to make, but on the few occasions when Peel had had occasion to investigate irregularities—motoring offences, drinking after hours, dramatic performances in a hall which had no licence for same—he had come up against the communal answer, "I don't know." It had been the same over Nancy Bilton's death: no one knew anything, and Peel was perfectly certain that quite a number of people knew quite a lot, but no wiles of his own could break down that unanimous ignorance of a village which was an integral whole. When he had received the news of Sister Monica's death, Peel had fairly jumped to it. Milham in the Moor had diddled him once over a big case, and it wasn't going to happen again.

He had arrived to find the two doctors, Venner and Wilson and Bob Doone all together close by the bridge. Hedges had been hurrying away after his agitated cows, who were not used to being honked at on their way to milking. No driver in the village ever honked at milking cows—it was bad for milk production. Peel had shouted at Hedges to come back and Hedges had disregarded the voice of the law, while Venner, Wilson, and Doone had all told Peel to "let mun be." Cows had got to be milked and Hedges didn't know aught about this here. Which negative statement set the old theme of not knowing.

After his first routine enquiries, Peel had agreed that the body should be moved to Dr. Brown's house. There was no object in waiting for the photographers, for the body had already been lifted from the water and its position gave no information. The sergeant was favourably disposed towards Dr. Ferens, for the simple reason that he was a newcomer to Milham in the Moor, and things had gone fairly smoothly, except that Peel was incensed because Jim Rigg, who had first found the body, was not at hand to be questioned. Jim Rigg worked at the Manor Farm and was now milking Sir James Ridding's pedigree Jerseys—and the Jerseys, Peel was given to understand, had to be milked to the clock and no dilly-dallying. "Him'll tell you all him knows in good time," said Venner, who had the Devonian's persistence in using an accusative for a nominative and vice versa.

Eventually Peel, who had plenty of commonsense when he wasn't being given information about dairy cattle, had decided that the best thing he could do was to search the immediate environs of the bridge. He could interrogate natives later, but any delay in searching might mean losing valuable evidence. The ground was fairly soft, and, for all Peel knew, somebody's cows might be driven all over the place before he could stop them. The sergeant knew who had been at the bridge since the body had been found: Rigg, Venner, Wilson, and Hedges, all in labourer's boots, Dr. Brown and Dr. Ferens in good country shoes. Rigg and Venner had lifted the body from the stream, Wilson and Hedges had turned up just after the body had been laid by the bank, and they had all come from the south side of the bridge. Dr. Ferens had come from the north, down the park. Peel and his attendant constable began to search the ground, the hedges and the grass, seeking for any object or sign which might indicate the presence of any other person who had been at the spot. When they had been at this job for some quarter of an hour, Inspector Carson of Barnsford arrived, together with two of his own men and a photographer. Peel saluted his superior officer, and while the constables continued searching the ground, the two seniors stood on the bank and Peel gave a brief description of events as far as his information went.

"I reckon we must make a job of it this time," he said. "I wasn't happy in my mind over the last case, and I reckon this proves I was right."

"What have you got in mind, Peel?"

"I believe there's a murderer in this village. That girl Nancy Bilton was a bad lot and she got into trouble with some chap here. I daresay she made a nuisance of herself to him and he pushed her into the mill stream. We never found out who he was, but I shouldn't be at all surprised if this Sister Monica had some sort of idea about his identity."

"Then why didn't she tell you?" asked Carson. "She swore in the witness box she didn't know the chap's identity and she was a religious body. You're not telling me you think she told lies?"

"No, I'm not, though I reckon she was queer—too religious, you know. Takes some women like that. I know she thought herself next door to the Almighty, for all her show of humble-pie. My own idea is that she had her own suspicions and wouldn't put 'em into words because she'd no means of proving it. And the chap knew she'd got an inkling of who he was and she was going round trying to ferret things out in that clever-belike way she'd got."

The Inspector grunted. "More than a year ago, isn't it? Not likely she'd have found out anything now."

"I don't know: this village is a queer place. Maybe somebody let something out to her, thinking it was all over and done with. Anyway, my guess is she met the chap down here and charged him with it sudden like, and he heaved her into the mill-race like he did the other. They do say she wandered round here of nights. Must have been some reason made her do it."

Again the Inspector grunted. "Well, you've evidently had the last case on your mind, Peel. What's your idea?"

Peel looked cautiously round the sunlit spot where they were standing, and lowered his voice even more. "Strikes me things went on pretty quietly in this village until two or three years ago. It's the sort of village doesn't change much from generation to generation. It was after that new estate manager came, three years ago, there seemed to be upsets."

"I see," said the Inspector. "Well, it's worth looking into. And about these folk in the Mill House here."

Peel interrupted with an exasperated snort. "There's none so deaf as them that won't hear. I reckon this spot is a sort of lovers' lane. As you see, you can come round the mill from the village street and walk up the park by that steep path there. The village folk are allowed to use that path, but not to go through the Manor garden. They can get out again, into the village square, by a gate beside the walled kitchen garden. In other words, you can take a walk down the village street, turn into the park by the mill here, walk up the park and get to where you started. The gates aren't locked. I bet any money the Venners know who's in the habit of walking through here: they know Sister Monica used to walk here after dark. Stands to reason they know who else does."

The Inspector nodded. "We'll see to that. And now what about finger-printing the hand rail of that bridge? It's worn smooth enough. We might get something there. I reckon there's been too much trampling around for footsteps to help, and it's too much to hope that we'll find anything left around. Not that you weren't right to start here. And we'll have those gates shut and see to it that no one comes through."

"Very good," said Peel. "Let 'em see we mean business from the word go this time, and not so much about the poor soul brooding and throwing herself in. Brooding my hat."

CHAPTER V

1

"Her come over dizzy, poor soul. That be it. Terrible dizzy Sister's been these weeks past. Only Sunday 'twere she fell flat as never was, and the little maids did all hear mun fall. And yesterday again, her did slip on stairs and knocked back of her head a real crack."

It was 'Nurse' Barrow giving evidence, treating Sergeant Peel to a wealth of detail over Sister Monica's dizziness, until the sergeant felt it would have been a relief to knock Hannah Barrow flat, and give her reason for dizziness herself. Hannah Barrow, aged 62, assistant at Gramarye since 1929, called 'Nurse' by courtesy, devoted admirer and servant to Sister Monica—"the most garrulous old fool I ever heard," groaned Peel. The worst of it was that she had corroborative evidence, lashings of it. Emma Higson, aged 59, cook at Gramarye since 1939, upheld every word Hannah Barrow uttered. "Her come over dizzy like, poor soul," she wheezed. "Her head, 'twas. Sister, I says, it's new glasses you're wanting. And what's the

National Health for, I asked her—you get some new glasses, Sister, I says. Them as knows can tell you wrong glasses do make folks dizzy. And a terrible fall she had, terrible. Sunday 'twas…"

Emma Higson was even more tiresome to listen to than 'Nurse' Barrow, for Emma was of Welsh parentage, reared in London, whose Cockney speech was variegated by a Welsh lilt, the whole rendered more formidable by a veneer of Devonian idiom, picked up in eleven years' association with Devonians.

"Her fell while her was watching water, that's how 'twas," said Hannah Barrow, sucking her false teeth back into place. "Her was unaccountable fond o' that bridge, a thing I don't rightly understand," she went on, "but then Sister was a proper saint, not common earth such as you and me." Her glance indicated that saintliness was very remote from the police force. "Her'd pray for hours," said Hannah reminiscently. "Terrible taken up with praying for us sinners was Sister."

Peel got the conversation back to the topic of Sister Monica's habit of wandering in the park after dark. "Iss, many a night she'd go out," said Hannah. "Her said her could meditate proper when the world was all still and dark and nought to come between her and her thoughts. 'Twas then she wrestled for righteousness," she added, "and there's no knowing the good she did a-communin' with spirits and souls of the righteous, and if her was took in the midst of 'oly thoughts, it was all for the likes of us."

"That's as may be," said Peel, and transferred his attention to the three young serving maids—Alice, Bessie, and Dot. Here he found the same unanimity of purpose. They had all heard Sister fall on the stairs, and had rushed to see what had happened. She had been sitting with her head in her hands by the time they got into the hall, and she wouldn't hear of having a doctor, like Nurse said she ought. "No, I'm not hurt, just shaken a little," she said. "I'm afraid I wasn't looking where I was going, and my foot slipped."

"And I don't wonder at it," said Dot, who was the talkative one of the three Abigails. "Look at the way Sister made us polish them stairs, fair glassy they are and the lino's old anyway and been polished for life-times. Then she wore them flat shoes about the house, soft shoes, so's you never could hear her coming. But there, she was a saint, so it's no use wondering she wasn't like the rest of us."

"How long have you been here?" asked Peel and she looked at him for a second with a bright and unregenerate eye.

"Fifteen months. I shall be eighteen come Christmas."

Peel knew what that meant. When she was eighteen Dot would be independent and able to choose her own job. "Are you girls happy here?" he asked.

It was a false move. Dot lowered her eyelids and clasped her hands and became a virtuous automaton again. "Ever so happy," she said smugly. "Sister Monica was wonderful. It'll never be the same again."

It was Nurse Barrow who took Peel over the house, pointing out again and again how spotless it was, and frowning over the marks made on the polished linoleum by Peel's damp and heavy boots. He knew the lay-out: the two dormitories where the children slept, with Sister Monica's bedroom opening out of one dormitory and Nurse's bedroom opening out of the other. Peel stood and stared at Sister Monica's room: it was like a nun's cell apart from its clutter of holy pictures and plaster angels. White-washed walls, a narrow iron bedstead, a chair, a little prayer desk and a wash stand and chest of drawers combined. That was all. He glanced into cupboard and drawers with Nurse's disapproving eye upon him.

"Where did she do her writing?" he asked.

"In the office, downstairs. Sister said bedroom was for sleeping in, and her bedroom's the same as ours. Same beds, same bedding. Never no luxuries for her."

Peel saw again the rooms where the maids slept: two rooms, opening out of one another: the senior maid had a room to herself, the other two shared one, and Emma Higson's room was next door, she being in control of the domestic staff. Peel remembered the maids' rooms. They had narrow casement windows, with a stone mullion between the lights. At one time they had been barred, but orders had been given to remove the bars in case of fire, and a fire escape ladder had been fixed at Sister Monica's window. The room in which Nancy Bilton had been locked had a very narrow window, and Sister Monica had said in evidence that she had thought the window was too small for anybody to get out of. She had had little knowledge of the athletic abilities of girls to-day. Again and again Emma Higson gave voice to her own opinion about Sister Monica's end. "Her turned dizzy, poor soul: fell backwards maybe and knocked herself silly and rolled into water."

Peel sent her away after she had shown him the office, and he sat down and went through the contents of the desk, using the keys which had been on a ring in the pocket of Sister's cloak. Everything was tidy and businesslike and in order. Neatly written books gave detailed descriptions of children who had been or were now in the home: similar details about the maids: account books, recipe books, inventories of linen and blankets and clothes and stores, all written in the same admirably legible hand with the same wealth of detail. Here were all the records anybody could possibly demand so far as the running of Gramarye was concerned: account books and analysis of accounts, costs per week, costs per child, wages, food, clothing, equipment, set out legibly and meticulously in a manner to rejoice any accountant's heart. But Sergeant Peel was not interested in accounts, or in the economics of running a children's home. He wanted to get to grips with the personality of the dead woman, to know something of her dealings as a human being, apart from her abilities as Warden. He went through every drawer and cupboard, every file and pigeon hole, without discovering a single letter or paper of a personal kind. "Damn it, the woman must have had some personal contacts," he said to himself. "Most religious-minded old maids are bung full of sentiment: they keep letters and photos galore and bits about their families and their young days and all that."

He sent for Hannah Barrow again, and asked where Sister Monica had kept her private letters and papers. Hannah told him that everything Sister possessed was either in her bedroom or in this office. There was nothing anywhere else. He could see the parlour, but there was nothing there. It was only used when visitors came.

"Do you know anything about her family—next of kin?" asked Peel.

"Her had no family, poor soul. Her was alone in the world," said Hannah smugly, with the air of one repeating an oft told tale. "One sister, her had, name of Ursula. Her died 'way back. Jubilee year 'twas. 'Now I'm alone in the world so far as kith and kin goes,' her said. I mind it same as if 'twere yesterday. 'My family's here now,' her said, 'the little ones, Hannah, and you and the others: you're my family and blessed I am to have you all.'"

"That's all very fine and large," said Peel to himself, "but there must have been some papers I haven't found. The woman was paid, presumably. She'd have been paid by cheque, I take it. She must have had a banking account, or a savings bank book. There's something damned odd about the whole set-up."

2

Peel's next call was at the Manor House. For twenty years Lady Ridding had been chairman of the Committee which controlled Gramarye, and it was to be presumed that she knew all that there was to be known about the deceased Warden.

The sergeant was conscious of acute discomfort when he and his attendant constable were shown into the morning-room at the Manor. Theoretically, Peel had no undue reverence for the gentry. In the eyes of the law, a witness was a witness, to be treated with neither fear nor favour, but Lady Ridding had given away prizes at the police sports, beamed upon competing police teams in the ambulance competitions, received bouquets from policemen's small daughters and salutes from sergeants and inspectors. It was Peel's duty to collect all the available evidence for his inspector, and information about the financial position of deceased, to say nothing of her next of kin, had obviously got to be obtained, but Peel knew in his heart that he could not really deal with Lady Ridding. If she joined in the 'I don't know' tactics of the village she could defeat him, not by a display of intransigence but by graciously worded regrets for her inability to help him.

Her ladyship (the title was accorded to her by all the village folk) swept superbly into the small room.

"Good-morning, Sergeant, Good-morning, Constable. Please sit down. This is indeed a sorrowful occasion. Sister

Monica's death is a tragedy, and I feel it deeply. I have had the privilege of knowing her for thirty years, and I cannot tell you how profoundly I grieve at her loss. Now I know that it is your duty to make a detailed enquiry into the circumstances of her death, but I do beg you to remember that I, and all who knew her, are mourning her loss. I ask you to be brief, Sergeant."

This speech was delivered with all the virtuosity of one skilled in addressing committees: moreover it indicated subtly that Peel was intruding into a house of mourning, and made him feel even less at ease. Essaying a few words of apology and sympathy, Peel started on the easiest question he had to put—the matter of next of kin.

"I have already discussed that with Sir James," replied Lady Ridding. "The plain answer is that there is no next of kin. Sister Monica told me years ago, after the death of her parents, that she had only one relative remaining in the world, her sister, Ursula Torrington. Ursula died in 1935. I remember it well. Sister Monica went to her funeral. Since then, believe it or believe it not, Sister Monica has never been away from Gramarye. She refused to take a holiday. Her very soul was in her work, Sergeant. She had no other life. Her home, her friends, were here, in this place."

Peel then got on to the rather more difficult matter of 'deceased's estate.' He said that he had been unable to find any private papers, any bank statement, any cheque book. Lady Ridding interrupted him here.

"She had no bank account. Sister Monica was utterly devoid of any interest in money. She despised money. She came to Gramarye thirty years ago, Sergeant. Wages were very different in those days. She was paid forty-eight pounds a year, plus her living expenses, laundry, and insurance. She asked to be paid monthly, in cash, and this method of payment has been adhered to. It was only with difficulty that she was persuaded to accept increases in salary. She was a selfless woman, Sergeant."

"Do you mean that her salary was still forty-eight pounds a year, madam?" enquired Peel, and saw the constable's eyes goggle over his notes.

"Of course not," said Lady Ridding tartly. "We did not exploit her unworldliness. Her salary was raised by regular increments of four pounds a year until it reached ten pounds a month. That was in 1940, during the war, and Sister Monica came to me and said she did not wish for any further rise. She wanted to make her own contribution to the financial sacrifices we were all making. At her own wish her salary has remained fixed at that sum—one hundred and twenty pounds a year. It was too little, of course, but it was what she wished."

"And she was paid in cash?" asked the sergeant.

"As I have told you," said Lady Ridding coldly. "I, as chairman of the Committee, am empowered to draw cheques on the Gramarye account, together with a signature from the vicar. I paid Sister Monica ten pounds on the first of every month, in pound notes. She once told me that after she had paid any necessary outgoings—uniform and so forth—she gave the remains of her salary each month to various charities. She was an amazing woman, Sergeant."

"She must have been," said Peel. He dared not meet Lady Ridding's eye, for the most heterodox thoughts were going through his worldly mind. A hundred and twenty pounds a year...and any good cook could get three pounds a week... had somebody been making a bit out of the Gramarye funds? Her ladyship was said to be as hard as nails over a business deal.

"You will realise that charities dependent on invested funds are finding it increasingly difficult to carry on," continued Lady Ridding, exactly as though she could read Peel's thoughts, and he felt his face getting even hotter. "And now, Sergeant, are there any further questions which must be dealt with at this very moment? I do not wish to impede your enquiries, but I have much to arrange."

"Quite so, madam. Could you tell me if Sister Monica had any old friends, outside this village?"

"I cannot give you a precise answer either way," she replied, "but think for yourself. If you had made your home in one place for thirty years, identifying yourself with the life of that place, giving all your affection and loyalty and devotion to the work you had made your life, is it not probable that other interests and friendships would have slipped into the background? I think this was so in the case of Sister Monica. To the best of my knowledge and belief she neither wrote letters nor received them, apart from those concerning her work at Gramarye. That was what I meant when I said it was her life."

A few minutes later sergeant and constable were walking away from the house, across the garden of the manor house.

"What's your opinion of all that, Briggs?" asked Peel. He knew Briggs well, and trusted him.

"Well, since you're asking me, Sergeant, I reckon she laid it on a bit too thick," said the constable. "I'll make allowances: deceased was a rum 'un, we all know that, but I can't swallow all this selfless stuff, if you see what I mean. Too much of it, if you ask me. Makes you wonder."

"Too much of all of it," thought Peel. "Too much dizziness. Too much devotion. Ten pounds a month…paid in cash. Doesn't sound natural, somehow. None of it."

3

"If you won't take it amiss, doctor, I'm coming to you for a bit of straight plain commonsense," said Sergeant Peel, and Raymond Ferens grinned sympathetically.

"Have a glass of beer first, and then tell me your troubles," said Ferens.

"Well, thank you kindly, sir. I reckon I could do with it," said Peel. "All this high-falutin's got my goat. There's not a soul in the place can even mention deceased in an ordinary voice. They clasp their hands and lower their eyes and tell you she was a saint.—Thank *you*, sir," he added, taking a deep draught of well cooled ale. "What do you make of all this saint stuff, sir?"

"It's no use asking me, Sergeant. I'm sorry, but it's not my province. As you know, the children's home was not in my care. Dr. Brown retained his position as M.O. there. My own contacts with Sister Monica were of the brief and casual variety—time of day, the weather, and such like. And I'm not going to repeat gossip."

"Very good, doctor. Are you willing to answer this question: so far as your observation of her goes, was she a normal, healthy creature?"

"I've no ground for opinions about her health. From the look of her, I should have judged her to be physically strong; she looked tough to me, but my opinion is of no more value than your own. As for normal in the usual sense of the word, no, I don't think she was. Her appearance was eccentric and her manner studied. She was a bit odd. But women who stick to the same limited environment for thirty years, and are in absolute authority in a small establishment, do tend to get odd." He broke off, and then added: "I take it you've seen Dr. Brown?"

"Yes, sir. I mean no disrespect to Dr. Brown when I say this. He'd known her for so long that he couldn't see her as she really was. You understand what I mean when I say a person can become a legend. They all say, 'She was a wonderful woman.' Dr. Brown said it, too. I came to you because you're a newcomer, sir. You saw this place with a fresh eye, and if I'm anywhere near the mark, you're not one who'd be hoodwinked by a legend."

Sergeant Peel was trying hard to express what was in his mind without giving offence, and he mopped his face as he spoke, while Ferens chuckled.

"Very astute of you, Sergeant. You're quite right. I'm not impressed by legends. Say if you tell me what you're really trying to get at. I'm quite trustworthy. I won't repeat anything you say, but I'll tell you if I think you're barking up the wrong tree."

"Thank you, sir. You couldn't put it fairer than that. You ask me what I'm getting at. It's something like this. I've got a feeling they're all putting on an act, and it's the same act. Sister Monica was a saint. Well, sir, was she?"

"I suppose it depends on what you call a saint," replied Ferens. "I've never met one. I shouldn't know."

"This village has always kept itself to itself," went on Peel. "We never heard anything much about it at Milham Prior, but since the older children have been sent down to our schools, it's been a bit different. Children chatter to each other, and a bit of what they chatter about gets through to the parents. The children don't think Sister Monica was a saint. Some of them were frightened of her. They said she knew everything. The fact is, sir, I've reason to believe she was one of those women who nosed out secrets."

"I shouldn't be surprised, Sergeant."

"No, sir. I reckon you wouldn't. Now being a nosy parker isn't my idea of being a saint, for all they say. And I reckon deceased was knocked over the head from behind and then shoved into the stream."

"So you may. But you've got to remember there's another possibility. There's evidence to show that deceased has been suffering from giddiness lately. She's certainly had one or two tumbles."

"Do you reckon it was possible she fell, knocked herself silly, and then rolled into the stream, sir?"

"It's possible, yes. If she were standing on that bridge, came over faint and went at the knees, there's a chance she might have knocked the back of her head on the hand rail behind her as she fell, and her body might have slipped backwards under the hand rail into the water. I'm not saying that's what happened, but it's a possibility."

"Maybe it is, sir, but somehow I can't see it happening like that, not unless she'd got some actual disease which made her liable to tumble—epilepsy, or something of that kind. They'll find that out at the autopsy, I expect. As for all this dizziness, well, it seemed to me they all laid it on too thick, like her ladyship did with her saintly stuff. You'll excuse me if I'm putting it crudely, sir, but there's such a thing as overdoing it."

"I get you, Sergeant. Methinks the lady doth protest too much."

"That's the size of it, sir. And not only the lady. Those two women at Gramarye—Barrow and Higson—they simply echoed each other. 'Her came over dizzy: terrible dizzy Sister was.' And those bits of servant girls—cheeky pieces they'd be if they acted natural—all casting their eyes up and saying Sister came over dizzy. I tell you it put me in mind of a Greek play they did at that queer school Dartmouth way—fates or furies or some such all chanting in chorus. That's what it was like, sir, sort of chorus of fates."

"Very cogently put, Sergeant. You've got an analytical mind, but it's worth remembering this. Sister Monica was a dominating woman. I've no doubt she trained all those domestics to be faithful echoes of herself, and it hasn't worn off yet. They'll come natural later on, when they've got over the shock of her death."

"Maybe they will, sir, but I feel bothered about the whole thing. There was that other case of drowning—the Bilton girl. I never believed we got to the bottom of that. And I'm not going to take anything on its face value this time."

Ferens sat very still: he recognised the Sergeant for what he was: an honest, painstaking officer, by no means devoid of intelligence, capable of a more imaginative and analytical approach than might have been expected, and the Sergeant was appealing to him—Ferens—for help, on the grounds that an intelligent newcomer to the village should be able to give some helpful counsel.

"I entirely agree with you," said Ferens quietly. "You've got to examine everything both sides, so to speak. You've come to me to ask me for help—an honest opinion, or information if I've got any. Don't think I'm holding out on you. I'm trying to be honest in my turn. I have no first-hand information, and I've told you I won't repeat hearsay. Village gossip is the devil. I'll think the whole thing over very carefully, and if I think of anything which bears on the matter and which it is my duty to tell you, I'll let you know."

"Very good, doctor. That's all I want. I've gone farther in talking to you than I'd've risked with anyone else, and I'll tell you what's really bothering me. They all say she was a saint, but if I know my onions the woman's death has been an almighty relief to the lot of them, high and low alike."

"I think you're probably right, Sergeant. But keep a sense of proportion. You've talked to me off the record, so to speak, and I'll do the same to you. I've known people who were described as saints, especially after their death. And I've often been aware of an element of thankfulness mingled with the tears in the house of mourning."

Peel allowed himself a quiet chuckle. "Does me good to hear you talking, doctor."

CHAPTER VI

1

"This is going to be one of those tiresome cases where we suspect everything and can prove nothing," said the Barnsford Inspector to Peel. "My own feeling is that deceased was a bit bats. I think she was regarded as a menace in the village, but they'll none of them admit it, and this story of her tumbling just about makes it probable that she *did* fall in the river herself."

"Something'll turn up," said Peel doggedly.

It was Peel who produced the next item of evidence. The observant sergeant had noticed that the letter box at Gramarye was a very solid and businesslike affair, a stout box firmly screwed to the back of the front door, its lid secured by a padlock, the key of which had been on the key ring found on Sister Monica's body. Peel, on the principle 'you never know your luck,' had gone to Gramarye on the morning of the 25th to see if any letters had arrived. His luck was in. He found a typewritten envelope addressed to 'Miss Torrington.'

Inside it was a half-yearly dividend warrant for £12-10-0 from the South West Building Society, and Peel promptly sat down to think and to do a little arithmetic, to the tune of 'this is a very different cup of tea.' The sergeant had been puzzled by the absence of any personal accounts. Despite Lady Ridding's firm statement of the cash basis of all Sister Monica's monetary transactions, Peel felt that there must be some records of her personal expenditure. He could not believe that a person who had kept such detailed and elaborate accounts of the institution she ran could have refrained from keeping accounts of the spending of her own income. Peel sat and pondered. He had some money invested in a building society himself and he knew the current rates of interest. £12-10-0 for the half year—that meant interest on a capital sum of £1000, a sum which took a bit of saving, thought Peel to himself. Could she have saved it? Pencil in hand, he worked out sums on the basis of Sister Monica's salary over a period of thirty years. It was obvious at a glance that it meant saving an average of £33 a year over all that period. "I suppose it's possible if she was one of the careful kind," thought Peel, "and she hadn't many expenses. But we shall have to find out how she paid it in, whether it was by little instalments at first and then bigger ones year by year, or whether it was in several hundreds at a time. Of course, there was the sister who died…she may have left her the money. That'll mean searching at Somerset House."

Peel sat and thought for some time, and by the time he met his superior officers who had come to make arrangements for the inquest, Peel had a number of ideas to put forward, including the suggestion that deceased might have had 'other irons in the fire'—further capital in addition to that in the Building Society.

The Divisional Inspector looked at the sergeant with a thoughtful eye. "What's in your mind, Peel?"

"Two things, sir. First I'm pretty certain something's been stolen: an attaché case or cash box, maybe. That dame—meaning deceased—must have kept personal records of some kind. Where's her Building Society book for one thing, and her cheque book or savings bank book? Second, when a woman's told everybody she despises money and then turns out to have a nice little sum invested, I want to know where she got it from. Maybe I'm doing a bit of fancy thinking, but deceased was a very queer party indeed, to my way of thinking."

2

The Deputy Chief Constable, the Divisional Detective Inspector and the Milham Prior police met for consultation that evening. Major Rootham, who was acting as Chief Constable during the illness of the permanent C.C., gave it as his opinion that the whole case indicated dirty work, and not in one direction alone.

"Deceased has been paying £10 a month into the Building Society over a period of eight years," he said. "The money was paid in pound notes, posted in registered envelopes. That is to say, she paid her entire salary in since 1943. Yet she must have paid out money for clothes and other personal expenses. This indicates that she had other means, of which at present we know nothing unless we assume she spent nothing but the interest on the capital sum."

"I think Sergeant Peel's got a suggestion to make there," said the Milham Prior Inspector. "He's only got rumour to go on, but it's a very suggestive rumour."

"Well, sir," said the sergeant. "Ever since the outbreak of

war, when collections for various funds were run in most localities, deceased organised all the collections, apart from National Savings, of course. There were any number of good causes during the war—Red Cross, prisoner's comforts, help for bombed areas, refugees and evacuees, to say nothing of the funds of the village Institute and various collections in connection with the church. I'm told that none of these accounts was audited, or examined by anybody in authority. Sister Monica was trusted to run the whole thing: she was so good at collecting money, and it saved everybody else trouble. It's worth noting that in the last year or so she has been relieved of all these extra duties. They've got a new treasurer for the Institute, and the churchwardens have taken over all the collecting for the church. Now I'm ready to admit that I've got these stories from sources which couldn't be used as evidence—but I reckon it's worth looking into."

"What you really mean is that deceased helped herself from the collections?" asked Major Rootham.

"Well, sir, I believe that other people think she did," said Peel, "but I'm wondering if she did a spot of blackmail as a side line. We don't know yet what other investments she's got. But one thing I'm certain of: she must have had some private papers in that house, and probably some cash as well, and we can't find a trace of anything of the kind."

"You think somebody in the house robbed her?" asked Rootham.

"I think somebody robbed her," said Peel, "but it's not easy to see how they disposed of the proceeds if it was anybody in the house who did it. There's the three young servant maids. I wouldn't put it beyond any of them to steal, but I don't think they'd commit a murder, and you've got to remember that deceased was a big strong woman. Then there's this to it. Hannah Barrow cleaned that room deceased used as a study: the maids were never allowed into it except when the Warden sent for them. Hannah says there's nothing missing."

"But deceased wouldn't have kept her private papers in a box anyone could snaffle," said the Inspector. "She'd have kept them locked away somewhere."

"Yes, sir," agreed Peel, "and if that's the case, how did someone open the drawer or cupboard where she kept them? Her keys were in the pocket of her cape when her body was found. I found them there myself, including the keys of all the drawers and cupboards in the house."

"I agree with Peel that that is a problem," said Major Rootham. "The theory at present is that deceased was stunned by a blow on the back of her skull, and then pushed into the mill stream. I'm willing to believe a murderer who knew that deceased habitually carried her keys in that pocket might have taken them out of the pocket, but if that were the case, why were the keys found in the pocket when the body was taken out of the water? Have you identified all the keys on that key ring, Peel?"

"Yes, sir. Every one. There are eleven keys: front door, garden door, store room: roll top desk, two cupboards and petty cash box in office: medicine cupboard, linen cupboard, stock clothing cupboard and bookcase. I haven't found any other cupboard, door, or box which is locked, except the pantry and such-like, and the cook has those keys."

"Then it looks as though there must be a hiding place in the house you haven't spotted, Peel," said Rootham. "It's a very old house. There are probably hiding places which it would take an expert to find. I agree that deceased must have had some private papers somewhere. We've no grounds for supposing they're stolen: that's only a supposition."

"I thought myself that there might be a hiding place in the house, sir. I asked the bailiff about it—Sanderson. He's been over the house with the estate joiner and mason. They all say there's no hiding places in the fabric. And the loft is clean as a whistle and the cellars, too. Never seen a house with so little junk in it. It's a puzzle and no mistake."

"Look here, Peel, we're in danger of getting confused by considering too many details," said Major Rootham. "I think it'd be a good idea to have a restatement of the whole case and see if there's anything we can eliminate. You have a go at it, Peel. You've put in a lot of work and you know the background. I often find it helps if you state a problem clearly, in your own words."

"Very good, sir." Peel waited for a minute, thinking hard, then he began: "The minute I heard of Sister Monica's death, I thought of the other case—Nancy Bilton was drowned in that mill stream, also at night. I was never satisfied that we got at the truth over that, and I had a feeling that Sister Monica knew more than she admitted. I know that feelings aren't any good as evidence, but I believe that in police work you develop a sense which helps you to sum up witnesses. You know when someone's holding out on you, even if you can't prove it."

The Divisional Inspector put in a word here. "I know what Peel means, sir. I think he's right. You can always tell the straightforward witness, who pours out all he knows with a mass of irrelevant detail, from the witness who's cagey and watching his step."

Peel threw him a grateful glance and continued: "I tried to sum the woman up. I knew she'd been in a position of trust for half a lifetime, and that she'd been in complete control at that home. I thought she'd gone a bit queer. Some women do as they grow old, especially if they've been undisputed bosses in a small world of their own. Because I wasn't satisfied about the Bilton case, I've been trying ever since to find out a bit more about conditions in this village. None of the village folk would talk—what they didn't know would fill a book. Now I've got a boy and girl of my own at our school here, and they've made friends with some of the children from Milham in the Moor, and I've listened to those kids chattering. According to them, Sister Monica was a know-all. There was nothing went on in the village she didn't get to know about, and the kids played a snooping game they called 'Sister M.' Now I reckon when a woman takes to spying on her neighbours there's likely to be trouble sooner or later. My own belief is that Sister Monica found out who'd got Nancy Bilton into trouble, although she denied knowing anything about it. It seems to me that the same person who shoved Nancy Bilton in the mill stream may have tried his luck again when he found Sister Monica somewhere near the bridge."

"You mean that Bilton was killed by the chap who'd got her into trouble," said the D.D.I., "and that he believed that Sister Monica knew what he'd done—or are you thinking she blackmailed him in a quiet way?"

Major Rootham put in a word of protest. "You're making out that Sister Monica was a thoroughly evil woman," he said. "I can't see that you've got any evidence at all to support the theory."

Peel got very red in the face, but he stuck to his guns. "I think she went queer in the head, sir. Religious mania is like any other mania, it makes people unaccountable for their actions. They think that whatever they do, it must be right. All this praying for hours, and going out at night to meditate in the dark, it's mania, nothing else. Then the fact that she had a sense of power added to it. She dominated everybody at Gramarye: the old nurse and the cook and the young maids, I reckon she almost hypnotised them. It's bad enough for anybody to get a sense of power like that. No one had ever stood up to her, they were all afraid of her."

"I'm willing to believe she dominated her household and got the village under her thumb because she knew too much," said Major Rootham, "but I'm not willing to believe she dominated Lady Ridding and the rest of the committee. They're not fools."

"No, sir," persisted Peel, "but I can see that Sister Monica was very useful to Lady Ridding. Her ladyship's always taken a pride in Gramarye—old family charity, unique in its way. And I know Lady Ridding's right when she says such charities are hard put to it to cover expenses these days. Sister Monica ran that place cheaper than anyone could believe. Nurse Barrow and the cook work for a fraction of the wages any other domestics get, and the young maids were delinquent juveniles in training. Lady Ridding's said to have a hard enough head when it comes to business, sir, meaning no disrespect."

Major Rootham looked troubled, as well he might. Lady Ridding's flair for business was becoming famous in the county. The D.D.I., who had no inordinate respect for county families, put in a word here.

"I can see Peel's point, sir. The Warden at Gramarye was a competent manager and a very economical one—there's no denying that. I've no doubt she soft-soaped Lady Ridding and the committee very cleverly, so the latter folks disregarded any signs of queer behaviour in the Warden and upheld the saint story. They're not going to change their tune now."

Major Rootham sat and cogitated. Then he said: "What

indisputable evidence have we got that there has been foul play?"

The D.D.I. answered before Peel had a chance.

"It's worth considering these facts, sir. Two women have been drowned at the same spot, both at night. They were both inmates of the same house. The first case resulted in a verdict of suicide. The question is, are we going to be satisfied with a verdict of accident in the second case? There's evidence that deceased had been suffering from attacks of giddiness: Peel has collected unanimous opinions about the probability of her having fallen over, knocked her head, and rolled or slipped into the stream. There's no evidence against that theory, but there's a possibility that deceased's private papers may have been stolen. It's up to you, sir."

"Yes. I see your point all right," said Rootham. "You feel that further investigation is called for. I agree. But it's not going to be easy. Country people can be very obstinate. Peel says the customary answer is, 'I don't know' or else 'I can't remember.' In other words, the village folk won't help. It's very odd, that."

"You've got to realise the sort of village Milham in the Moor is, sir," said Peel. "They've always been cut off, kept themselves to themselves. We say in Milham Prior, when we've got a fête or a dance of a collection, 'No use asking those folks out there on the moor to help,' and they say, 'Milham Prior's done nought for us. Us won't do nought for Milham Prior.' It's not actually a feud, it's a habit of mind, going back for centuries for all I know. They diddled me last time, over the Bilton case, because they were solid against outside interference." Peel mopped his face and then added stubbornly: "It's as though the moor's in their blood. Something hard, and something different from folks who're used to the give and take of town, and law and order that's part of their lives. It's as though they're trying to be a law unto themselves," he concluded.

3

"I'm disposed to put this business to the Yard, Grey," said Major Rootham later to the D.D.I., after Peel had left. "I see your point about the two deaths looking fishy. We can't leave it alone. But it looks like being one of those long jobs. You've got your hands pretty full already, and I don't think the chaps here have got time for this job: neither do I think they can get to the bottom of it."

"I agree with you there, sir, but all the same I think Peel's done pretty well. He jumped to it: he got all the routine evidence, timing, position of contacts and so forth. He examined the ground and he went over that house. In addition to all that, he thought out the possibilities involved and some of his ideas are worth following up. But I don't think he'll get any further. It's not his fault. It's the peculiarity of those two places. I thought he put it pretty well when he described that village as a law unto itself, but he's got a bias. They've put his back up, and that means he's put their back up."

Rootham nodded. "That's it. I think a newcomer would have a better chance: would see the thing more in focus. Of course I could take you and your chaps off that job you're on."

"I'd be sorry if you did that, sir. We've put a lot of work in with the excise officers and I think we've a chance of getting it cleared up. It's a sizeable racket and it involves a lot of local knowledge. This business here is concentrated into a limited environment, if you see what I mean. And I think there's this to it. The Milham in the Moor folk are holding out against the Milham Prior police. They've seen them before and they reckon they've sized them up. They may feel quite different when a Yard man tackles them. And that goes for all of them, the quality as well as the villagers."

Major Rootham's eyebrows shot up, but the Detective Inspector went on: "It seems to me, sir, that Lady Ridding must have known her Warden was getting a bit odd, to say the least of it. I've every sympathy with Peel when he gets hot under the collar about all this 'saintly' business. There's several people in that village who'd be none the worse for knowing what it feels like to be pinned down to hard facts by an expert investigator."

"You may be right," agreed Rootham, "and if that's so, well, someone from London might tackle the job with a more open mind, if you take me."

The D.D.I. grinned to himself as he went back to his car to get busy on the job he'd been working at for weeks.

"If they're to be bullied, let the Yard wallahs do the bullying. I bet they will, too, saints or no saints."

The Deputy Chief Constable sat and thought very deeply after he had parted with his officers. Rootham could not help being conservative by nature, in his general approach to a problem as well as in his politics. It was ingrained in him to trust and respect the 'right people,' and he felt uncomfortable about the D.D.I.'s comments on Lady Ridding, and still more uncomfortable when he remembered that phrase, "It's up to you, sir." Did Grey think he was going to shut down on an enquiry because its continuance would cause discomfort to the Riddings? But Rootham was honest enough to admit to himself that he would feel relieved if this case were to be handled by C.O., and not by the County men. It would have been very uncomfortable to have a sense of divided loyalties, a desire to save 'the right people' discomfort and a desire to back up his own men, no matter which way their enquiries led them. "Probably all a mare's nest, but there may be some mud slinging," he thought to himself.

The thing which nagged uncomfortably at the back of Rootham's mind was that he believed he had a faint glimmering of what might have been going on so far as the mystery of Sister Monica's finances were concerned. Lady Ridding had paid the Warden's salary, in cash. Officially that salary was £10 a month, all of which had been thriftily paid into the Building Society. Had Lady Ridding augmented the salary, unofficially? Rootham remembered hearing a woman friend of his wife's say: "You can always get a little extra from Etheldreda Ridding." Mrs. Rootham had promptly changed the subject. Cream, was it, or butter? pondered Rootham. Had the Warden of Gramarye tumbled to it? A trivial thing, but unpalatable. Of course, Major Rootham didn't really know anything about Lady Ridding's affairs: he'd only overheard a remark—and ignored it. He had not been Deputy C.C. at the time, and a man can't snoop on his wife's friends.

Major Rootham stretched out his hand for the phone. "I'll ask for a first rate man," he said to himself.

The upshot of Major Rootham's request to the Commissioner's Office was that Chief Inspector Macdonald was detailed to investigate the matter of Sister Monica's death.

CHAPTER VII

1

Macdonald enjoyed his drive down to Devonshire. He took Detective Inspector Reeves with him, and they left London at 5.30 a.m. on June 27th. At that hour, the London streets were almost deserted, and Macdonald drove south-westwards through Chelsea and Mortlake and then on through Staines before the inevitable lorries had set out in any great numbers. It was a glorious morning and Reeves sat in happy companionable silence as Macdonald's well serviced car slipped easily along the sunlit roads. They drove by Basingstoke and Andover, and then increased speed over the fine Wiltshire roads to Amesbury, with Salisbury Plain to their right, and the chalk downs beyond. Reeves gave a grunt of surprise when he first saw the stone circle of Stonehenge in the distance. It looked so small—like a model of the familiar reality.

"I've never seen it before," said Reeves.

"High time you did," said Macdonald.

He pulled the car up, and they walked towards the mighty

stones. Reeves stood and stared, and at last he asked a question: "Where did they get them from, originally?"

"The outer circle, the sarsen stones, from the Wiltshire downs: the inner ones, the blue stones, from Pembrokeshire."

"How the heck did they move them?"

"When you're tired of detecting events concerned with the unruly wills and affections of sinful men, you might find it refreshing to try to answer that 'How?'" said Macdonald. "The most probable answer is by floating them here, and to do that they would have had to excavate canals connecting up existing rivers."

"Some job."

"Yes. Some job. As a variation, you can think out the mechanics of moving them on rollers, invoking such assistance as the law of the lever might give, bearing in mind that there were no roads and that stone age Britain was pretty thickly covered with forest."

"Yes. Quite a nice problem," said Reeves. "Seems to me it'd be simpler to concentrate on Who killed Sister Monica? plus How and Why? But I'll keep your tip in mind. It'd make a nice change of thought some time when I'm browned off."

"And when I retire, I might write a monograph, for private circulation only, on the subject of stones," said Macdonald. "Stonehenge, the Dale Stones in Lunesdale, and the London Stone."

"Not forgetting the item from Scone," chuckled Reeves.

"I hadn't forgotten it, but let sleeping stones lie," replied Macdonald. "If you've stared enough, what about some coffee? We've made good time. 78 miles in two hours isn't bad going, remembering we started from Westminster."

They drove on through Taunton and reached Milham Prior in time for an early lunch at the George, Reeves studying the Victorian decor with lively amusement. After lunch they drove to Milham Prior police station to consult with Sergeant Peel and the Barnsford Inspector.

2

"There's something wrong there," said Peel, after he and Macdonald had discussed the report which had been sent to the Commissioner's Office. "I know it's no use guessing, and our deputy C.C. said, 'Leave it to the Yard,' so I've left it. But my opinion is that every single witness I interrogated could have told me more than they did. They just shut down, and that goes for the Manor House as well as the cottagers: old Dr. Brown, the Rev. Kingsley, the estate agent—Sanderson— they all know more than they admitted."

Macdonald looked at Peel's carefully typed lists. "I have a feeling that the fellows who were there when you first arrived on the scene ought to be able to give a bit more factual evidence than they have," he said. "If I've got things right, all those chaps were closely associated with that bit of the village nearest to the mill stream. There's Samuel Venner, who lives at the Mill House, Bob Doone, who's foreman at the saw mill close by, George Wilson, who's electrician in charge of the generating plant, and Jack Hedges, cowman at the farm close by the Mill House. Jim Rigg, who found the body, is second cowman at the Manor Farm, but he lives in a cottage by the bridge over the river. Am I right in saying that all of them would be likely to use that footbridge over the mill stream at any hour of the day or night?"

"Correct, sir," replied Peel. "Cowmen have to look to their beasts at calving, no matter what the hour may be. George Wilson's got to keep an eye on his storage batteries, and I know for a fact he often goes to inspect the plant late at night, especially when a lot of current's been used up at the Manor. Doone's often been known to work at the saw mill after dark. He does some trading of his own with the farmers, and he or his son will cut posts for the farmers, or saw logs for them when they've been felling their own timber. Young Doone's got a tractor outfit of his own and runs a saw from the engine in the evenings. But I'd give them all a clean bill so far as character is concerned. The only thing I'd say is that they're pretending to be stupider than they are."

"Well, it's with them I shall start," said Macdonald. "Now, tell me this. You say deceased used to be treasurer of this, that and the other. What reason is given for her being relieved of those activities?"

"'Her was tired out. Terrible tired Sister was,'" quoted Peel sardonically. "'Old Dr. Brown said Sister was wearing of herself out and us was properly ashamed to've put upon her so.' You sort that one out, Chief. It sounds easy but it isn't. Butter won't melt in their mouths."

"Well, I'll have a shot at melting it," said Macdonald, "and the sooner I get going the better."

"And good luck to you," said Peel. "Now where are you going to stay, sir?"

"At the Inn at Milham in the Moor. I think this is one of the cases when it is salutary for everybody concerned to know that the C.I.D. is very much on the spot, and that it will remain on the spot until something turns up. Reeves and I will adopt wearing-down tactics."

Reeves chuckled. "It does work, you know. They get to hate the sight of you, and somebody loses their temper eventually, and says something they wish they hadn't. Haunt them, that's the idea, day and night."

"Haunt them," echoed Peel appreciatively. "You've got something there. They're superstitious in their own way."

"Don't tell Reeves so. He's quite capable of borrowing a nurse's cloak and providing apparitions which aren't regulation," said Macdonald. "For myself, I'm out after chapter and verse, hoping somebody will slip up eventually."

The two C.I.D. men drove out towards the moor, both keenly aware of the fragrance blowing in at the open windows: new mown hay, flowering beans and clover, so that Reeves sniffed like a pointer. When they saw the church tower and roofs on the hill-top, Reeves said: "Quite a place. It's different from anything I've ever seen."

Macdonald said: "Hill-top villages are the exception rather than the rule in England. Perhaps an unusual site makes for unusual people."

"Uppish?" hazarded Reeves, his eyes fixed on the piled up roofs, one above the other on the steep hill side.

"No. Not uppish. Isolated maybe," said Macdonald. "Isolated communities tend to a communal defence mechanism. Sorry. That's hideous jargon."

"Is it? I shouldn't know," said Reeves, "but I get the idea. All for each and each for all and to hell with interlopers."

Macdonald drew up outside the Milham Arms and went in to find the landlord, whom he asked for two single rooms. Simon Barracombe shook his head. They weren't expecting visitors just now, he urged, washing his hands.

"In that case you had better take some of those A.A. and R.A.C. signs off your walls," said Macdonald. "I am an officer of the Criminal Investigation Department of Scotland Yard. I want two bedrooms. Can you accommodate me or not?"

Simon Barracombe had another look at the lean dark

fellow whose quiet voice did not sound very 'accommodating,' and decided not to be awkward.

"Very good, sir. We will do our best. I am sorry things aren't quite as I could wish, but we don't have many visitors at this time. I'll take your bags up, sir. Could you tell me how long it would be for?"

"I can't tell you," said Macdonald, "but I'll take the rooms for a week to start with. We are here on duty."

Some five minutes later, the two C.I.D. men strolled down the steep village street towards the Mill House, and Reeves said: "Order of the day: brass tacks and plain English."

"That's it," said Macdonald. "Consciously or unconsciously—my bet's on the former—this village has been developing what's called a 'mystique' by some people. It involves saintliness, other-worldliness, general vagueness over matters of fact and inattention to detail."

"Hocus-pocus. I looked that one up on your recommendation," said Reeves.

"You're a diligent chap. Well, the first thing to do is to clear the air, and let them see that we're not going to be fuddled by the village technique. This must be the Mill House. You can go and consider the footbridge."

"Right," said Reeves. "I will meditate on fits, dizziness and giddiness, and work out the chances of hitting the back of my own head on the hand rail if I go at the knees. She was five foot eleven, wasn't she? You might co-operate later."

3

"Mrs. Venner? I am an officer of the Criminal Investigation Department of Scotland Yard, and I am here to investigate the death of Miss Monica Torrington. There are some questions I want to ask you, so may I come in?"

White-haired Mrs. Venner looked as startled as if a squib had been let off under her nose: she looked up at the tall, lean officer, realised that his voice, though deliberate, was courteous, and she tried to hedge.

"Well, I've told all I do know to sergeant, and that wasn't much. The fact is I don't know anything to help."

"I want to make it clear that I am starting this enquiry afresh," said Macdonald, "right from the beginning. It's my duty to get answers to my own questions, not to rely on previous answers. You can refuse to answer if you wish, but that will only mean a longer examination for you in court."

"Oh, I don't mean I'm refusing to answer, only that I've nought to tell," she replied, "but come in, and I'll do my best."

She was a stout, middle-aged, kindly-looking woman, the type of countrywoman Macdonald liked at sight, and she led him into a tidy parlour, one of those little-used rooms which country housewives are proud of. Macdonald started on an interrogation which he knew he would have to repeat again and again.

"Did you know Miss Torrington personally, Mrs. Venner?"

"Why, yes, of course. We all knew her. Sister, she came and nursed me when I had the pneumonia. During the war, 'twas. A wonderful nurse was Sister."

"You mean she was very good to you and you were grateful to her. You felt you could trust her." Macdonald was very much aware of the glance Mrs. Venner shot at him, but she replied:

"Her was a wonderful nurse, was Sister. Never tired of helping others."

"When did you last speak to her?"

"Well, I couldn't rightly say."

"Was it shortly before she died—a day or so? Or more like weeks?"

"Well, a few weeks maybe. 'Tis a steep hill up to village and Sister wasn't so young as she was. No more am I. I don't go up top more'n I need."

"It is a steep hill—I've seen that for myself," said Macdonald, "and it must be just as steep going up by the park."

"'Iss. 'Tis—and rougher going."

"But Miss Torrington used to come down that hill at night sometimes, didn't she?"

"So they say."

"Did you never see her by the mill stream or in the park at night?"

"Well, yes. I did see her the once. And surprised I was to see her."

"When was it that you saw her?"

"Quite a while back that was. I can't rightly say when."

"Well, let's try to get the time fixed. You're a country woman, Mrs. Venner. The seasons mean much more to countryfolk than to townsfolk. Are you going to tell me that you can't remember if it was spring, summer, autumn or winter when you saw Miss Torrington in the park at night?"

Mrs. Venner flushed uncomfortably, paused for a long time, and then said: "'Twas springtime."

"Not this year, because you said 'quite a while back,'" persisted Macdonald.

"Well, then, 'twas last year," she said. "I went out late, after twelve 'twas, because my young dog had gone straying, and I was worried. The farmers don't like dogs straying."

"Especially when there are lambs in the fields," said Macdonald. "You lamb early in Devon, so it would have been early in the spring."

"Yes. 'Twas—and what difference do that make?"

"The difference it makes is that Nancy Bilton was drowned in the mill-race a year ago this April, Mrs. Venner. You had seen Miss Torrington wandering in the park at night early in the spring—before April, that is—but no mention was made of that fact at the inquest on Nancy Bilton."

"No one asked me, and 'twasn't my business. Sister Monica was asked questions, same as all of us. It was for her to tell on what she did herself."

"It's the business of every honest man and woman to tell everything they know in a police enquiry. Did Miss Torrington know you saw her?"

"I don't know. I never spoke to her about it. And we always called her Sister Monica. I get moithered with your Miss Torrington. I can't think of her that way."

"I think it'd be much better if you did," said Macdonald crisply. "Then you might think straight about her. This 'Sister Monica' you talk about is a being who is all wrapped up in make-believe. You say she was 'wonderful,' and you've gone on saying it until you've forgotten that she was a real person. You're trying to make out to yourself and me that she was a cross between a plaster figure and Florence Nightingale."

"Well, I never did…" expostulated the stout dame. "That's no way to speak of the dead."

"I'm not talking about the dead. I'm trying to get an idea of what Miss Torrington was like when she was alive, and you've already told me quite a bit about her, Mrs. Venner."

"I told you her was a wonderful nurse."

"Yes. She nursed you when you were ill. We get used to summing people up in my job, Mrs. Venner. It's my belief that you are a kindly person, as well as a truthful one, and I don't think you'd be ungrateful. Yet when I ask you what was the last time you spoke to Miss Torrington you can't remember. It must have been quite a long time ago. When you saw her out in the park after midnight, you didn't speak to her. That seems very odd to me. You'd reason to be grateful to her: you must have thought it strange to see her out like that. In the ordinary way, wouldn't you speak to a neighbour if you saw her out after midnight, and ask if anything was amiss?"

"I don't know what you're getting at."

"I think you do. I'm trying to find out what made you change in your attitude to Miss Torrington. You say she was 'wonderful,' but you seem to have avoided her for some time past. Why did you avoid her?"

Mrs. Venner sat very still, her rubicund face troubled. At last she said: "I'm not saying I avoided her. It just happened like that. And what 'tis to do with police I just can't see."

"Why do you think I have been sent here from London, Mrs. Venner?" asked Macdonald. "We have plenty of police work there, you know."

"I can't see for why," she said obstinately. "Sister, her came over dizzy and her fell in the mill-race. 'Twas plain accident."

"The only thing that's plain is that two people were drowned at that spot," said Macdonald. "The verdict on one was suicide: you say the second was an accident. I'm here to try to find out if it *was* an accident, and to do that I've got to find out all that I can about Miss Torrington. One of the things I want to know is why you didn't speak to her that night you saw her in the park after midnight. Was it because you'd seen her there before?"

"No. I'd heard tell her wandered…" Mrs. Venner broke off. She was quite unused to protracted arguments, and her distress showed in her face. Sergeant Peel had asked questions, but he hadn't picked her answers to pieces as this London detective was doing.

"Do you know where she went?" persisted Macdonald. "Did she cross the footbridge or go into the village street?"

"I don't know."

"You sound very sure about that," replied Macdonald, "but you haven't answered my question. Why was it you didn't speak to her?"

"Well, if you must know, her had gone queer. She'd changed like. Doctor said she found work too much for her and her wasn't well. When a woman of Sister's age gets overdone and won't give up, her do get snappy and tiresome like. I knew her was queer."

She broke off as she heard a footstep in the passage outside, and she said quickly: "That'll be Venner, wanting his tea." The door opened and a big grizzle-haired man stood in the doorway, looking at Macdonald as Mrs. Venner said hastily, "'Tis a detective from London, that C.I.D. they're always telling of, and I'm fair moithered with all the questions he do keep asking."

Macdonald stood up. "My name's Macdonald, Mr. Venner. Chief Inspector C.I.D. There's no need for me to tell you why I'm here."

"That there isn't," said Venner, "but we've told all we do know to sergeant, and a-worrying of us isn't going to make us tell no more."

"Well, I'm going to tell you just what I've learnt since I've been here," said Macdonald, speaking easily and deliberately. "The first thing is that though you knew more than a year ago that Miss Torrington walked about in the park after midnight, that fact wasn't mentioned at the inquest on Nancy Bilton, though it certainly ought to have been. Second, when Mrs.

Venner saw Miss Torrington out in the park late one night, Mrs. Venner did not speak to her, as you'd have expected a good neighbour to have done. Finally, Mrs. Venner says that Miss Torrington had changed: she had become queer."

"Well, so she was," agreed Venner. "Her'd got awkward like."

"Very well," said Macdonald. "She was queer. And part of her queerness was wandering late at night. You knew she was in charge of small children. Did either of you report to the committee of the children's home or to the doctor, that the Warden had 'gone queer'—was behaving in an abnormal manner?"

Venner answered that one. "Folks in village don't go reporting things," he said. "We live and let live. Life wouldn't be worth living if us got telling on one another."

"Live and let live. In this case it's been die and let die, hasn't it?" said Macdonald.

4

It was some time later that Macdonald came out of the Venners' house, and turned down the path that led to the footbridge over the mill stream, less than fifty yards away from the Venners' windows. Reeves was standing on the bridge, looking down into the swirling water. Macdonald went and joined him there and Reeves said promptly:

"I've no use for this idea that deceased hit the back of her head on that hand rail. She was too tall and the hand rail's too low." Macdonald nodded and Reeves went on:

"When a person falls in a faint, in my experience they more often fall forward than backwards, but if they fall backwards their head goes back first, of its own weight. If she fell backwards, the rail would have caught her somewhere in the small of her back. She might have toppled backwards into the water, but she wouldn't have hit her head."

"But she might have slumped down like a sack, weak at the knees," said Macdonald.

"All right: that means she slipped into a kneeling position—you've got to fold up somewhere. The knees go forward, the feet back. In order for her to have hit her head on the hand rail she must have been facing the water, either up or down stream. If she'd gone at the knees, wouldn't she have grabbed at the hand rail?—it'd have been almost a reflex—you grab at anything when you're dizzy. In which case her weight would have gone forward, not back. Finally, assuming she slumped down on her knees and toppled backwards, her head still wouldn't have hit the hand rail because she was too long in the back. You try it. She was only a couple of inches shorter than you."

"I'm not sure that's a valid argument, because a body slumps at the waist as well as at the knees," said Macdonald, "but I think you've got one point. If she went on her knees first, even though she did hit her head somehow on the hand rail she wouldn't have hit it hard enough to make the bruise described. There wouldn't have been enough velocity. It'd have been a flop, not a crash."

"The only other way she could have bruised the back of her head was if she fell flat on her back while walking over the bridge," added Reeves. "In which case I don't see how she rolled into the river without assistance. The bridge isn't that narrow, and it's perfectly steady."

"Yes. I agree with you there."

"We might offer a prize to any near-six-footer who succeeds in banging his-her head on the hand rail when they go at the knees on this bridge," said Reeves. "Seeing's believing. How much could the folks in the Mill House hear of what goes on out here, Chief?"

"They couldn't hear any ordinary coming and going, nor voices speaking conversationally. The sound of the water prevents it. They could have heard a scream, I imagine. Also it's worth while remembering that farmers develop an uncannily quick ear for hearing any unusual sound at night. It's second nature to them to listen for any disturbance among their stock—and that house on the other side of the footpath by the Venners' is a farmhouse."

"I don't believe anybody batted the woman over the head while she was on this bridge, Chief. It's too close to the houses and the road."

"Yes, and it's an awkward spot to swing a stick or a cosh," said Macdonald. "Added to which, footsteps are much more audible on a plank bridge than on solid ground. But nobody would have wanted to lift deceased's body if they could help it. She was too heavy."

Macdonald walked across the bridge and stood on the far bank facing the stream: behind him was a hedge of thorn and dogrose, elder, blackthorn and bramble: to his left the path led on to the saw mill, to his right the hedge was broken by the path leading up through the park. There was a five-barred gate across the path, latched but not padlocked.

"I think it must have happened here," he said. Reeves, who had followed him, nodded.

"I agree, but where was she going? I'd got it into my head she'd have been walking across the bridge, towards the street, but she must have turned off here, and gone left a bit, by the stream."

"The point we want to decide is 'what was she doing here?'" said Macdonald.

Reeves looked at him enquiringly: "We're cutting out all the stuff about 'Sister was queer like, awful tired Sister was and her turned dizzy, poor soul'?"

Macdonald nodded. "I think so. I shall know better when I've seen her account books and the rest. Nervous disorder nearly always shows in a person's handwriting and arrangement of the page, as well as in precision or lack of it: mistakes, erasures and the like. If I find, as I expect to find, that her recent book-keeping has the same precision and legibility as that of past years, I shall assume that she was in normal control of her faculties."

"All right," said Reeves. "My guess would be that she came here to meet somebody, or else to spy on somebody. She may have been one of those dames who get a thing about courting couples."

"Quite possibly, but I favour the former rather than the latter. You see, the village knew she wandered at night, and villagers share their information among themselves. Courting couples would have avoided this spot."

"Yes. There's that," agreed Reeves, "but if she was meeting somebody, why the heck come right down here? There must be plenty of meeting places in the park where nobody would have been likely to see her at all, and it's the devil of a steep path, isn't it?"

"I imagine so. Let's walk up through the park," said Macdonald.

"And call on the quality," said Reeves, a grin flashing across his keen dark face.

"Not yet. I'm going to leave them till last," said Macdonald.

"That'll annoy them no end. Gentry expect to be priority," said Reeves. "Didn't you sense that Peel believed the gentry was on in this act?"

"I think he felt that they'd been reinforcing the village technique," said Macdonald, as they went through the five-barred gate and turned up the path which had been cut in the steep hill-side. To their right the ground dropped almost sheer to the river: to their left it rose to the ridge where the village street ran.

"It'd be the hell of a path on a dark night," said Reeves thoughtfully.

CHAPTER VIII

1

When the two C.I.D. men reached the little plateau at the top of the hill, Reeves said: "That's quite a climb, Chief."

Macdonald nodded, his eyes on the Manor House and the church tower beyond. "As you say—and that's a lovely house. The smaller one over there would be the Dower House. I think I'll go and talk to Dr. Ferens, if he's at home. According to Peel, he's the one person in the place who talks plain commonsense."

"Right. If it's all the same to you I'll go and buy stamps at the post office and shoe laces at the general store and maybe some seeds for my garden."

"It's too late in the year to sow seeds. They ought to have been in two months ago."

"They're for next year," said Reeves. "What can I sow for next year?"

"Try wallflowers. Are you playing at being the Royal Navy?"

Reeves hitched up his dark eyebrows. "R.N.? Oh, I see. Showing the flag. Those were the days."

He grinned as he turned left, along a path which led by the walled garden to the village street, and Macdonald opened a handsome gate, strolled across a wide lawn and entered the garden of the Dower House by the gate in the yew hedge. A slim sunburnt girl, bare legged, bare armed, dark headed, clad in a cotton frock whose pattern of cerise and viridian put Macdonald in mind of Gauguin, was cutting Mrs. Sinkins pinks. When he said "Good-afternoon," she replied:

"Do you know what to do with Mrs. Sinkins after she's stopped flowering? She's threatening to monopolise the border."

"Cut her back, hard," said Macdonald firmly. She faced him, holding an armful of snowy flowers whose fragrance was intoxicating.

"Speaking as one having authority?" she enquired, her dark eyes bright and mirthful.

"No. As the scribes," replied Macdonald promptly, "but if you don't cut them back they will certainly monopolise the border. I apologise if I've come in the wrong way; is Dr. Ferens at home?"

"Yes. This village is unreasonably healthy. He's in his surgery, in the old coach house, writing up hay fever. I'll take you there. Chief Inspector Macdonald, I presume?"

"Correct. Is it Mrs. Ferens?"

"It is. As you're probably aware, the very bees are buzzing C.I.D. It'll do them a power of good, you know."

"The bees?"

"No. The village. They've been making a cult of latter-day saints. Are you used to villages?"

"I've known a few, but I've never been a villager. I know enough not to generalise...well, not to over-generalise."

"You're a Scot, aren't you? I think you'll have your fun. This is the surgery, though you might not think it." She opened a door without ceremony and called: "Raymond. Here's Scotland Yard. I'll leave you to it."

She withdrew and Macdonald crossed a small waiting-room to an open door as a voice called, "Come right in."

Macdonald went in and saw a leanish, pleasant-faced fellow sitting at a desk covered in sheets of manuscript.

"Good day," said Ferens. "Do you ever have hay fever?"

"No. Never," said Macdonald firmly, "so if you want a guinea-pig you'll have to buy one."

"They're no good for this. Still. Sit down. What's your trouble?"

"Miss Monica Torrington, deceased."

"Congratulations. Do you know you're the first person who's ever used the woman's proper name to me? 'Sister's this and that' they say. 'Sister Monica'...A compound redolent of nunnery and hospital ward. It's hypnotic. I was hoping that Peel would discover her real name was Maggie...or Maudie."

"It wasn't," said Macdonald. "Her name was Monica Emily. Born 1888 in Kilburn, London, N.W.6. Daughter of a green-grocer, one Albert Torrington, a bandsman in the Salvation Army. A very good chap, I understand. We've found some of his one-time neighbours. He had five daughters: Monica, Ursula, Teresa, Dorcas, and Lois."

"Well, well. You've been very diligent."

"We've got the chaps to do the looking up," said Macdonald. "That sort of thing's easy. Now—"

"Yes. I know. But just tell me this. Did Albert, Ursula, Teresa, Dorcas, or Lois ever leave Monica a nice little packet?"

"No. Not by testamentary disposition. Besides, they're not all dead: or at any rate Somerset House has no record of the deaths of Dorcas or Lois and it's believed they all remained single."

"Did they? Singleness evidently ran in the family. Before you start the Torquemada effect on me, give me some further gen on the woman's background. I'm enormously interested."

"Born in Kilburn in 1888—if that conveys anything to you," said Macdonald. "Went to the National elementary school, called Board School in those days. Left at the age of eleven and became a nursemaid in 'good service.' Which meant wages of £10 a year. We've got all this from an octogenarian charlady who is still going strong and earning good money. In 1914 Monica Emily became a V.A.D. She must have been an educable girl, and she'd done well as a children's 'Nanny.' In 1917 she was appointed as assistant at an orphanage in Watford. In 1921 she was appointed assistant Warden of Gramarye. She was then thirty-three—"

"And passing rich on £48 a year," murmured Ferens. "Thanks very much for telling me. It's very enlightening: did you hear anything about her mother?"

"The mother, according to our octogenarian, was very respectable, very thrifty, a holy terror to live with, and believed that sparing the rod spoilt the child. She belonged to one of those obscure religious sects, probably the Peculiar People." He broke off and then added: "I know it's a perfect text-book case: jam to any psychiatrist who dabbles in writing, but I'd like to say this. You've noticed for yourself that the 'Sister Monica' business almost hypnotised the people in this village. It's been going on for a long time. You, as a newcomer, contrived to see it objectively, so perhaps you will understand me when I say that not only do I refuse to be hypnotised by the Sister Monica stuff, I also refuse to be obsessed by the psychiatrist's approach. A woman named Monica Emily Torrington was drowned in the mill stream here, and I'm not going to get that woman muddled up with halos or lamps or complexes or inhibitions or defence mechanisms, or any of the other jargon which is two-a-penny to-day."

"Duly noted," said Ferens, "but I'd like to ask one question. If you don't believe a person's background affects their mentality in riper years, why have you bothered to collect all that information about her childhood and upbringing?"

"I didn't say there was no effect. What I do want to keep clear in my mind is that her death occurred here and she'd been living here for thirty years. This is a local problem. I don't go back to Kilburn to discover why the woman was found drowned at Milham in the Moor."

"I got you," said Ferens. "You're doing what the bomber pilots did, weaving to avoid the flak till you get a pointer on the target."

"Very neatly put. Now I know that you have only been here three months, but I should be very glad if you would give me your own opinion of Miss Torrington, as far as you formed an opinion."

"Oh, I formed an opinion all right. I disliked her at sight. It was the religious pose which got my goat." He hesitated, pulled out a packet of cigarettes and pushed it across to Macdonald. "Stop me if I get too verbose. Medical men see a lot of nurses. I respect nurses: they work damned hard and up till now haven't had much of a deal. But unfortunately there has been in times past a tendency for a nurse's training to develop, in some of them, the quality of tyrants: it made them dominate their patients, their probationers, their patients' relatives—everybody they have power over. And when that realisation of power is reinforced by a belief they're chosen vessels in the religious sense, I'm very allergic to it. My first impression of Miss Torrington was that she had the dominating power of the worst type of old-fashioned hospital matron, plus the religious fanaticism which makes the most hypocritical sort of egoist."

"Were you satisfied for her to be Warden of that home?"

Raymond Ferens thumped the desk with his fists. "It wasn't my business. Do get that clear. If I'd had any evidence at all that the children were ill-treated, I'd have raised Cain about it. I hadn't any such evidence. Neither had anybody else. My dislike of the woman was a personal idiosyncrasy. I disliked her get-up, her mealy-mouthed humility, her fanatic's eye and her physical presence. She was a grenadier of a woman, with enormous hands and feet. I expect the psychiatrists would tell you that I resented the fact that she was much bigger than I am myself and looked down at me—down her nose at me, too."

"Do you think that she resented you?—the fact that you were a newcomer, and that you didn't regard her with the awe that she thought was her due?"

"She had no reason to. I made it quite clear from the outset that I took no interest in Gramarye and that I had no intention of interfering. But dislike is generally mutual. The fact that I disliked her probably awoke reciprocal tendencies. But I don't quite see where this is getting you. I didn't bat her over the head, you know."

"I wasn't supposing that you did," said Macdonald, "but I was wondering if the fact of your arrival here had any indirect effect on her behaviour?"

"How so?"

"She would have known that your patients would probably confide in you. Sergeant Peel tells me that you are well thought of in the village and she would have known that. Did it occur to her that you might eventually learn something that would make her own position here untenable, and that she was making a last bid for power and pushed somebody too far?"

"Well...might be," said Ferens. "The whole situation was pretty complicated, as I saw it. Miss Torrington was strongly upheld by all the authorities here, and it would have taken something pretty drastic to discredit her."

"She may have been strongly upheld by the authorities, but it's my belief that someone did bat her over the head," said Macdonald, "and it must have been something 'pretty drastic' that made them do it."

Ferens grinned. "Oh, quite. You're asking me if I've any ideas on who was irritated enough to do the batting. I don't like repeating gossip. Some of the old Biddies in this village pour out floods of tripe, but most of it isn't true: however, there are a few side-lights on Sister M.'s mentality which I might repeat. Her long suit was suggesting a fact by denying it. For instance, there's John Sanderson, the estate agent, a very decent kindly bloke. Sister M. had her knife into him. She went round saying she was sure it wasn't true that it was Sanderson who got Nancy Bilton into trouble. That was her method; the result was that some people went round saying that it *was* Sanderson who got Nancy Bilton into trouble. Sanderson ignored it. It's not everybody who would have done so."

"Agreed. Why did Miss Torrington get her knife into Sanderson?"

"You'd better ask him. He's a very straightforward chap. He came fresh to this place after being in the Army and a refresher course at an Ag. Col. and he saw the woman as I did. He had to superintend post-war redecoration at Gramarye, so he saw it from the inside. He didn't like what he saw—but he never suggested the children were ill-treated. However—you go and see him."

"I will. Is he married, by the way?"

"No. But don't go getting ideas into your head on that account."

"I don't get ideas of that variety into my head," said Macdonald. "I'm allergic to them. Also I'm a bachelor myself."

"Are you, by Jove. Seems a pity... Incidentally, here's another Torrington-ism. Sister was quite sure there was nothing wrong when Anne—that's my wife—asked Sanderson to this house to have a drink when I was out. I'm justified in repeating that one, because it reflects on Sanderson and me fifty-fifty, but I think you'd better find another source for others of the same kind in case you think I'm an interested party."

"Right. Now for a few questions. You said Miss Torrington was strongly upheld by authority here. Did she ever use her negative technique against what you call 'authority'?"

"No. Never. She was no sort of fool." Ferens paused a moment and then went on: "The only one of the gentry who was included was old Miss Braithwaite, who used to be on the committee at Gramarye. She put down a motion that Sister Monica be retired at the age of sixty, and a younger Warden be appointed. After that, a story seeped round the village that the girl child whom Miss Braithwaite adopted in 1920 was *not* Miss Braithwaite's own infant. Sorry if that sounds involved, but that's how it went."

"I see. You say Miss Braithwaite used to be on the committee. Did she resign?"

"Yes. I imagine she was asked to resign. Lady Ridding and the vicar and the M.O. all had full confidence in the Warden and did not want to lose her."

Macdonald sat in silence for a moment and his next question was unexpected. "Who was it who did get Nancy Bilton into trouble?"

Ferens' eyebrows shot up. "I wasn't here at the time," he said. "I never saw Nancy Bilton."

"I know you didn't, but from what you've told me it's plain enough that one of your patients told you all the current 'Torrington-isms,' to quote your word. I know the way news seeps around a village like this one, and I know how determined villagers are not to share their news with outsiders, but a doctor very soon ceases to be an outsider. In the nature of things confidences come his way, as they've certainly come yours."

"To a certain extent, yes," replied Ferens guardedly.

Macdonald chuckled: "Meaning an uncertain extent. I argue this way. It's obvious you were interested in the Torrington situation. So should I have been. It had a fantastic quality, because the woman herself was fantastic. The most dramatic thing that happened in this village for years was Nancy Bilton's death—Milham in the Moor has an unusually clean sheet in such matters as suicide and sudden deaths—. Nancy Bilton was a maid at Gramarye, under Miss Torrington. Can you honestly say that you never asked your gossip-patient who was the seducer of Nancy Bilton, Dr. Ferens?"

"Well, there you've got me," said Ferens resignedly. "I did ask."

"I was sure you would have. I should have myself in the same circumstances."

"You've done a perfectly logical piece of argument," said Ferens, "but it's not going to help you much. My gossip-patient, as you call her, died a fortnight ago. She was aged seventy-nine and she died of cancer. I saw her every day for the last few weeks of her life, and the one thing she enjoyed was a nice gossip. But I don't know how truthful she was, let alone accurate. She told me some pretty weird stories, some of which were certainly untrue." He broke off, and then added: "You can't check up on any of this. It's not evidence, only hearsay."

"I know that. I'm not asking you for evidence to enter in court. I'm asking you which way the wind blew, to help me to shape a case."

"It's not going to help you, because the chap's dead. He was a National Service man, and he was killed in a plane crash. I haven't tried to get any corroborative evidence of this, but I think it's probably true," Ferens added. "If the chap responsible for her condition had been in the village or locality at the time of the girl's death, I think his identity would have been admitted, or at any rate there'd have been such a lot of gossip, it'd have got round. But since the chap was overseas and couldn't have had any hand in the girl's death, no one would name him. According to my old Biddy, the argument went, 'He couldn't have killed the girl. Naming him would only make more trouble for those who're alive'. "

"Yes. I follow that," said Macdonald, "but there's another point. If the chap's identity was known in the village, how was it that Miss Torrington didn't get wind of it? I gathered she was one of those females who pries out secrets."

"She certainly was. Thinking it out, it's my belief that Miss Monica Emily Torrington did know, but thought it more profitable to keep her information to herself. I may be quite wrong there, but that's my guess. And when the chap was killed, about six months after Nancy Bilton's death, that was that."

"Was it?—or did she try to make trouble with his family?"

"How could she? It was all over and done with. Country folk don't make heavy weather of such little slips, you know. The lad marries the lass if he's let her in, and nobody thinks any the worse of either of them. The infant is born in wedlock and the time which elapses between the wedding day and the lying-in is nobody's business. In any case, there was no family for Monica Emily to make trouble with. Only a widowed mother who lives on her widow's pension." He turned and looked at Macdonald, his eyebrows tilted up. "I suppose you won't give me any peace until you've got the name, but don't go worrying the poor old girl. She's Mrs. Bovey—Mrs. Susan Bovey. She lives in one of those picturesque hovels across the bridge. The boy's name was Stephen. He had an older brother who was killed in Burma in 1945 and Mrs. Bovey's left all by herself. If you're seen on her doorstep the whole village will start buzzing, and I think she's had trouble enough. Let the dead bury their dead is sound counsel."

"Not in criminal investigation," said Macdonald dryly, "though I agree with you that no detective has any right to cause avoidable distress. You're probably aware that Sergeant Peel thinks the two deaths are connected—Nancy Bilton's and Miss Torrington's."

"What evidence has he? That's only Peel's little idea, and it's the sort of idea which leaps to the mind all too easily."

"Peel's no fool, you know," said Macdonald reflectively, "and his little idea has some foundation in the accumulated experience of police work. A murderer who has pulled one job off successfully has been known to repeat himself."

Dr. Ferens moved restlessly: a movement of discomfort which did not escape Macdonald's notice.

"Peel's got an idea that there's what he calls a killer in the village," said Ferens. "I don't believe it."

"But Monica Emily Torrington was murdered," said Macdonald quietly. "At least, that's what Reeves and I believe. Perhaps you'd like to enter for Reeves's competition and demonstrate how to knock yourself silly by hitting your head on the hand rail of that bridge when you come over dizzy. Do you really believe a woman the height of deceased could have done it?"

"No. I suppose I don't. But neither am I prepared to say it's impossible," replied Ferens. "Casualties do some funny things. Incidentally, I haven't heard the result of the autopsy. Am I allowed to ask if they found any cerebral abnormality to account for her famous dizziness?"

"No. They found something much more unexpected. This is in confidence, of course. There were traces of alcohol. Deceased must have lowered some potent tots some few hours before her death."

Ferens lowered his fist with a bang on the table. "But, good God, that's ludicrous. The woman was a rabid teetotaller. It's unthinkable..."

"Possibly, but it happens to be true," said Macdonald placidly, "and the fact may account for the well-attested dizziness suffered by deceased."

"Well, that's the last thing I ever dreamt of," said Ferens, "though I suppose the same thing's been known to happen before. Elderly women of irreproachable character sometimes take to drink quite inexplicably." He broke off and sat in deep thought, his chin in his hands, and Macdonald did not interrupt him. At length Ferens looked up with a start: "Sorry. I was thinking. The whole thing's altered by that piece of evidence, isn't it?"

"Is it?"

"Well, damn all, if the woman was drunk it accounts for

everything. She may have had a fall some time before she toppled into the stream."

"I didn't say she was drunk. I said they found traces of alcohol," said Macdonald. "She hadn't taken anything for some time before she died. One of the things I want to know is where she got the stuff from, or who gave it to her, likewise where she kept it. But that all comes under the heading of routine—domestic enquiries. One routine question for you, doctor. You were out at a case on the night Miss Torrington was drowned?"

"Yes. I didn't get in until about two in the morning. I was out at a maternity case on the moor. I drove back up the vil- lage street, past the Mill House. Not a soul about, not a light showing anywhere, and a midsummer night to dream of, by gad. I don't think it got really dark all night, and the village street was white under the moon. You could see as clearly as in daylight." He paused, and then added: "I did think of park- ing my car by the smithy, way down the hill, and walking up through the park, just because it was such a gorgeous night. If I'd done so, I might have been more useful to you."

"Who knows?" said Macdonald meditatively. "Well, I've kept you away from your hay fever for long enough. In con- clusion, is there anything you'd care to add, or opinion you'd like to express?"

"Nothing of any use to you," said Ferens. "In my own mind I think it's probable that the Torrington woman did shove Nancy Bilton into the mill stream. That is to say, deceased was unbalanced. If she'd taken to drinking that in itself shows she was abnormal; it was such a startling departure from the hab- its of a lifetime, and I'm the more disposed to believe that she got herself drowned without assistance from anybody else."

2

When Macdonald left the Dower House, he found Reeves looking out for him in the little square on the hill-top.

"Had a successful shopping expedition?" he enquired.

"Very," said Reeves. "I've sent my missis some Devonshire cream. Got it at the Manor House Creamery. Very high hat. D'you know what it costs? Ten bob a pound including postage—and the tin. I liked that bit. A very nice specimen in the way of land girls there. I said I'd go in again to-morrow. You can pay for the next lot. Send some to the old man. How was trade with you?"

"So-so. The things which weren't said were more enlightening than those uttered—as usual. Now I'm going to see the bailiff, Sanderson. Would you like to come too?"

"Not unless you want me. I'd like to prospect in the park. Learn that path off by heart and find just what you can see and what you can't see. Shall we be doing the Gramarye place later?"

"Yes. In an hour's time. The children have been packed off, but the nurse and the cook are still there."

"O.K. I'll be there. I have a feeling the things *they* haven't said are more interesting than those they have. Exert a little leverage."

"First find the lever. 'Give me a lever and a place to stand on and I will move the world'. "

"Who said that?" demanded Reeves.

"The same bloke who said 'Eureka,'" replied Macdonald.

Reeves knew that one. "Have you?" he enquired.

"No, but I've got the glimmering of an idea," said Macdonald.

CHAPTER IX

1

John Sanderson lived in a beautiful little stone house not far from the park gates at the top of the hill. It was an early Georgian house with a porch whose classic gable was upheld by slender Ionic columns, elegantly fluted, and there were Ionic pilasters on the house front.

Sanderson himself opened the door: he was a big fellow, Macdonald noted, squarely built, with a square face whose low forehead was lined as though he were given to worrying. He looked a countryman, not a townsman, though he spoke without any accent whereby you could place him.

"Yes. Come along in. Chief Inspector Macdonald, isn't it? I'm having tea. Will you join me?"

"Thanks. I'd be glad of a cup," rejoined Macdonald, and while Sanderson fetched another cup and plate, the C.I.D. man took in the small dining-room. Good old furniture of the right period, pleasant curtains, some good etchings and pewter tankards and plates. "I envy you your house, Mr. Sanderson."

"You're not the only one. It's a good house and I like houses of this period. It happens to have been the bailiff's house ever since it was built. Sugar?"

"No thanks. Part of my job consists of taking an interest in other people's. I should think yours is a very satisfying job."

"Yes. It is. I'm interested in buildings and in the land. I couldn't ask for a better job than I've got here. Which brings us on to your job. The late Warden of Gramarye would have got me sacked if she could. You might as well know it first as last."

"Why did she want to get rid of you?"

Sanderson laughed a little. "It was mutual. I knew she was a damned hypocritical humbug and not fit to be in charge of either young children or young maidservants."

"Any evidence to support the statement?"

"Yes. I'm responsible for the fabric of Gramarye. It's an ancient house and needs constant attention, so I go there quite often. She didn't beat the children, but she locked them up when they were tiresome: sometimes in a small room, sometimes in a dark cupboard. In my opinion that's no way to treat small children. I reported it. She denied it. So there you were. I was told to mind my own business. Sister Monica got her own back by reflections on my character."

"I've heard a bit about Miss Torrington's methods," said Macdonald. "Now you've probably heard that Sergeant Peel has a theory that the two cases of drowning in the mill stream may be connected. I have an open mind on the subject, but I want to get any information I can about Nancy Bilton. Did you ever speak to the girl?"

"Oh, yes." Sanderson answered quite easily. "I was supervising a job on the roof of Gramarye and I was in and out there pretty frequently a month or so before Nancy Bilton's death. Neither she, nor the other maids, were supposed to speak to me: they were under orders not to, but girls like Nancy Bilton don't obey orders of that kind. She made opportunities to get in our way. She was a bad lot, you know, but I think her tendency to throw herself at any man's head was aggravated, not lessened, by the atmosphere at Gramarye. Her line with me was to appeal for help to get out of the place."

"I'm surprised she didn't run away," said Macdonald.

"She tried to more than once, but this isn't an easy place to run away from. She had no money: her wages were being saved for her by the Warden. If she'd got on a bus she'd have been seen and reported. It's a ten mile walk to Milham Prior, and Nancy Bilton was no pedestrian and she hadn't much stamina. She tried it once, at night. She walked seven miles before blistered feet made her sit down by the roadside to cry, poor little wretch. She'd been missed by that time, and the Warden got old Dr. Brown to get his car out and go after her. He brought her back. After that, they locked her into her room at night and put another girl to sleep with her. I was surprised myself that she managed to get out of that window. It took some doing."

"What was your own opinion on the matter? Did you think she drowned herself?"

Sanderson waited a long time before he replied; then he said slowly: "I don't know. I simply don't know. I accepted the verdict at the time. I knew the girl was miserable and I think she probably dreaded being kept at Gramarye until it was time to send her on to some other home for the birth of her child. She might have killed herself in a fit of depression. But thinking the matter over since—and God knows I've thought about it quite a lot: I found her body, you know—I've doubted whether the suicide verdict were the true one. You see, she wasn't a miserable penitent. She was still chock-full of original sin: she enjoyed being naughty—at least that's my opinion. And I don't believe she'd have taken all that trouble to scramble out of that narrow window in order to kill herself. She got out of the window because she'd thought out a plan for some future devilment."

"I think that's probably sound reasoning," said Macdonald, "but the query is—what devilment? Had she made contact with any other lad in the village?"

"I don't think so. There'd been too much fuss about Nancy Bilton already. They'd all have fought shy of her. My own idea is that she meant to try another bolt and was caught by the Warden, and got shoved into the stream in the ensuing scrimmage. I may be quite wrong, but I think that's more probable than suicide. You see, at the inquest nobody mentioned that Sister Monica had taken to wandering at night."

Macdonald nodded. "Yes. That's quite a point. It was early in the morning when you found the girl's body, wasn't it?"

"Yes. Seven o'clock. I walked down to the saw mill to see if Doone had got some planks cut ready for loading. It was a beastly business." He sat in silence for a while, his brow frowning, his eyes downcast. Then he looked up at Macdonald, suddenly: "Obviously you're wondering whether I shoved the Warden into the mill stream. Sergeant Peel believes I did, and Nancy Bilton into the bargain. I can only tell you I didn't. I've no alibi. I live here alone. I was in bed both nights, but I've no means of proving it."

"Neither have I," said Macdonald, his voice as equable as ever, "but it's my business to get both pros and cons. It seems reasonable to me to suppose that Miss Torrington did not share Sergeant Peel's opinion—if it be his opinion—that you killed Nancy Bilton."

"Why not?" demanded Sanderson.

"If she had known, or believed, that you or any other man had pushed the girl into the mill stream, she would have avoided the chance of the same fate happening to her. In other words, she would have shunned that spot after dark, or taken great care that she wasn't caught unawares. The fact that she went on going there after dark indicates to my mind that she thought she was safe in doing so."

"Well…thanks for the crumb of comfort," said Sanderson dryly. "I should like to add this. I've got to know the folks in this village pretty well. They're odd: secretive, and suspicious of strangers, but I don't believe there's a murderer among them. The only person I've ever met here whom I thought might be capable of murder was the Warden herself, and that's because she was unbalanced. She'd got a power complex, and she was cruel. There are more ways of being cruel than by violence."

"Admittedly, but murder is no way of restoring the balance. I believe myself that Miss Torrington was murdered. You say you know the people in this village. I ask you, have you any idea at all who murdered her?"

"No. None whatever." The answer came quickly, and Macdonald was pretty sure that Sanderson had anticipated both question and answer. "I can't see any point in having murdered her," went on the bailiff. "Her power was on the wane, you know. It wouldn't have taken much more in the way of gossip and disapproval to have got rid of her. She was obviously too old for the job and even Lady Ridding was saying that poor Sister Monica was getting over-tired. Old Brown is pretty doddery now, and I think it'd have been only a matter of months before he gave up Gramarye. Once Dr. Ferens took over, he'd have got rid of her anyway."

"He's been saved that trouble," said Macdonald dryly.

"Now I shall obviously be enquiring about the general routine at Gramarye, but it would help if I got some previous information to check by. So far as you know, were the maids at Gramarye given time off in the usual way and allowed out alone?"

"Not out of the village. I do know that. They went shopping, and to the cinema very occasionally, in Milham Prior, but they were always accompanied by one of the old servants—Nurse Barrow or the old cook. I know the bus conductors made a joke about it; I've heard them gossiping. The girls were allowed out in this village by themselves, and Lady Ridding let them go into parts of the Manor House garden, or to tea with her own servants. Incidentally, their times off were so arranged that they were not out by themselves on the days the buses run. That's only on three days a week."

"Did you ever hear of any other troubles among the maids, apart from Nancy Bilton, during the time you've lived here? Any runnings away, or carryings on in the village?"

"No. It's obvious enough that the Warden was successful in imposing her discipline. People said she was 'wonderful' with the girls—you've probably heard that one already. I can well believe she was capable of terrorising them. She was terrifying to look at, you know, and she had a great power of imposing her will on people. She was an extraordinary woman. I can believe she was capable of almost hypnotising people. Then she ran quite a skilful system of rewards. The good girl had many inducements to be good and the recalcitrant girl had a very poor time, no freedom, no outings, no sweets, no pocket money."

"How did you get to know these details?"

"The whole village knows. Mrs. Yeo and Mrs. Barron at the village shop knew what money the girls had and what free time they had. The general opinion was that the Warden managed them very capably, and it was true. I didn't like her methods—too much of the oldtime workhouse matron or prison wardress about her."

Macdonald sat and pondered. "It's a problem with a lot of possibilities. One wonders if any girl who hated Miss Torrington in time past came back to square up the account. But the objection to that is that they couldn't have known she'd be at that particular spot at that particular time."

Sanderson considered that for a while and then said: "How about this for a suggestion. I said it wasn't easy for the girls to run away. They were dressed in uniform and they'd have been spotted anywhere; but any smart girl could post a letter without being seen. Could one of them have got to know that the Warden went out at night on certain occasions and have written and told somebody else about it?"

"It's worth looking into," said Macdonald. "I shall get a policewoman up and see what we can make of the three girls who were at Gramarye. Well, thanks for your help. I shall probably be looking in again some time, if further questions arise."

"Do," said Sanderson cordially. "I'm generally at home in the evenings and I shall be glad to see you any time. I admit that Sergeant Peel put my back up. He regards me as his hope of promotion, but you've been both fair and reasonable and I'd gladly talk to you again."

"Thanks. But don't be too hard on Peel. He put a lot of hard work into this job, and his report was an honest effort, not a biased one."

2

Reeves was ready when Macdonald approached Gramarye: not exactly waiting; Reeves wasn't the sort of fellow to stand outside a house and wait for a senior officer unless there was some point to be served in so doing. He had been prospecting, and he was able to give Macdonald a description of the entrances and exits to Gramarye.

"The front door opens on to a drive, and the drive has a gate into the park," said Reeves. "I imagine it was used by riders, because the gate opens on to a bridle path. There's another gate into the Manor House garden, and a small gate into the Manor kitchen garden. The back of the house opens on to that flagged yard, which has a door in the wall which is locked: inside the yard there's a door to the kitchen premises, which tradespeople use, and a side door as well."

"It seems to be well supplied with ways in and out," said Macdonald. "Two ways into the square, by the drive or the yard. A gate into the park, two others into the Manor Gardens."

"That's it. And none of the gates on the park and garden side can be overlooked from the house because there are too many trees and clipped shrubs and hedges. And that steep path down the park isn't overlooked anywhere. It's an interesting lay-out."

The two men went up the drive and knocked at the front door proper, where they were admitted by Hannah Barrow in impressive array of severely starched cap and apron, a blue cotton frock also starched as stiff as cartridge paper, black shoes and stockings and glazed collar and cuffs. She had a wrinkled old face, and her grey hair was strained back off her face. Macdonald knew that she was only sixty-two years of age, and he knew plenty of women of that age who might pass for forty-five: why was it, he wondered, that this specimen looked so much like a wizened and elderly monkey? He stated his name, rank and business, and Nurse Barrow accepted the information without any show of interest or surprise.

"Please to walk in," she said, and led them into the parlour, where she stood as erect as a ramrod, though Macdonald noticed she walked as the elderly walk, and guessed that her severe black shoes pained her quite a lot. He asked her to sit down, but she remained standing. (Reeves, noticing her stiff skirts, knew that Nurse Barrow had not sat down since putting on her clean frock: there wasn't a crumple in those formidable skirts.) Macdonald began by asking questions about the late Warden's health.

Nurse Barrow replied: "Sister had very good health. All the years I've known her she never took to her bed. She kept to her room sometimes, if she'd got a cold, but that was to avoid spreading infection. Sister didn't hold with people coddling themselves. You can keep well if you've the will to keep well, Sister said. A wonderful powerful will Sister had got."

"But what about this dizziness she suffered from?" enquired Macdonald. "People don't tumble about if they're quite well."

"It was her eyes, poor soul," said Hannah. "Sister wouldn't never have them seen to. She had a pair of glasses for reading, but she got them from the Market, same as I did before the National Health. That'd be it, you mark my words. 'You can't see them stairs like you used, Sister,' I said. 'We're none of us so young as we were'. "

"Who cleaned her bedroom?" enquired Macdonald.

"I did. I always done it, ever since I come, and it was the easiest room in the house to clean, Sister being that tidy. Never a thing left about."

"Do you know if she took any medicine? Were there any medicine bottles in her room?"

"That there were not. All the medicine in this house is kept in the medicine cupboard. If Sister took a dose at times, it wasn't my business to dose her."

Macdonald next asked about the routine of the house in the mornings. Nurse Barrow was first up. She rang a bell on the landing at 6.15 sharp every morning. The maids were allowed a quarter of an hour to dress. At 6.30, one went down to lay breakfast and help cook. One came to Nurse Barrow to help wash and dress the children. Some days Sister Monica came in to assist and inspect, some days she didn't, but breakfast was at 7.30, winter and summer alike, and Sister was always there to the tick to say Grace.

"Did you take the Warden a cup of tea up to her bedroom?" enquired Macdonald, and Hannah Barrow repudiated the idea with scorn.

"You don't understand about Sister," she said loftily, her speech slipping more and more into her natural idiom. "Her never had nothing we didn't have. Tea in bed? Never. Sister's brought me a cup of tea in bed whiles I've been poorly, but her never had none herself, and often enough she'd be outdoors before breakfast, a-communing on holy thoughts."

Hannah Barrow told Macdonald the routine of the household, together with the free times of the two maids. An hour off every day they had, she said, afternoon or evening, and a free afternoon once a week: Hannah or Cook took them shopping and church on Sundays. Hannah Barrow said proudly that she never worried about time off herself "and no more did Sister. Her work was her life, Sister said, and as for holidays, her never wanted holidays." At night, Hannah went to bed at nine o'clock and so did Cook and so did the young maids. Sister locked up. What Sister did after the others went to bed was no business of Hannah's, but she knew Sister often went out for a walk after dark, "after her had finished all her writing and accounts," Hannah added. "Her did all that of an evening after supper."

While she ran on, increasingly garrulous as she got used to the strangers, Macdonald pondered over the life she had led. For twenty-two years she had worked in this austere house, rising at six, working the clock round, apparently contented, worshipping Sister Monica. Was it as simple as that, Macdonald wondered?

"I see you came here in 1929, Miss Barrow. You were then forty years of age. Had you done work in a similar institution before?"

The thin lips suddenly shut tight and the pale eyes looked wary. "I'd been in private service," she replied. "In Exeter 'twas, and then in Barnsford. Children's nurse I'd been. Sister, her looked into everything, my character and that. Her took me on trial. Sister often laughed over that. 'You're still on trial, Hannah,' she'd say, after I'd worked for her years and years."

"On trial." Macdonald repeated the words slowly, watching the wrinkled face. Then he said: "I'm afraid I've kept you a long time. I should like to see round the house next. I think Inspector Reeves has written down the main facts you have told us. Will you read it through and sign it, if you are satisfied it is correct?"

Reeves got up and laid his notes on the table. They were very simple and written in an admirably clear hand. Nurse Barrow stood and studied the sheet of paper until Macdonald asked quietly, "Shall I read it to you?"

"If you please. My eyes aren't that good."

Macdonald read the statement aloud: then he said quietly, "You can't read, can you?"

She flushed, the dull red covering her face. "I never had much schooling," she said, "but Sister, her knew I did my work. Her never found nothing to complain of."

"You've worked for her for over twenty years. That speaks

for itself," replied Macdonald. She took Reeves's pen and signed her name, slowly and laboriously. Then she turned to the door.

"Please to step this way," she said. She was obviously accustomed to showing people round the house.

3

"I'll lay any money Nurse Barrow has been 'inside'," said Reeves reflectively, as the two men left the house and went through the gate in the clipped yew hedge which divided the Gramarye drive from the park.

Macdonald nodded. "I'm with you. We'll have to get on to Records. It's curious how it came out: she made a perfectly spontaneous anecdotal statement: 'You're on trial, Hannah.' That remark had become a joke and she repeated it without thinking and then suddenly became aware of the form of words she'd used."

"I know. I saw her eyes contract and her jaw tighten as you repeated her words," said Reeves.

"It'd have been so much in character," said Macdonald slowly. "Monica Emily Torrington liked to have people about her whom she'd got a hold over. It's quite possible she got Hannah Barrow through one of the Prisoners' Aid Societies. Got her, kept her, and dominated her. I can well believe that if Hannah Barrow showed any signs of rebelliousness when she first came here, the Warden would just say, 'You're on trial, Hannah,' and the double-edged words became a sort of joke as the years went on. I wonder what she was tried for."

"For her life," said Reeves. "It's over twenty years ago, and when you repeated 'on trial' she was shaken to her boots, poor old trout. A little thing like a sentence for petty larceny never kept its terror for twenty years."

"I think you're right there, Reeves. I may query your navigation occasionally, but when it comes to a judgment of that kind, you're more often right than any magistrate I ever met."

"Old lags," said Reeves meditatively. "I'll go out of my way to talk to 'em whenever I get the chance. And I've sometimes felt I'd turn the job in. These high hats talk a lot of hot air about reform. The system does something to 'em, but it doesn't reform them. It drives the devil which possesses them under cover, deep down, and clamps it down with fear."

Macdonald stopped and stared at the other. "So you feel like that about it?"

"Yes, chief. So do you. That old trout's worked her fingers to the bone for over twenty years. I wish one of these social welfare dames had fitted a pedometer to Hannah Barrow's flat feet and noted how many miles a day she walked in that penitentiary she's so proud of. Twenty years—and at the end of it the sight of you and me, making her remember, turned her stomach. Oh, I know someone's got to do our job and it's a good job by and large, but I often feel we've slipped up somewhere when I see the mixture of cunning and fear on an old lag's face."

"Cunning and fear," said Macdonald reflectively. "How much fear was there and what was she afraid of, past or present?"

Reeves stopped by a trail of wild roses, stared at them as though fascinated, and then took out his knife, snipped a flower off and put it in his button hole. "I hardly believe in them," he said. "There's something about them. Sorry. About the old trout. I agree the worm may turn. May get suddenly browned off and run amok. I've been learning quite a bit about this Monica Emily. Twenty years of her. Twenty years of being alternately sweated and prayed over. Twenty years of saying, 'She's wonderful' and then running amok over some small silly thing. I agree it's in character. But look at the size of the little cuss. About five feet nothing. She'd have had to stand on tip-toes to reach Monica Emily with a coal hammer. And the old trout puffs like a grampus and her stays squeak with every breath she takes and she sucks her teeth. Likewise she's got shocking corns, not to mention bunions and her eyesight's about as good as a bat's."

"All quite true," said Macdonald, "particularly about the stays. But she could have taken the stays off."

"That's right out of character," said Reeves firmly. "Women like the old trout feel lost without their stays, and they never realise they squeak because they're conditioned to it. My grandmother-in-law had squeaky stays but she said they didn't. My missis told me so." Reeves suddenly laughed, his thin keen face boyish in his mirth. "I hand it to you for high-class quotes, chief, to say nothing of the law of the lever and items like radio-active isotopes, but when it comes to stays I can leave you standing. And her corns aren't irrelevant, either. This path we're on is steep and rough. I bet the old trout never comes down here. It'd be pain and grief to her with those feet. Where do we go from here?"

"To see the Medical Officer responsible for Gramarye," replied Macdonald.

"Old Dr. Brown," said Reeves. "He's highly thought of in the village. This is where I do my silent act. Incidentally it was pretty snappy of you to spot that Hannah Barrow can't read. It all adds up."

"Yes. It adds up—to a portrait of Miss Monica Emily Torrington."

"Some of the high-ups are going to get a bit of a shock," meditated Reeves. "Or aren't they? The person I'm looking forward to seeing is Her Ladyship, as the village has it. If she didn't know, why didn't she?"

"It's often more convenient not to know," rejoined Macdonald.

CHAPTER X

1

"Sister Monica was an exceedingly obstinate woman," said Dr. Brown. He spoke wearily, and his voice, despite the conditioned note of professional certitude, sounded disillusioned.

Macdonald and Reeves were sitting with the old doctor in the latter's consulting room. Reeves, doing his 'silent act,' was very much aware of his surroundings. Even on this day in midsummer the room was dim and dank and green. "Like a new-fangled aquarium with the lights turned off," thought Reeves; "we might all begin to swim in a minute, like deep-sea fishes."

Green walls, green paint, green curtains, green carpet, all faded to despondency: green aspidistras in the fireplace, green rhododendrons and laurels and yews too close to the windows: green mosses and algae in glass tanks and beakers and test-tubes, for Dr. Brown had turned naturalist in his retirement, and was writing a treatise on fresh water algae: ("spirogyra and hydrodictyon? See dictionary," noted Reeves.) "I'd hate to be doctored by him: this room must be a real breeding place for bugs. I shall be getting a sore throat myself next," thought the hardened Cockney while Dr. Brown went on:

"Of course she was too old for the job. I admit it and I admit I knew it. But when you're old yourself you find it hard to be censorious about people who're a dozen years younger than yourself. She'd run that place for nearly thirty years, and she'd run it well, efficiently, wisely, economically. When younger folks complained she was old-fashioned and harsh in her methods, I reminded them that that house had a better record for health than any other children's home I know of. She'd worked non-stop, unsparingly, without holidays and without diversion. Unwise of her? Maybe, but I come of a generation that respects hard work. She'd worked herself out, like an old cart-horse. She didn't want to give up and I didn't want to be the one to tell her to pack up. I was wrong. I admit it—but I'm not ashamed of it."

"I respect your point of view, sir," said Macdonald quietly, "but I have been sent here to get facts. The most important facts you can give me are those concerning Miss Torrington's health. You were her medical adviser."

The old man snorted. "Yes. I was her medical adviser. During all the years I've known her she's never complained to me about her health, never asked for physic, never taken to her bed. I said just now she was like a horse, and she was as strong as a horse. Barring looking at her tongue, peering down her throat, taking her pulse and taking her temperature—which she was quite capable of taking herself—I've never examined her. Never so much as seen her with her uniform frock unbuttoned. No need to. She's had colds, she's had throats, but she's never been really ill. Not up till this last six months. And then it wasn't disease. It was anno domini, tiredness, frayed nerves, and the knowledge that she herself was failing. I knew it couldn't go on, but I'd set a term to it in my own mind, and I'd told her so. This was the result. It preyed on her mind and broke her up."

"Will you enlarge on that point, sir?" asked Macdonald, and the old man cleared his throat noisily.

"You know I retired last spring. I kept on Gramarye at Sister Monica's request. She didn't want a change, not at her age. For over a quarter of a century, barring my own holidays, I'd been to that house at eleven o'clock every Monday morning. The drill was always the same. Hannah showed me up to the little dispensary where Sister Monica was waiting, and Hannah paraded those tots past me, each taught to say 'good-morning, doctor' and 'thank you.' If there were any cot cases, those two women would march me up to the dormitories, regulation hospital fashion. I've seen them through their measles and mumps and chicken pox, prescribing the same medicine and treatment, which Sister Monica knew as well or better than I did. At the end of it Hannah would march me to the front door—always the same, Monday after Monday. Sister Monica, and Hannah too, knew all about the treatment for children's ailments, knew it by heart. They didn't want any bright young fellow with new ideas coming along, turning everything upside down." He broke off and sighed: a heavy, old man's sigh, and then went on: "When I retired, I thought I'd live out my natural span here, pottering about with algae and fossils, but it wasn't so easy. That young chap, Ferens, he's a capable fellow: up to date, *au fait* with all this hooey over glands and hormones and vitamins and antitoxins and antibodies and all the rest. Quite right, too. But his very existence up there was an implicit criticism of all I'd ever done. I'm not criticising, mind you, and I'm not grumbling.

But when old Anna Freemantle lost her husband—my wife was a Freemantle—when Anna suggested she'd got a big comfortable house and not too much money to run it on and why not come along and share the expenses and the comfort, well, I thought it was a good idea."

He cleared his throat again and said: "I'm rambling on, but let me tell you my own way. I'm too old to learn new tricks."

"I ask nothing better than for you to talk in your own way, sir," said Macdonald. "You're giving me a vivid picture of things which I'd only guessed at."

"You're a good listener, Chief Inspector. Shows your wisdom and your manners, too," growled old Brown. "Where was I?"

"Anna Freemantle," prompted Macdonald, and he went on:

"Yes. Anna. 75 last year, but spry as they make 'em. In Wiltshire she lives: nice place, nice stretch of river, a bit of fishing, and a good housekeeper and gardener. Worth thinking about. So I told her I'd pack up here round about Michaelmas, sell most of the furniture and take a few bits along and have a little comfort for my last year or so. Well, there it was. I told Sister Monica what was in my mind and said: 'Why not retire? Lady Ridding'll see you have a good cottage and a bit of a pension, and Hannah Barrow will be only too glad to stay with you and look after you.' She just said: 'I don't wish to retire. When it's time for me to retire the Almighty will make it clear to me.' You can't argue with that, you know. Once a woman gets it into her head she's being guided, there's no use talking to her."

"True enough," agreed Macdonald. "Now you said that Miss Torrington was tired and her nerves were strained. Did you prescribe anything for her?"

"I did. Wilson, the chemist in Milham Prior, sent the stuff up. I gave her a sedative—the usual bromide. Wouldn't have hurt a baby. And a bismuth mixture: more peppermint than anything else in it. She'd got a sort of nervous indigestion. Hannah told me about it. Faithful creature, she is. For all I know Sister Monica poured the stuff down the sink."

"I don't think she did that. The analyst found traces of bismuth in her organs. He also found traces of alcohol."

Dr. Brown sat staring at Macdonald, his old face contracted into an amazed frown. "Good God," he said slowly. "I never thought of that." He broke off, and then added: "I'm too old to be surprised by the aberrations human nature's capable of, Inspector. I've seen too many queer things done by ordinary people. Drink? It's not the first time I've heard of a respectable woman falling into that snare... It might explain a lot."

"Where did she get it from?"

"Depends how much she had. Have you looked into that medicine cupboard at Gramarye? Yes? I thought so. Was there a bottle of brandy there?"

"No, sir."

"There's been one there for years. Good brandy, too. I sent it up myself. During the war they took evacuees into the house, and there was one old soul who was in a bad way. A heart case. I prescribed brandy to keep her heart going, a matter of a few drops. After the heart case had been moved on to hospital, Sister Monica wanted me to take the brandy away. I said, No. She ought to have it in case of emergency. She ran our Red Cross unit and casualty station. It was never in action of course. She kept the brandy in the locked section of the cupboard labelled 'poisons'—though she'd not got anything that'd poison a babe in arms."

"It's not there now," said Macdonald.

2

"Why couldn't she have given up?" growled old Brown sadly. He had had a respite from talking, mixing himself a modest whisky and soda with hands that shook. He looked a weary unhappy old man, and Macdonald had offered to go away and resume the conversation later, but Dr. Brown had replied: "Let's get it over. The whole thing's been a shock. I've known Sister a long time: worked with her, trusted her, respected her sterling qualities, aye and told her my own troubles, many a time. They'll tell you in the village it was my fault she wasn't pensioned off. That's not true. I've advised her time and again to give up this last year or two, but I wasn't going to see her packed off like a worn-out suit. After the years she'd worked at that place, she'd earned the right to choose her own time to retire. That's how I saw it."

"Did she talk to you about her own affairs, sir? Her family and connections, her savings and business dealings and so forth?"

"Savings? She can't have saved much, poor soul. I told Etheldreda Ridding she'd got her pound of flesh all right. Not that Sister ever mentioned money to me. She'd got her own rigid code, you know. You couldn't get past it. In actual fact she never talked to me about her own affairs. Never got personal. The fact was, she'd got a pose as well as a code. She was other-worldly. That's how she saw it. I'd say, in confidence, she was a bit simple and a good bit of a snob. I don't say that unkindly, but I suppose her origins were pretty humble. That's guess work, because she never told me, but I do believe that she put great store on being talked to confidentially by Lady Ridding. So Sister lived up to it, part mystic, part perfect lady. No harm in it. She didn't have much in the way of luxury, God knows."

"But wasn't there another side to her, sir?" asked Macdonald. "Not mystic: not ascetic: not perfect lady. Isn't it true that she could set malicious gossip in train, too?"

"Maybe. I've never known a woman who didn't," said the old man tartly. "No one's ever repeated gossip to me. It's a thing I can't abide, and if anyone tried tale-bearing about Sister Monica, I dealt with them in the only way I know. Told them to hold their tongues. Maybe she did chatter, but she wasn't malicious. If she said a thing she thought it was true." He paused, his face working unhappily. "Of course I know what you mean," he admitted. "She'd turned people against her. She'd got a sort of reformer's bug into her head. You try reforming a village and see how popular you are. Villages are all alike, made up of human beings who love and lie, who're unselfish one minute and self-seeking the next, who're faithful one day and fornicators the next. Human nature's a mixed bag. I've lived thirty years in this village and I don't expect too much of anybody. I've too much sense."

"Wouldn't you agree that if would-be reformers are too zealous they make enemies, sir?"

"Of course they do. We all make enemies. I've made plenty myself. I'm a damned cantankerous old man and I know it. But when you make enemies in a village like this, you don't murder one another. It was that fool of a sergeant who started this murder idea. Damned nonsense. I'm willing to admit anything within the bounds of reasonable possibility. I'll admit Sister Monica may have taken to the brandy bottle, improbable though it seems. And if she did, you've got a logical explanation of the way she behaved and of the fact she fell down, knocked herself silly, and rolled into the mill stream."

The old man was working himself up into a temper, as old men do, and Macdonald changed the angle of his questions.

"Getting back to Gramarye, sir. Can you tell me anything about Hannah Barrow?"

"Hannah? She's been there for twenty years or more. I can tell you she's a hard worker, a conscientious children's nurse, and an ignorant, superstitious woman. Not that that made any difference to her work. She's one of the sort who'll work till they drop. Not like the youngsters of to-day, always out for their own enjoyment."

"Do you know where she came from?"

"Came from? She's Devon bred. I think Sister Monica got her by recommendation from some home or other. She was a domestic to start with, and they took to calling her Nurse when she was promoted. No training of course: no education. Just got a knack of managing children. She's been invaluable."

"You don't remember what sort of home she came from?"

"I never asked. Not my business. May have got landed in trouble—Sister Monica always liked reforming people. Makes me laugh to think of reforming Hannah. Ugly little cuss she was when she came and couldn't say boo to a goose." He cocked an eye at Macdonald. "Not thinking Hannah took a coal hammer and knocked Sister Monica over the head, are you? Why not say I did it—it'd make just as much sense. Hannah worshipped Sister Monica. She'd have cut off her own hands rather than cause Sister any distress." He stirred fretfully in his seat. "I expect you know how children's homes are run these days. Trained nurses, trained psychologists, trained welfare officers, trained social reformers, trained nursery teachers. Gramarye was run in the main by two women who'd had about as little training as women can have: they ran it by commonsense, rule of thumb, and hard work: two women of humble origin, one of whom was nearly illiterate. But they did the job. And after a quarter of a century detectives come along and suggest one of those women was murdered and the other murdered her. I don't want to be offensive to you personally, Inspector: you strike me as a fellow with plenty of commonsense, but melodrama's never been in my line. We're commonplace folk in this village."

"Would you really have described Miss Monica Torrington as a commonplace person, sir?"

"Under the uniform and the mumbo jumbo, yes. She played a part, but considering how hard she worked and how little relaxation she had, it wasn't surprising she put on a few frills and pretensions."

The old man yawned, and Macdonald got up to go. "You're tired, sir."

"I'm damn tired, Inspector. Not used to talking so much. And you've given me a few knocks. I thought I knew our Sister Monica, saw through the pious trappings to the human being underneath. Now you tell me she'd taken to drink. I ought to have spotted it. I didn't. I'm an old fool and you're justified in telling me so."

"I didn't say that she'd taken to drink, sir; I said the analyst found traces of alcohol in her organs. We don't know at all in what circumstances it was taken, and there was no sign at all that she was an addict. The reverse is true. But as a detective, I can't help being aware that a stiff dose of alcohol, taken by one unaccustomed to it, may have had some bearing on her death."

"And what about the bottle of brandy, Chief Inspector? You say it's no longer there. It was kept under lock and key, and whatever defects Sister Monica may have had, careless-ness and forgetfulness were not among them. Did you find her keys, by the way?"

"Yes, sir. Her keys were in the pocket of her uniform cloak when her body was found."

"That's clear enough, isn't it?" growled old Brown.

3

It was after nine o'clock that evening when Macdonald got his car out, saying to Reeves: "There's a rhyme to the effect that a policeman's lot is not a happy one. I've always maintained that there are good points about the job, and we're going to prove it this evening. Hop in, Pete."

"Where are we going?"

"We're taking a couple of hours off duty, and we're going to drive to the highest point of Exmoor and see the county of Devon from sea to sea: from Bideford Bay in the north to the Exeter gap in the south. It's as near the summer solstice as makes no difference, and we'll see a midsummer evening over Exmoor."

"Suits me," said Reeves.

Macdonald turned northwards: they drove at first through deep lanes with high hedge banks, warm and fragrant with the incense of midsummer, while already tall foxgloves flowered in serried ranks and the lush green foliage of oak and beech nearly met overhead. Then the hedge banks dwindled away and the bonnet of the car tilted to an unaccustomed angle as they mounted to the moor. White owls swept across the road, and as they drove on a great hawk flew in front of them and came back again and again as though to protest against their intrusion into his territory. The north western sky was still lambent, glowing with pale golden light, and when they reached the summit of the rough road the very air seemed drenched with the aftermath of sunset. Macdonald pulled the car on to the rough verge, and they got out and walked over close turf, starred with flowers and tangle of blaeber-ries, until they reached a ridge where two mounds stood out against the sky.

"Long barrows," said Macdonald: "your ancestors and mine, maybe. A good spot to be buried."

Reeves stood and stared: some moorland ponies stared back and then bolted in a wild stampede of flying hooves and manes and tails. To the far west, Lundy Island hung like a cloud on the horizon: Bideford Bay was one great curve of reflected light from Hartland to Morte. To the north the head of the Lynn valley showed a sinuous green among the dark green of heather. Turning about, Reeves looked beyond and below the moor to a chequer of farmland and woodland, the rich earth of south Devon spread out to the river Exe and the distant hills behind Exmouth. Having stared his fill, he sat down beside Macdonald, who was gazing out to Hartland and remembering the coombes that cleft that rocky coast—Welcombe, Marsland Mouth, Coombe Valley, and Moorwinstow.

"Well, thanks for this," said Reeves, as he gazed at the first white pin-prick of starlight. "I shan't forget it in a hurry."

They sat in silence and listened to the call of the moorland birds and watched kestrels hovering until the light faded and the northern sky paled, misted to faint amethyst and then to lilac grey. Reeves lay on his back and watched the stars strengthen, while his mind inevitably went back to the problem they had come to solve. It wasn't that he didn't value this high solitude of air and sky and distant sea, but an active mind cannot easily ignore a present problem. Sensuously he was aware of near bird call and far constellation, of fragrance and the chill of evening air, of the reflection of headland lights flashing out from hidden lighthouses: intelligently he was aware of a conundrum in which human motives made a criss-cross of pattern, moving inevitably to the cold rush of the mill-race.

They stayed there for a long time, each busy with his own thoughts, the smoke of Reeves's cigarettes mingling with the mellower smoke of Macdonald's pipe, while rustles in heather and bracken told of unseen small beasts busy on nocturnal occasions, and the last bird call died away in sleepy cuck-cuckings, save for the mournful hoot of owls. When Macdonald got up and stretched himself, Reeves could see his tall straight figure like a void against a sky which was still vaguely pale, though myriad pin-points and scintillas of golden starlight quivered from horizon to horizon. Reeves got up and stretched too, and found his coat was misted with dew.

"You can see it's round when you're at sea, but you don't often see it's round when you're on land," he said.

Macdonald considered the cryptic phrase and turned slowly the full three hundred and sixty degrees. They were so high above the rest of the moorland that they had their own uninterrupted circle of horizon. "There's something satisfying about a full circle," he said. "It seems to settle the infinity argument. This is where we go back, in time as well as in space. I'm going to drop you about half a mile from the mill. I shall go on up to the top and walk down through the park. We will each follow our own devices and discuss results when we get home. There's a moon for you—like a dinted green cheese."

They went back to the car, turned the headlights on and bumped down the steep descent, lighting up an occasional white owl, and once a hawk flew in the beam of the head lamps, every pinion displayed in its great wing spread. Back into the tunnel of the lane they drove, and on till the first thatch gleamed in the moonlight at the bottom of the village street. Here Reeves got out and Macdonald drove on up the hill to the little plateau between inn and manor and church.

Every south-facing wall was white in the moonlight, white as milk: every thatch gleamed with the faintest tinge of gold on its well-combed surface, and beneath the eaves the shadows were purple black.

CHAPTER XI

1

Macdonald walked across the village green to the entrance gates which closed the drive of Gramarye. They were tall wooden gates and they were bolted on the inside. Having noted their solidity, Macdonald put his hands on the top of the gates, pulled himself up and got over the top without any difficulty at all. The drive was dark, shaded by ilex trees, and the Chief Inspector walked silently along the tunnel of gloom until he could see the garden front of the old stone house. It looked very beautiful and serene in the moonbeams, its mullions and flat Tudor archways showing clear in the witching light. Every window was closed, despite the warmth of the midsummer night, and the narrow leaded casements had a dark, secret look. The sunk lawn was smooth and white now, but anybody leaving the house could get immediately into the shadow of clipped shrubs and hedges. The conditions to-night, Macdonald pondered, were the same as on the night when Monica Emily Torrington had walked down to the mill, and when Dr. Ferens had driven up the village street to the Dower House.

Leaving the drive by the gate he and Reeves had used that afternoon, Macdonald moved on into the park. He paused after he had descended a hundred yards of the steep declivity. To his right, the scarp rose sharply to the line of the village street, the houses hidden by the trees on the slopes. To his left, the ground fell away steeply to river level, so steeply that it was probable that if anybody took a false step and slipped from the path, he would roll helplessly down the long bank, faster and faster, till he reached the bottom. Despite the fact that he was not many yards away from the village street, no houses were within sight. Away and below, across the river, woods banked darkly, and beyond them again the ridge of the distant moorland showed against the sky. It was midnight, but it wasn't dark. It wouldn't be dark all night, thought Macdonald. Everything was plain to see, though the colours of day had faded out. White and black, or grey and lilac, the great sweep of parkland and woodland was like an aquatint, its half tones treated with a wash of some faint tertiary colour which blurred some of the outlines but never hid the detail.

Macdonald walked on: the path was straight now and offered no cover: anyone walking either up or down could be seen clearly and would have no means of concealment. He stood still for a while and listened; the only sound came faintly from far below, the perpetual plash of water over the weir. Macdonald had gym shoes on, for he found they were quieter than any other form of footwear and gave better foothold on a slope. He picked up a small stone and tossed it. As he expected, he got an echo from the scarp to his right. Every sound was amplified on this path. "She had acute hearing," he pondered to himself. (The conscientious Peel had noted this down.) "Even the rustle of a cotton frock would sound loud here. Surely no one would have risked following her down this path. She would have heard them, and once she had turned, she would have seen them."

He walked on, thinking hard. "She must have gone to meet somebody. If she had only been walking for the pleasure of a walk in the moonlight, or to induce some sort of semi-hysterical trance, she wouldn't have gone on through that last gate to the workaday jumble of mill house and saw mill and generating station. And if you wanted to meet someone surely you wouldn't choose to meet them on this path. It's not wide enough for two people to walk abreast without fear of slipping; it's steep and toilsome, and not particularly safe. If she went to meet somebody, she'd have chosen level ground at the top or level ground at the bottom."

He walked on, slowly and silently, down to the five-barred gate which shut off the park from the level space by the river. There were trees overhanging the path here, and a big elder tree, covered in flowers, looked fairylike in the moonlight. Macdonald wanted to know what Reeves was up to. He would be down there somewhere, near the bridge, watching and listening, as Macdonald himself had been watching and listening. Reeves would be quite capable of doing a practical experiment to discover what happened to a person who tripped up on the bridge, and Macdonald thought it not improbable that one or other of them would end up in the mill stream, the betting being that he (Macdonald) would have to swim for it. The fact that Reeves was there, unseen and unheard, but certainly watchful, acted as a sort of stimulant, and Macdonald began to test his memory about the approach to the bridge, recollecting what there was in the way of cover where an assailant might hide. There was an open space of level ground on either side of the bridge, and while he stood visualising this, Macdonald suddenly thought: "Being Reeves, he'll probably get under the bridge somehow. It's a wooden bridge and there must be beams of some sort to act as stays: it's too wide a span to have no supports. If somebody grabbed your ankle or got a crook round your leg while you were on the bridge, the result might make hay of all our arguments about what happens when you go at the knees. Well, here's his chance for a demonstration."

He had just put out his hand to loosen the chain on the gate when he caught a sound on the farther side of the stream. It was a slight clatter, as though a stick had fallen on cobbles. Macdonald drew back into the shadows: he could see right across the bridge and on to the moonlit space beyond it. The path which ran between the Mill House and the farm was in black shadow, and it was from here that the sound had come, as though someone coming towards the bridge from the village street had knocked a stick down. Macdonald's first thought was: "That wasn't Reeves." Reeves had the eyes of a cat, and a cat's neatness in avoiding obstacles. A moment later a man moved out of the shadows between the houses and into the moonlight. He walked quietly on to the bridge and Macdonald saw who it was—Sanderson, the bailiff. He was dressed in singlet and shorts and he was very obvious in the moonlight. Behind, in the shadows, was another man, unidentifiable in the gloom. Whatever Macdonald antici-pated, the next event took him entirely by surprise. Sanderson measured his length on the bridge, if not with a resounding crash, with a thud which was not far removed from a bang. Then his big form rolled over and fell in the water with a smack and a splash which made a great deal more noise than Macdonald would have believed possible. Immediately there was an outburst of barking from the dog in Venner's house, and the calves in the nearby byre bawled their protest at being woken from sleep.

2

Macdonald said afterwards that something in his subconscious mind told him the whole thing was a put-up job. When Sanderson fell, his limbs did not seem to lose control as do the limbs of a man rendered suddenly senseless. It was a good fall, and in addition to the thud on the echoing planks, the timber of the bridge creaked and groaned in reverberation. The lively uproar following the noisy flop into the water was reinforced by the sound of a window being flung violently open and Venner's voice calling, "What's that? What's that?"

It was then that another voice spoke from the shadows, the calm sensible voice of Raymond Ferens.

"All right, Venner. Sorry if we startled you. Don't wake the whole village. We were only trying an experiment. Come down here a minute."

Macdonald, peering from the shadows, decided to hold a watching brief, and assumed that Reeves was doing likewise. Sanderson, who was evidently a good swimmer, had reached the bank with a few powerful trudge strokes across the current, and by the time he had scrambled out, Ferens was reassuring Farmer Moore, who had appeared in his night-shirt in a surprisingly short space of time, roused by the indignant voices of his young stock in the byre.

Venner came out of doors and turned on Ferens in a fury.

"You did ought to know better, doctor, giving we a turn like that. Us has had enough without you fooling like a zany—"

"Keep calm, laddy. We weren't fooling. Listen to a little

commonsense. If Miss Torrington had collapsed on that bridge and fallen into the water as is generally supposed, she'd have made as much row as Sanderson did. She was as large as he is. I never believed she could have slipped in without a sound, not if she fell from the bridge. She'd have made enough noise to wake your dog and the dog would have barked."

"The dog didn't bark," said Venner. "Us didn't hear a sound that night. I told you so, doctor. Not a sound did us hear, and if you don't believe me—"

"The whole point is that we do believe you," put in Sanderson. "What do you think I flopped into the water for? It was to find out how much noise it made. If anybody fell on that bridge at night, and flopped into the water, they'd make noise enough to wake your dog. Your dog barks and wakes the cattle, and the cattle wake Moore's dog, and so it goes on, like the house that Jack built. Half the village will have been woken up to-night, you mark my words. We've proved what we set out to prove. That's all. Now I'm going up to have a rub down. It's not so warm as you might think."

He turned towards the village street, jog-trotting, and Venner turned again to Ferens. "What good d'you think you've done, doctor?" he asked angrily. "If so be 'twas an accident, and I reckon 'twas, what's the use o' making it seem harder?"

"I tried to believe it was an accident, Venner. We all did," replied Ferens, his voice low and deep. "If the police had been willing to accept the accident theory, no one would have been gladder than myself. But the police don't believe it was an accident, and they've put Scotland Yard on to it now. Sanderson and I tried this experiment to prove the thing one way or the other. If your dog hadn't barked and the cattle hadn't bawled I'd have gone to the Chief Inspector and said, 'If you do fall flat on that bridge and flop into deep water at night nobody'd hear you.' Now I know that isn't true. You've got a trained watch dog and the dog wakes up at any unusual sound."

"And so you'll go to the C.I.D. man and tell him what you've found out?"

"No, I shan't. It won't be necessary. He'll try the same thing himself. The reason Sanderson and I took a chance to-night is that the C.I.D. men have driven out to the moor and I thought we should have the place to ourselves." He paused a moment and then added: "Look here, Venner. She didn't fall when she was on the bridge. She didn't knock her head on the hand rail. If you still believe it was an accident, how else did she fall?"

"Her come over dizzy, on the bank there, maybe, and her fell backwards and knocked herself silly."

"If she fell backwards, how did she roll into the river?" persisted Ferens. "That's what they'll ask, you silly old fool. If you can prove to me any way it could have been an accident, I'll back you till the cows come home, but going on talking about her being dizzy doesn't explain how her body got in the river. Put that in your pipe and smoke it. Now I'm going home to bed."

He turned to cross the bridge—they'd been standing on the Mill House side of the stream—and Macdonald squeezed back as silently as he could behind the elder bush, for it was evident that Ferens intended to come up the path through the park. Ferens spoke again as he reached the bridge:

"It's no use getting angry, Venner. I know you feel mad with me, but if you believe that woman drowned by accident, for God's sake use your wits and think out how the accident happened. Phoney explanations aren't any good. Sanderson and I have blown your blessed theory about the bridge sky high. You've got to think again if you're going to persuade that C.I.D. chap it was an accident. Good-night."

He crossed the bridge, opened the gate and chained it up again and set up the path at a good steady pace. Macdonald waited until he heard Venner shut the door and shoot the bolt before he emerged from the thicket which had concealed him so successfully.

3

"Talk about performing apes: I reckon I've proved my ancestry," muttered Reeves resignedly. The two C.I.D. men were sitting in the shadow of the saw mill shed.

"I guessed you'd be under the bridge, waiting for me," said Macdonald.

"I'd say I was. I heard you come down that path, for all you were as quiet about it as a tom on tiles," said Reeves. "There's an echo or something. You chucked a stone, didn't you? I got a foothold and handhold on the timbers underneath the bridge, close in by the bank, reckoning I could hold on for a brace of shakes. It seemed hours," he said, "and as for the row the chap made when he did his swooning act, you'd have thought the whole bridge had copped a V.1. Thunder also ran. I suppose water reflects sound back like any other surface. Then he fell in the stream with a proper belly flop and I was just going in after him when I saw he was swimming like hell, so I gave that idea up and held on till the curtain came down."

"It was a very convincing demonstration, and both those chaps have been using their wits," said Macdonald. "The swooning act made much more noise than I'd have believed possible. They've proved their point, all right."

"But did they know we were there?" pondered Reeves. "When blokes start being clever, I always wonder how far the cleverness goes. And what will old Venner cough up as a variation on 'her was dizzy like'?"

"I don't know, but I think we can accept our first ideas as a basis of probability. I argued that she was killed somewhere near the bank of the stream because she was too heavy to carry: that it wasn't on the Mill House side of the stream because of the risk of being heard or seen: that it was a little upstream from the weir, because her body was found caught in the piles where the current makes an eddy. Her cape would have floated out in the current and it was the cape which hitched itself on the piles and anchored the body against them. It was one of those old-fashioned capes with loops for the arms, so it wasn't torn off her."

"So she was probably knocked out close to where we are now," said Reeves. "It's good and dark here in the shadow."

"Yes, and about as light as day in the moonlight," said Macdonald. "That may have been an advantage from deceased's point of view. She could have been quite sure she wasn't being followed. That path is straight for quite a long stretch." He paused, and then went on: "I've been trying to work out reasons for the woman coming here. What's your guess, Pete?"

"Well, I might make quite a number of guesses: put them up to see if I can knock them down, like ninepins," said Reeves. "I think we've got to accept the probability that she'd done the same thing several times before. Mrs. Venner saw her, that's once. Maybe Nancy Bilton saw her—and that's the last thing Nancy Bilton did see. I'd have guessed deceased was spying on someone, but I don't think she'd have chosen bright moonlight for spying; she could be seen too easily. She might have been going to somebody's house, but to do that she'd have had to cross that bridge and go along the path between the farm and the Mill House, and there was always the chance she'd wake those dogs. And there was the moonlight again: if she'd gone into the village street she'd have been so obvious if anyone had happened to be around. No. I come back to your original idea. She came here to meet someone. She'd put around this blah about meditating in the peace of the night, so if anybody did happen to see her on that path she could say afterwards she was wrestling with the devil or whatever it was she did say, and to make her date she'd only got to come through that gate and take a few steps along to the cover of these shacks. As to why she met anybody here, well, I reckon Peel wasn't far out when he suggested blackmail. To collect her loot—that might have been the idea. And the payer-up got fed-up, and that was that."

"I've been playing with the blackmail idea myself," murmured Macdonald. "We don't know yet what her assets are. She's probably got some other funds besides those in the building society. My own idea is that she'd become a miser. It'd be in keeping with her character. We shall get information about that sooner or later. But why should she have come to this spot for her date, as you call it?"

"Search me," said Reeves.

"I'll offer one or two suggestions," went on Macdonald. "Neither party would go to the other's house, and the post-mistress in this village may be a nosy parker. They often are in small village post-offices."

Reeves chuckled, the faintest of mirthful murmurs. "You've got that right. The dame in the post-office here is definitely interested. I saw her sorting the afternoon mail and she didn't half quiz them. A nice registered packet of pound notes has got quite a feel to it."

The two men were sitting close together on a huge tree trunk which lay close up against the shed in the shadows. Their voices were only the low, practised murmur which was inaudible to any save each other, and the plash and swirl of falling water made a background of covering sound.

"We've had a good evening," said Reeves. "A free demonstration provided, which saved you a swim, and we've got the feel of the place. You say it was a rum place to choose for a date. I think it's rather cosy, not far from home but quite hidden away."

"It has its advantages," agreed Macdonald, "and more than those you've mentioned. Call it a day. We've got a surprising lot of information in a very short time."

4

"What have you been up to, Raymond?" asked Anne. "You might as well tell me, and then you won't have to bother about every word you utter for weeks on end. You're tiresome when you're concentrating on keeping a secret."

Anne Ferens sat up in bed when her husband came in, and he chuckled at her words. "All right, angel. Sorry I'm so late. I went in to see Sanderson, and we got chewing things over. Both of us have been trying to think out some convincing theory which will prove the woman's death was due to accident and nothing but accident. I was always doubtful about that idea of her slipping into the water without a sound, because it seemed to me that a woman of her weight falling on that bridge was bound to make some noise, and Venner's got a very spry young house dog."

"So what?"

"I asked Sanderson if he'd come and do a reconstruction. Fall flat on the bridge and then flop into the water and see if there were any reactions."

"Did he agree?"

"Yes. Straight away—rather to my own relief, I admit. I expected him to argue and say it was ill-advised to go butting in, and so forth. He changed into shorts and we went down the village street. I didn't want to go down the park in case we ran into Sir James or Lady R."

"But heavens above, Lady R. doesn't go rambling in the moonlight."

"Not so sure, angel. Everyone's nerves are rather playing tricks just now—but never mind that. Sanderson did his stuff all right. He fell like a hero, an absolute pitcher. I couldn't have done it if I'd tried, and the row he made was unbelievable, shook the whole bridge. Then he rolled over and pitched into the stream, raising a sort of water spout. Whereon Venner's dog barked like mad and woke up Venner and the calves in the byre, and Moore's dog began barking as well. What you might call a good reaction. Venner came out and pitched into me; he was properly furious and we had quite a party. But it convinced all of us of one thing: it couldn't have happened the way everybody said. That wooden bridge makes too much row, and a big body flopping in the water makes too much splash, just like a flat dive. It makes a real smack and splother."

"Oh dear..." said Anne.

"Yes. I know. But it's better to get things straight. My first idea was right. Somebody gave her a good whang from behind and rolled her into the water. And they didn't do it from the side of the stream by Venner's house. It had to be on this side, and a bit away from the bridge."

Anne sat up, with her knees up to her chin, her hands clasped round her ankles, and her face was troubled. "Ray, did you feel it was worthwhile, this experiment of yours?"

"Yes." He spoke without hesitation. "It's cleared up some

possible misapprehensions, and I know you realise what I mean. Perhaps inquisitiveness isn't a very admirable quality, but you've either got it or you haven't. I wanted to get one or two things clear."

"You've proved that she didn't tumble all in a heap on the bridge. You haven't proved that she didn't commit suicide by slipping quietly into the water."

"Angel, you don't get an enormous welt on the occiput by slipping quietly into the water. The only way she could have bruised the back of her head like that was by collapsing in such a way that her head struck the hand rail as she fell. I was willing to maintain that that *might* have happened until this evening. Now I know better."

"So let's put it quite plainly. You believe somebody murdered her," said Anne, "and that means somebody in this place. It's not a comforting thought."

"I quite agree. But it's better to look the fact in the face."

"Well, don't you go getting a great whang on your occiput, Ray. Leave it to that rather pleasant cop. He looked pretty competent to me. I wonder where he was when you were doing your reconstruction act."

"He told Simon Barracombe he was driving up to Stone Barrow: but for all I know he was somewhere around by the bridge. If so, he saw a very competent demonstration of what didn't happen."

"In that case you'll get ticked off tomorrow. Pros don't like amateurs butting in," said Anne. "Let's go to sleep and forget all about it."

"Shouldn't be hard, angel," said Raymond sleepily, as he slipped into bed beside her.

CHAPTER XII

1

"Isn't the real fact of the matter that you accepted Miss Torrington at her face value, madam?" enquired Macdonald evenly.

He was talking to Lady Ridding, who had already tried several varieties of technique on the Chief Inspector, without seeming to make much impression. First, her undoubted charm had been well to the fore.

"It was so wise of the Chief Constable to put the matter in your hands, Chief Inspector. I was very worried about Sergeant Peel. He showed a tendency to jump to conclusions—and very unwise conclusions, too. Between you and me, I'm afraid he's rather a stupid man."

"I have found Sergeant Peel a most able and conscientious officer," said Macdonald quietly.

"Ah, but you wouldn't know the extent to which he has upset the village," said Lady Ridding. "There people are *our* people. I know them all, and know them well. Knowing them as I do, it seems outrageous to me that any police officer should imagine that a crime of violence could have been committed by any of them. And Sister Monica—"

Macdonald let her babble on uninterrupted for a while. Saintliness and halos, self-abnegation and devotion, floated in the air like incense, until Macdonald put his abrupt question. Lady Ridding flushed and drew herself very erect.

"I *knew* her, Chief Inspector," she replied. "She had worked faithfully for me for thirty years."

"Nevertheless, I think that, apart from the qualities she made a show of, you knew very little about her," persisted Macdonald, "but there is another point I should like to raise first. Have you any knowledge of the antecedents of Hannah Barrow, known as Nurse Barrow at Gramarye?"

"Nurse Barrow has been at Gramarye for over twenty years," said Lady Ridding coldly. "I have no recollection of where she came from, because Sister Monica engaged her and made all the necessary enquiries. Sister was a genius at training domestic servants, and I left the engaging of them to her judgment. Of course we had village girls as domestics at Gramarye in the old days, but it got increasingly difficult to persuade girls to go into service. We were very lucky in having Hannah, who was a very hard worker."

"Yes. I think she has worked hard," agreed Macdonald. "I am going to tell you Hannah's history, because it throws light on Miss Torrington's character. Hannah was brought up in an orphanage in Bristol. She was trained as a domestic servant and placed in a job with a woman who was a very harsh and cruel employer. I need not go into all the details, but in 1918 Hannah Barrow was arrested and charged with the murder of her employer. Eventually the charge was reduced to man-slaughter, and Hannah Barrow (or Brown, as her name was then) was sentenced to ten years' penal servitude. There were extenuating circumstances, as she had been abominably treated, but she certainly killed her employer. Some time after her release, Hannah was engaged by Miss Torrington. Were you aware of these facts, madam?"

Lady Ridding looked horrified, but she kept her poise. "I knew nothing of this," she declared. "Nothing. Sister Monica was very wrong to keep me in ignorance, but she doubtless did so from motives of charity."

"She did so from motives of self-interest and to indulge her own mania for domination," said Macdonald quietly. "She liked having people about her whom she had a hold over. I have had a woman police officer interviewing Hannah Barrow. She has been terrorised for twenty years. She is a very simple, ignorant, credulous creature, and her one abiding fear was to be turned out again into the world with the stigma of her conviction made known. There was certainly no charity about Miss Torrington's dealings with Hannah Barrow."

"But Hannah worshipped Sister Monica," protested Lady Ridding, her voice rising in pitch in her agitation.

"Hannah's worship was not unlike that of a rabbit towards a stoat," rejoined Macdonald. "She had a small repertoire of phrases: Sister was wonderful. Sister communed with the spirits and souls of the righteous: Sister went out into the peaceful night to think holy thoughts. These latter were doubtless learned by heart, after many repetitions by their originator. Now that Hannah Barrow has been told that her own history is known to us, the phrases she uses about Miss Torrington are less stereotyped."

Lady Ridding opened her mouth to reply, but no sound came. She remained sitting with her mouth open, and something about her silver hair and pink mouth reminded Macdonald of a white rabbit. He went on politely: "I agree with you, madam, that the Warden of Gramarye had no right to engage a woman with a history like Hannah Barrow's on her own responsibility alone. The matter should have been brought before the Committee, but, if my judgment is right, Miss Torrington had a very low estimate of the Committee. She knew she could manage the Committee. That is one of the things I implied when I said that you took Miss Torrington at her face value. This, as has been frequently repeated, was 'wonderful.'"

Lady Ridding had not been Lady of the Manor for thirty years without having developed a technique for dealing with difficult and tiresome people, and this C.I.D. man was, in Lady Ridding's opinion, being excessively difficult and tiresome.

"Your implications are beside the point," she said tartly. "The whole matter is one of profound distress to me, and I will tolerate neither flippancy nor impertinence from you."

"Believe me, I am very far from feeling flippant over the condition of affairs at Gramarye," replied Macdonald. "If I have any personal feelings about the matter, they are more like horror and astonishment that a Committee of responsible persons could allow themselves to be hoodwinked by the pose of an unprincipled and exceedingly competent employee. As for impertinence, I maintain that everything I have said was pertinent. As Chairman of the Committee, it is desirable that you should learn and face both the facts and their implications. They are very far from being pleasant facts, madam."

"I shall be indebted if you make your statement with all possible brevity, officer, and without redundant comment," said Lady Ridding.

There was a rustle of paper from the corner of the room, as Detective Reeves turned over a sheet of paper rather more noisily than he need have done. Reeves was a highly skilled amanuensis, who noted down conversations at a speed unattained by the majority of police clerks. He apologised for his clumsiness as Macdonald glanced round, repeated "without redundant comment" and waited with pencil poised.

"As is customary, the essential parts of this interview are being put in writing," explained Macdonald to Lady Ridding. "To continue with my facts. I understand that Miss Torrington was paid £120 a year, in cash, £10 monthly. Is that correct?"

"It is. I paid her myself. She refused any further rise in salary."

"Have you any knowledge of her private means, madam?"

"She had no private means. She told me so explicitly. Sister Monica cared nothing for money," replied Lady Ridding loftily.

"Yet during the past ten years Miss Torrington paid into various building societies the sum of over two thousand pounds, this money being paid in cash, monthly, in pound notes. The sum she invested was much larger than her total salary for that period. If she had no private means, can you suggest how she acquired this sum?"

"Two thousand pounds?" gasped Lady Ridding, "two *thousand* pounds—but that's preposterous." She broke off, almost with a gasp, as though she had suddenly checked herself, and a deep colour flooded her face. "I can't believe it," she added helplessly.

"Did you, at any time, give Miss Torrington any money over and above her salary?" asked Macdonald.

Lady Ridding moved unhappily in her place. "An occasional present, a pound at Christmas and on her birthday," she admitted, "but nothing, *nothing* in comparison with the sum you mention. I can't understand it. She told me she had no means..."

"But it seems she had some source of supply," said Macdonald. "The obvious suggestion, of course, is blackmail."

Lady Ridding sat and stared at him, her plump white fingers fidgeting with a long gold chain which she wore round her neck. That she was surprised, and very much upset, seemed plain enough, but it also seemed to Macdonald that there was some sort of calculation going on in her mind.

"Can you make any sort of suggestion in connection with this part of the problem, madam?" he asked.

She shook her head, very decidedly. "I am absolutely at a loss to explain or understand it," she said, and paused for a moment. "You suggest the possibility of blackmail. I am appalled by such an idea." She drew a deep breath and went on: "You have been explaining to me, in terms which admit of no misunderstanding, that I have been deceived in this woman. That she deceived us all. It is a shocking and humiliating thought, Chief Inspector."

Without turning his head, Macdonald was aware that Reeves had looked up. Reeves, while younger than Macdonald, had had a lot of experience of men and women giving evidence. A *volte-face* (or, as Reeves would have said 'going into reverse') was a not unusual manoeuvre for an embarrassed witness, and both the C.I.D. men recognised the indications when such a move might occur. Reeves was alert to notice if this witness would 'crash her gears.'

"I blame myself bitterly," continued Lady Ridding. "Suspicion is alien to my nature, especially towards those who are in our service. For all these years, Sister Monica has run Gramarye with real ability. She worked very hard, she was always willing and anxious to help in any worthy cause. I realised, of course, that she was old-fashioned, but I myself am old, and I still think there is much that is praiseworthy in old and tried methods." She broke off with a profound sigh, while Macdonald sat in silence and Reeves wrote industriously. Seeing that she was to be given no help by the words of sympathy and agreement which she obviously expected, Lady Ridding plunged in again.

"If ever I had any suspicion that Sister Monica was not all that she appeared to be, I put such thoughts away from me as unworthy," she said sadly.

"Miss Torrington was certainly not what she appeared to be," said Macdonald quietly. "Have you any idea if, or when, she was married?"

"Married?" gasped Lady Ridding. "Do you mean…married?" Her last enquiry came in a gasp. (As Reeves said later, "She wasn't slow to tumble to that one.")

"I think you know exactly what I mean, Lady Ridding," replied Macdonald evenly. "The pathologists who carried out the post mortem reported that she was not a virgin."

Poor Lady Ridding dropped her face in her hands. When she raised her head again, her face was very white, but she replied with a dignity which was real this time.

"I am more horrified than I can say, Chief Inspector. When I spoke of suspicion, I did not mean that I questioned Sister Monica's moral character. I accepted that without a thought…I am afraid I must ask you to excuse me any further questions just now. I am so much upset that I feel incapable of forming reasonable answers."

She got up resolutely, and Macdonald got up also, saying: "I am sorry, Lady Ridding. I realise you have cause for distress, but you have got to face the facts. I am quite willing to defer any other questions until such time as you feel able to answer them. Meantime, might I speak to Sir James?"

2

Sir James Ridding was a man of seventy, lean, erect, very neat, clean and vigorous looking. He was dressed in a checked tweed jacket, stock, and excellently fitting whipcord breeches and well polished riding boots. He came to the point promptly and without embarrassment.

"My wife is very much upset, Chief Inspector. She is an exceedingly nice-minded woman. I am not a nice-minded man. Stock breeding doesn't leave much room for ultra refinement. So let's accept the facts without fussing. It would save you from barking up the wrong tree if you could believe that Miss Torrington has never, in all these years, been any affair of mine." He looked Macdonald straight in the face and added: "If she'd ever attempted to blackmail me she'd have found herself in Queer Street. But she knew just how far her sphere of influence went. It did not include me."

"The question is, whom did it include?" asked Macdonald bluntly.

"I've nothing to tell you that will help you, Chief Inspector. In all the years she's been at Gramarye, I've never done more than pass the time of day with the Warden. I couldn't abide her. I believed her to be competent at her job, I knew her to be clever at managing people. I knew my wife made use of her, particularly in the realm of getting village girls trained into competent servants." He paused, and then added: "My wife's probably given her an occasional fiver, but it didn't go farther than that. We've a joint banking account and we're both methodical people over money. Have to be, these days. A coupla' thousand pounds, even over a period of ten years—No. You can take that as read. Or you can see our bank statements if you want to. I'm not a fool. I know you're not here to be polite to us."

"I'm here for one reason alone, sir—"

"Quite, quite. Fact finding. Got to be done, I know that. It's the hell of a mess, all the same. I could never understand the hold the woman got over people. Uncanny, absolutely uncanny. I told my wife years ago it'd be better to shift her. She was always nosing around, nobody's business was their own. But she was competent, gad, she was competent. That place ran on oiled wheels."

"I think the cruse has been failing a bit lately, sir."

Sir James chuckled. "Thank God for a spot of flippancy. The whole thing's frightful, and the saintly stuff's got me down. Hushed voices and odour of sanctity. I knew in my own mind the woman was a damned humbug. Altruism my hat. She stayed here because she liked it. She'd got the Committee eating out of her hand, the Vicar where she wanted him, the M.O. trained to her ways, and most people indebted to her for service rendered. And now she's gone and got herself murdered on my property. A pretty kettle of fish. What's this story about old Hannah Barrow? My wife had got it all haywire."

Macdonald told him.

"Poor old Barrow!" said Sir James. "And now I suppose you're bound to suspect that poor old bit of God-help-us, arguing she'd had enough and to spare, so she borrowed a golf club and got busy. Would a golf club have done the job? I've mislaid my favourite putter."

"I shouldn't have chosen a putter myself, sir. And I'm quite sure that Hannah Barrow wouldn't have. A police truncheon would have been handier."

"Would it? I've got one somewhere. It was issued to my grandfather. Chartist riots, was it? Something of the kind. I'll make sure it's still around," said Sir James pensively. "I hope you've no real reason to suspect that Hannah did the job, though I'm bound to admit that it would be a relief to know that she did. Sounds brutal, I know, but any good counsel could show a jury that Hannah's not quite a hundred per cent, if you get me. I don't suppose she'd work any harder 'during detention at His Majesty's pleasure' than she's done at Gramarye."

"She'd work considerably less hard," agreed Macdonald, "but I think it'd be a good idea if you deleted from your mind that we are here to serve anybody's convenience, sir."

"Oh, quite, quite. But human nature's human nature. I'm fond of the village folks. I should hate to see any of 'em run in, my cowmen or shepherds or ploughmen, or the chaps who work the saw mill and the generator. It's probable that quite a number of them hated the deceased Warden. She ought to have been pensioned off years ago. I know it. I've only got myself to blame. The fact is, I like a quiet life: as the hymn says, 'give peace at home.' Lady Ridding could only see Sister Monica's good points. So there it was."

"You say 'a number of them hated the Warden,' sir. Why?"

"Why? Devil take it, you must have learnt a bit about the woman. She wormed herself into people's confidences. She learnt all the little shoddy secrets which exist in every village community. If a husband was unfaithful, if a wife were in debt, if tradespeople didn't abide by the rationing laws, if a farm-labourer did some poaching and a farmer's wife made butter on the quiet and sold it—she got to know somehow. She always has done, but it's only in the last few years she's taken to dropping veiled hints where the hints would do most damage. Damn it, I'm told she's even said malicious things about that nice girl at the Dower House—Ferens' wife. And as for John Sanderson, she did her best to discredit him. And he was right, you know. He said the woman wasn't fit to be in charge of anything."

"I take it you knew that Miss Torrington was relieved of her duties as treasurer and collector for various funds?"

"Yes. I knew all about that. I had a few words with the Vicar and the Church Wardens—all very guarded. Maybe she did dip into the bag a bit. More than probable. But not to the extent of two thousand pounds over a period of ten years. Nearly four pounds a week. That's more than all the cash collections lumped together, a lot more. You can't imagine Venner or Moore, or Rigg, or old Mrs. Yeo, paying out sums like that. Seems to me you'll have to look further afield, Chief Inspector. You can never tell what a woman like that got up to. May have blackmailed somebody in writing. She was clever, y'know."

"In my own belief, the essentials of the matter are here, sir, not farther afield at all. One of the points which is firmly established is that deceased hardly ever went out of this village. It's an easy point to establish. Milham in the Moor is too far away from any other place for her to have walked, and we know she didn't ever go in the bus of recent years. As for letters, I've no wish to get your postmistress into trouble, but I think she is a very observant body. She knows quite well what letters deceased posted in the area of the Milham in the Moor post office, and there were no letters suggestive of the sort of private correspondence which indicates blackmail by post."

Sir James Ridding treated himself to a quiet chuckle. "I always post my own letters at Milham Prior or Barnsford," he said. "Incidentally, I can't help being interested in the late Warden's financial transactions. Did she have a banking account?"

"Not so far as we have ascertained up to the present. Interest on her share accounts was reinvested in the companies concerned. Notice was sent to her of dividends paid, of course, but these notices were posted in envelopes supplied and addressed by Miss Torrington herself."

Again Sir James chuckled. "She was nothing if not thorough. She worked out a method which gave nothing away. She chose investments which were tax free, or rather on which the tax was paid by the companies before the dividends were issued, so she reduced to a minimum any correspondence with the Inland Revenue, and the addressed envelope system gave the postmistress precious little satisfaction. But how did she post the cash for investment?"

"By registered post once a month from Milham Prior central post office. Hannah Barrow posted the letter and brought back the receipts, and Hannah Barrow is illiterate. But she knows it was only one letter she posted monthly, 'the register letter' she calls it."

"Thorough, the late lamented," observed Sir James. "I always knew she was intelligent."

"Her intelligence didn't prevent her from being too thorough," said Macdonald dryly. "She ended by driving somebody too far. Now, sir, you have a pretty clear idea of the main facts. I put it to you, have you any information which can assist this investigation?"

"No, thank God, I have not," said Sir James. "I have always carefully avoided any discussion about Sister Monica. I disliked her, and I have told you so frankly, but my wife valued her and wished to retain her services. I left it at that."

"But you were aware that discussion of deceased might have landed you in difficulties, sir?"

Sir James rose to his feet with an air of finality. "I thought she was a canting old hypocrite, Chief Inspector. I realise that she felt herself a person of importance, that she cherished her position here, and that at one time she threw her weight about too much in the village. But I also believed that villages like this one have the ability to deal with busybodies. The process is slow, but sure. I was not prepared to cause a domestic upheaval in my own house because I disliked the woman. She didn't seem to me to be important enough to warrant it." He gazed out of the window for a moment, fingering his stock, obviously in two minds whether to continue or not. Then he turned and faced Macdonald and added: "There are occasions in married life when, for one reason or another, a husband puts his foot down without regard to ensuing recriminations. The same is true of a wife. Sister Monica did not constitute one of these occasions."

3

"I enjoyed that, Chief." Reeves murmured his appreciation of the foregoing interview a little unkindly, for as he spoke he was enjoying the colour and fragrance of Lady Ridding's rose garden. From the clear yellow of Golden Dawn, through the orange copper of Luis Brinas, the flame of Madame Herriot, to the deep crimson of Etoile de Hollande, the roses flamed in a glory of rich colour, their fragrance seeming to quiver on the sun-warmed air of midsummer.

"All right, but you can't pick her roses," said Macdonald.

"I wasn't going to. I'm a cockney. We know it isn't allowed," said Reeves, "though if I were going to pick one I'd have the dutchman…Etoile de Hollande. That's a rose, that is. How much of all that did she know, Chief? She registered surprise quite snappily, but I wasn't really convinced."

Macdonald made no answer until they had left the Manor House garden and were in the park again. This time, the two men turned away from the steep narrow path which led down to the mill, and took a diverging path which led across the park to the woodlands.

"I don't know," said Macdonald reflectively, "but I think I was more interested in trying to assess how much Sir James knew. He didn't have to register surprise: his wife had told him the essentials. I can't judge Lady Ridding. I agree with you that something about her horrified astonishment struck me as accomplished."

"But she *is* accomplished," said Reeves. "You've hit on the right word. It means finished, doesn't it, complete, polished off. Product of a finishing school. She's got a veneer, and you can't get past it. Isn't that what you mean when you say you can't judge her?"

"Something like that. But I think there's something substantial underneath the manner, the courage, and the stability which are, to some extent, the result of being very sure of herself. If she *did* know the real Monica Emily, there must have been some very powerful factor which forced Lady Ridding to accept a situation which would surely have been intolerably distasteful to her. And look at her face, Reeves. Hardly a line on it. It's the face of a woman who's pleased to the point of complacency."

"Umps… Yes. There is that. No hair tearing or nerve racking about that dame, I grant you. But there's a type which kids itself by saying, 'I prefer not to know.' Turns away and doesn't look: very careful not to look. And calls not looking good taste."

"If ever you forget your technique in the witness box and give evidence in your natural idiom, may I be there to hear," said Macdonald, "but emulating your method, I'd say this. She might say, 'I'd rather not know. I'd rather not look,' but she'd know other people wouldn't be equally accommodating.

She's shrewd, and she'd hate her friends to say, 'Poor Lady R. How she was hoodwinked."

"Yes. She'd mind what other people say. She's found her Warden very useful to her all these years and she didn't want to lose her."

Macdonald chuckled. "The fivers mentioned by Sir James probably indicate Lady Ridding's gratitude for extra-mural services, so to speak. You know, in his indirect way he told us quite a bit. And there were the points he didn't mention."

"Yes. I've got him verbatim. We might chew him over in detail," said Reeves reflectively, as they entered the shadow of the beech woods.

Macdonald added:

"I'm convinced of one thing. Monica Emily had become a miser. She didn't spend. She hoarded."

CHAPTER XIII

1

On the same morning that Macdonald went to see Sir James and Lady Ridding, one of the foresters on the estate went into the bailiff's office while Sanderson was looking through his letters.

"Yes, come in, Greave," said Sanderson, "what is it you want?"

"It's about that hut of mine in Coombe wood, sir. You'll mind I spoke of it before. I keep some gear there, because it's an awkward place to get at. I can't get a van or tractor up there, and I've got a stove and so forth in the hut because it's right out of the way."

"Yes. I remember it," said Sanderson. "What's the trouble?"

"I want a good chain and padlock, sir, and maybe a hasp and staple so that I can bolt 'em through from the inside. It's been broken into again."

"Why, it's not so long since I had a new lock put on it for you," said Sanderson.

"That's right, sir. The old one was rusted rotten. But locking it be'n't good enow'. There's too much play on that old door, and you can lever it open."

"Who's been doing it?" asked Sanderson. "Have you missed anything?"

"My sharpening stone's gone, carborundum that be, and maybe some other gear. As to who, I reckoned it was some o' them dratted boys, after their birds' nesting, the last time. Nothing was took, just devilment I reckoned. But this time I'm not so sure. That's been forced open with a bar, that door has. I reckon it was that old varmint of a tramp. Hale, the keeper, warned he off the woods last month, but 'tis a lonely ride that, through Coombe wood, and one keeper be'n't enough to keep an eye on it. In the old days 'twas a different story. Four keepers Sir James had."

"I don't much like the sound of this, Greave. Game-keeping isn't my business, but your hut and gear is. I think I'll come along and see it, and if the place has been forced open as you say, and gear stolen, the police had better be told."

Greave looked unhappy. "Surely now, you wouldn't make a police matter of it, sir? We've had our bellyful of police, begging your pardon. I'd rather pay for the stone and padlock an' all than have that Milham Prior sergeant poking his nose where it's not wanted. We've had enough of he and to spare. And what can he do like? If so be that old varmint broke into my shed and stole my stone, him won't be sitting in a hedgerow awaiting for Sergeant Peel to search he."

"I don't suppose he will be, but thefts should be reported to the police," said Sanderson. "Look here, you come along into the yard and hunt out your padlock and staple and bolts—I know we've got some in store—and I'll get my car out and drive you as near as the ride will allow. Then I'll have a look at the damage, and you can get your hasp and staple fixed. You can borrow a brace from the joiner's shop."

"Very good, sir. I'll be right glad to get that fixed. I'll make a proper job of that this time. But don't you go bringing that Milham Prior sergeant here again. We be fair sick of he."

2

Thus it was that John Sanderson, having of necessity taken a round-about route to get his car to the woodland ride which approached Coombe wood, saw the two C.I.D. men strolling along the ride ahead of him. Sanderson pulled up and called to them:

"Would you like to come and exert your talents on a case of breaking and entering? Greave here says his hut's been forced open and some of his gear stolen, right away in the woods yonder."

"We should be most happy to assist," replied Macdonald cheerfully. "We shall be poaching, of course, but I expect I can square Sergeant Peel."

"Splendid. Get in behind, will you. Greave suspects a tramp. We get an occasional hobo, generally after eggs, but not very many. We're too far away from a high road."

Macdonald and Reeves jumped in at the back, and as Sanderson proceeded slowly over the unmetalled track, Macdonald asked: "Where does this lead to?"

"If you keep to the ride you come out at Hazeldown, just on the edge of the moor. There's a small mining hamlet there. The mine was disused between the wars, but they opened the workings up again in 1940, and the cottages are still lived in. But we shall turn off from the main ride, and leave the car. There'll be a bit of scrambling—rather rough ground,

I'm afraid. There was some felling done a while back. The foresters shifted the valuable timber, but there's a lot of small stuff left, and we shift it ourselves as best we can. Timber's the devil to come by these days and we don't leave any to rot."

They jogged along in the car for about twenty minutes before Sanderson pulled up, saying, "The hut is up on the rise, yonder. You can see where they felled the big stuff, on the scarp beyond. It was a difficult job getting it moved, but what some of those modern lumberjacks can do with a cat-erpillar tractor and cable is worthy of the Royal Armoured Corps—and looks nearly as hazardous to me. That's the hut."

It was a commonplace little wooden shack, having no windows, but a stove pipe projected from the roof at one end. The door had evidently been levered open, and the catch of the lock wrenched away.

"I reckon that was done with a bar," said Greave.

"A tyre lever would have done it," said Macdonald; "it's very much on the same principle as a jemmy."

"That's about it," said Reeves. He pushed the door open and looked inside. There was a rough bench along one side, an iron stove at the far end, and some sacks stuffed with bracken lying against one wall.

"I gets the lads to take them sacks along when they've got a tractor near enough to be handy like," explained Greave. "Bracken, that makes good bedding for my ducks when straw's hard to come by."

"That'd make good bedding for a tramp, too," said Sanderson, "and I'll bet that's what it's been used for. You can see that some-body's been lying on the sacks from the way they're flattened."

"Aye, that's true enow," agreed Greave, "the old varmint's been using my hut to doss down in, drat he, and made free with the sticks and logs I left for the stove, too."

"Oh, well, I'm afraid I haven't provided you with much of a problem, Chief Inspector," said Sanderson. "I think Greave is right—the sacks give it away." He kicked one of the sacks aside, saying, "You'd better get those shifted. Free bedding and firing is too much of a bait—"

"What's that there, sir? Him have left us a token, seemingly."

He was just bending down to pick something up when Macdonald said:

"Don't touch it. That never belonged to an old hobo. It must be stolen property."

"Jiminy!" exclaimed Greave. "That be—": he broke off and stood staring. Reeves turned the beam of an electric torch on to the floor, where a black object lay jammed between the lower sack and the match boarding. The object was a black leather hand-bag, a bulging, old-fashioned object, the sort of hand-bag which was once described as a reticule by old-fashioned gentle-women.

Macdonald pulled the sack away, and the bag slipped on to the ground and lay flat: both its straps were broken and its clasp unloosed.

"You know who that belongs to, don't you, Greave?" said Macdonald.

"It's the dead spit o' the one Sister carried," said Greave. "Her's had it for years. Put it down on our kitchen table many a time when her came collecting. Deary, deary me, I never thought o' nought like this."

"When did you come here last, Greave?" asked Sanderson, and the old man rubbed his head. He had taken his cap off, and stood looking down at the black bag as though it were mortal remains.

"That'd be a fortnight ago," he said slowly. "I came here to lop some ash branches, small stuff 'twas, but good enow' for posts for fencing. I marked mun, aye and sawed same into lengths to make a-shifting of 'em handy like. Then this morning, I got Joe Grant to bring his lorry as near as might be—seven o'clock we started—and we got the branches into the lorry and took 'em to saw mill to get 'em sawn up, ready for Mr. Moore. And 'twas this morning I saw the door of the hut had been interfered with. Joe saw it, too. And after my breakfast I went along to Mr. Sanderson's office to tell him I wanted a padlock and hasp and staple and that, to bolt from inside and make a job of it."

"Was the door and lock in order a fortnight ago?" asked Macdonald.

"That was, sir." Greave turned to answer the C.I.D. man, and at the same time pulled a key out of his pocket. "I was working here all morning, Joe gave me a lift in his lorry as far as he could, and I lit the stove to make me tea. I know 'twas all in order then, and I locked mun up meself when I left. I'd sharpened my saw to cut through a trunk—too heavy 'twas to handle—and I left my files on the bench there. I missed they at once, and my old iron pan I boil water in, that's gone too."

"Thanks very much. You've told me just what I wanted to know, and told it clearly, too," said Macdonald. "Well, I think this is our job now, Mr. Sanderson. If you'll take Inspector Reeves back with you, he can bring my car out here."

"Very good," said Sanderson. "I understand I'm to leave things to you, and not report elsewhere?"

"That's it," said Macdonald. "It would be better if neither you nor Greave said anything about it. Otherwise there'll be no end of stories going round."

"I shan't name it, sir, not even to Mother. Get a woman on a tale like this and her'll never leave off," said Greave.

3

It was the best part of an hour before Reeves came back in the car, complete with his own "gear," some Cornish pasties, two bottles of beer and a bunch of very young carrots, which he chewed with the enthusiasm of a donkey.

"I'll go hungry when there's any object in going hungry," he observed, "but I work better when I'm fed."

"In common with other domestic animals," agreed Macdonald. "All right. Let's sit on the far side of the shed so that we're not an exhibit if any happen to pass this way."

"'Happen' is good," said Reeves. "Thick and fast they came at last, meaning explanations. 'Her was dizzy' doesn't seem to meet the requirements after last night's little experiment. So a tramp is provided. Not a bad effort."

"Provided by whom?" asked Macdonald. "I agree with you that somebody's been being helpful, though we can't be certain until we've identified the finger-prints on that bag—if there are any to identify."

"If there aren't, that's proof the job's phoney," said Reeves. "Tramps don't wear gloves." He chewed away at his Cornish pasty and then said: "Rather neat the way Sanderson collected us and brought us along. Did it occur to you that he was being helpful?"

"I wondered a bit, but the plain fact is that Sanderson had no means of knowing that you and I were going to stroll through the woods arguing over evidence to date. We couldn't know ourselves. It was just chance. And I'd say Greave is honest. The way he told his story was absolutely straightforward."

"Yes. If he'd been on in this act, he'd have seen to it that Joe Grant found that bag, and they could have brought it along to

Sanderson with everybody's paw marks all over it. But it was Sanderson who saw to it that the bag was found under our very noses: and it was Sanderson who was helpful last night."

"Maybe, but it was Ferens who suggested the experiment on the bridge. As I told you, when I went and saw him this morning, Ferens was quite straight over it. It was his idea, and he persuaded Sanderson to co-operate—not that any persuasion was needed."

Reeves dealt with a bottle of beer to his satisfaction and then said: "You know, it's a pretty ingenious spanner somebody's thrown in the works. We shall find that the story of a tramp being warned off by the gamekeeper was true, and it's such a nice straightforward story. Devout dame, a bit weak in the upper storey, goes wandering in the moonlight at midsummer with a nice fat bag under her arm. Tramp sees her, bats her one with his cudgel, steals bag and rolls dame in river. Tramp retires to hide-out in the woods, empties bag, keeps coin of the realm and burns any papers in the stove."

"But why didn't said tramp burn the bag, too, or at any rate bury it or hide it in the woods?" asked Macdonald. "Since he knew he'd just committed a murder, would he have left the bag to be found? Of course he wouldn't."

"I'm not so sure, chief. How often have bags been found after being emptied of their contents? You know the answer to that one. And you can't burn a bag completely: the metal frame's almost indestructible."

"But you could bury it, or shove it down a rabbit burrow, or wedge it under a rock in the river," objected Macdonald. "To burn the papers and leave the bag argues a very silly tramp. However, if you've finished chewing carrots, come and do your stuff on the bag."

4

"Curiouser and curiouser," said Macdonald.

He sat and looked at the bag thoughtfully. When it had been new, initials had been stamped on it in gold—M.E.T. There was very little of the gold left, but the die stamp was still clear enough. There were no finger-prints on the worn surface of the leather, and the absence of them was explained by the fact that the bag had been immersed in water. It was dry now, but the temperature of the wooden shack at mid-summer was high enough to explain why it had dried. The lining was a bit damp, and its worn silk showed the stain from its immersion. The torn straps interested Macdonald: they had been good strong straps, and it must have taken a severe pull to tear them away from the bag.

"Might be called over-acting," he said. "I think the straps were torn away deliberately to give the right impression."

"Could be," said Reeves, and Macdonald went on:

"I keep on going back to our first assumption; she was knocked senseless somewhere close by the river, because her body was too heavy to be carried far. What we're supposed to argue from this bag is that the straps broke when the bag was tugged away from her. That implies she was holding on to it very tight. If she'd kept her grip on the bag like that when a tramp was trying to get it from her, doesn't it stand to reason that she'd have screamed? And if she'd screamed, the dogs would have heard her and barked. They didn't bark. If they had, half the village would have heard them. Whatever is the explanation of this bag, I'm pretty certain the woman was knocked out without knowing anything about it, silently."

"And if she'd been knocked out, she wasn't gripping the bag, because her grip would have gone as she lost her senses," agreed Reeves, "therefore the straps wouldn't have broken. I see that point all right. But we don't know exactly what happened: it's possible that the bag fell in the water with her body, and was washed downstream and found by somebody not connected with the original assault. The tramp, for instance. We've still got that tramp in the offing." He paused, staring down at the worn black reticule. "You said something to the effect that this village had developed a sort of mystical technique, chief. I'd call it a technique for mystification. At first it was the saintly stuff. Then that wore thin—you knocked the stuffing out of the Venners with plain commonsense. Then it was 'her went dizzy, poor soul,' and Ferens knocked that sideways by showing she couldn't have collapsed on the bridge and knocked her head on the hand-rail without making more row than was indicated. Now somebody's trying again. ''Tis a tramp surely, knocked Sister down and stole her bag. Iss, 'tis a tramp.' Can't I hear 'em at it."

"You're assuming that the village knows what really happened?"

"Yes. And they're going to prevent us finding out. I don't suggest the murder was a co-operative effort: co-operation in murder doesn't happen in our experience. It's my belief that the village knew the woman was a menace and feels justice has been done, but whether that's so or not they're going to protect whoever it was who did the job—one of themselves, that is."

"Query, does Ferens know what happened?" mused Macdonald.

"Might do. What do you think yourself?"

"I should say he didn't *know*, not as evidence goes. He's got that sort of professional probity which bars telling plain lies. It isn't entirely a moral quality. It's an awareness of the loss of prestige—professional dignity—if found out. That type would hate to be bowled out telling a lie: they prefer to stick to the truth. But Ferens has done some guessing, as you and I are doing some guessing, and it's my belief he staged that demonstration last night as a warning to somebody, or as a warning to the whole village. It was like saying, 'You can't get away with that one.' That's my belief, anyway, but he's not likely to admit it."

"What's the betting that this racket with the bag was worked last night—after Ferens' demonstration?"

"I think that's quite possible. If so, it involves the fact that somebody had this bag in their possession."

Macdonald broke off, and was silent for a moment or two. Then he went on: "We've got to square the discovery of the bag with the assumptions we've made on the earlier evidence. Peel argued that an attaché case, or a box containing documents, had been stolen from the office at Gramarye because he couldn't find any personal papers. It seems possible to me that deceased carried her personal papers about with her in this bag. It's large enough to contain quite a lot of stuff."

"That's reasonable enough," agreed Reeves. "Women do carry the most incredible lot of stuff around with them in their bags. I can quite see this Torrington dame being suspicious of everybody at Gramarye, and making a habit of taking this bag around with her whenever she went out of the house. She was evidently a methodical cuss, and a very careful one. She'd never have mislaid the bag, or left it about."

"Well, if we accept that, it seems probable to me that whoever laid her out would have taken the contents of her bag. We're arguing she was a blackmailer. If she carried that bag about with her habitually, it might well be argued that she'd got something valuable in it."

"O.K. The argument following that seems to be that the murderer pocketed the contents of the bag and then tore the straps off it to indicate that it had been snatched, and threw it in the stream—the safest thing to do with it. It might then have been washed down stream and found by somebody else. The latter party put it somewhere to dry, so that it was ready to plant in an emergency, so to speak. And planted it was."

"It's a possible reconstruction," said Macdonald, "but there could be plenty of variations on it. It was a neat enough idea putting it here, and I'm disposed to believe it could have been done last night, 'after the demonstration' as you say. Anybody could have known that Greave was coming out here with Joe Grant to pick up the timber for the posts."

"And some could have known better than others," meditated Reeves.

"Well, when you've finished your job here, we'll screw the door up. There don't seem to be any more souvenirs about," said Macdonald. "I'll put the bag in my attaché case, and try to find out when deceased was last seen carrying it in the village. After that I'll send it up to C.O. and see if the backroom boys can help. They ought to be able to tell us if it was ever in the stream at all, or merely held under a tap."

"Oh, they'll tell you a lot—age, place of origin, habits of owner, and force required to sever straps to three places of decimals," said Reeves, "but the village won't tell you anything. They'll run true to form with 'I can't rightly say. Maybe that is and maybe that isn't.'" He paused, as he put his insufflator and camera away. "I'm a bit surprised that Peel didn't get on to the fact that the bag was missing. He was very good at the routine stuff."

"We can't blame Peel any more than ourselves," said Macdonald. "A leather hand-bag was found in deceased's bedroom: it contained a purse, note case, handkerchief, and all the items you might have expected, including smelling salts and sal volatile."

"That was her Sunday-go-to-meeting bag," said Reeves promptly. "The smelling salts was to ginger up any toddler who tried to be sick in church. The Sunday bag was probably a gift from titled employers. You ask if it wasn't, chief."

"I will. You're probably right over that one."

"They do crop up, don't they?" said Reeves reflectively.

CHAPTER XIV

1

"Can you identify this bag, Mrs. Yeo?" asked Macdonald.

The Chief Inspector had put his attaché case on the counter of the village post-office-cum-shop, and felt rather like a commercial traveller as he raised the lid to display his wares.

Stout Mrs. Yeo stared: took off her glasses and stared afresh. "Well, I never did," she exclaimed, "if that be'n't Sister Monica's old bag. Years it was Sister had that bag. I do mind her telling me her had had that bag when her first come here, and that's a tidy time ago, as you'd know, sir."

"Can you tell me when you last saw her carrying it?" asked Macdonald.

"Now that be'n't so easy," countered Mrs. Yeo. "I mind she had it last Christmas, when her come collecting for a children's party. In Bristol, 'twas."

"But haven't you seen it since then?" asked Macdonald.

"Maybe I have and maybe I haven't," said Mrs. Yeo. "It's

like this, sir. Sister always wore that long cloak, and if so be she carried the bag under her cloak, you wouldn't notice like."

"But didn't she take her purse out of the bag to pay for her shopping?" asked Macdonald.

"Why, sir, Sister didn't do no cash shopping," said Mrs. Yeo. "Gramarye was registered here for fats and sugar and that, but Sister never did no little bits of shopping. A weekly order, 'twas, all very businesslike, Sister and Cook would make out the order every Saturday to be delivered Monday, and bill at the end of each month paid by cheque. And if anything was forgot 'twas Sister's rule they must do without till the next week. Very exact was Sister."

"Didn't she ever buy any stamps, or any sweets?" persisted Macdonald.

"She'd buy stamps ten shillings at a time," said Mrs. Yeo, "about once a month 'twas, and always paid for by ten shilling note. Nurse Barrow would come in, with a list, neat as anything, twenty-four twopence halfpennies, forty-eight halfpennies, thirty-six pennies. Always the same. I do know Sister's stamps by heart. And the little maids—the children—they'd send picture postcards home every other week, if so be as they'd got a home or an auntie to send to."

"And about the sweets," put in another voice from the back of the shop. "Sweets was ordered, too, every week, and the points pinned on the order all neat and correct. Boiled sweets mostly 'twas, and chocolate creams for saints' days and festivals. As good as a 'Churchman's Calendar' Sister's order was, her never forgetting no holy days."

"That's right," agreed Mrs. Yeo, "and the sweets went on the bill like the rest. Sister saying that sweets were part of the children's rations. But 'twas all ordered, no chance buying so to speak. If you'd care to step inside, sir, I could show you some of Sister's lists. A rare beautiful hand her wrote."

"Thank you very much, Mrs. Yeo. I should like to see them if you can spare the time."

"I can and welcome, sir," said the stout soul heartily. "If you'll come this way, Rosie can mind the counter a bit."

She lifted a bead curtain and opened a door which had glass panels in it and led the way into a comfortable stuffy little sitting-room, whose window was gay with the variegated geraniums popular in the village.

"Now do you sit down, sir," said Mrs. Yeo. "I'm glad to have a chance to talk to you, and that's a fact. Some o' the things they're saying in this village do keep me awake at nights. Such nonsense I never did hear. But first I'll show you Sister's lists, like I said."

She opened a drawer and pulled out some sheets, neatly clipped together, and handed them to Macdonald. "There they be, sir, and if everyone was as neat and tidy as that, Rosie and me'd be saved a lot of trouble. Rations for eighteen, as you see, all worked out in weights: twelve children, six adults— that be Sister Monica, Nurse, Cook, and the servant girls, and you'll mark as chocolate creams is ordered on the last list, that be for Midsummer, Saint John, he be midsummer saint. And the adding up done, too, and never no mistake."

"Miss Torrington seems to have taken a lot of trouble," said Macdonald. "Did she always bring you this list in herself?"

"Her used to, sir. Every Saturday morning, like clockwork, but this last year, her'd changed a lot. These last months, Sister often sent Nurse over with the order. Seemed as if Sister didn't want to come into village. Her'd be with the children in the garden and in the park, and her came to church same as ever: every soul in Gramarye came to church Sunday mornings, and they had a cold meal because Sister didn't hold with Cook working on the Sabbath. But somehow her had taken against coming shopping in the village. There was some foolish things said, sir, and some downright unkind ones, about Sister and the collections she made for charity. Maybe 'twas time her gave that up. I know me own memory isn't what it was, and Sister's wasn't neither. But there was no call for hard words."

"Are you quite sure of that, Mrs. Yeo? Haven't you ever spoken any hard words about Miss Torrington yourself?"

Mrs. Yeo's round face flushed up, but she didn't get flustered. "And if I have, sir, there's not many folks in our village I haven't got cross with, one way or another. Sister was bossy-like: she would do things her way, and she'd interfere in things that wasn't rightly her business, like the Mother's Union and the Choir outing and Sunday school treat. I know I've got proper mad with her at times. And we do seem to be more nervy-like than we used. I'm sick to death of this here rationing and Government orders and prices going up and all the rest. Sister was, too. Her was worried to death, poor soul, over costs going up all the time, and her that careful. Maybe I have got mad with her when she was alive, but I was taught to respect the dead, sir, meaning no offence."

"So was I, Mrs. Yeo," said Macdonald quietly, "but I am a policeman. The only way we can do our work is by getting at the truth: the truth, the whole truth, and nothing but the truth. And the idea underlying police work is to protect the innocent and punish the guilty. To respect the dead and thereby let the guilty go unpunished does not ensure justice, but the reverse."

"That's true enough, sir, but why you do make so sure that there's guilt in our village, I don't rightly see."

"Because I believe that Miss Torrington was murdered,

Mrs. Yeo, and it's my job—and yours too—to bring a murderer to trial. Whatever a person's just grievances may be, and no matter what threat is held over a person, murder is no way of settling the matter."

"God ha' mercy, need you tell me that, sir? I do know that as plain as you do. But how do you know her was murdered? Be'n't you guessing, like Sergeant Peel did?"

"No. I'm not guessing," said Macdonald, his quiet voice giving emphasis to his words. "Let's put it this way. You're used to judging weights—butter and fat and the rest. Your own experience tells you if a package is what it ought to be. I'm used to judging probabilities about sudden deaths. My own experience tells me when appearances aren't to be trusted. I haven't asked you to point a finger condemning anybody. But I do ask you to answer a few very simple questions."

"I'll answer them if I can, sir."

"Very good. You've told me that that bag was Miss Torrington's. You've recognised it. Did she always carry it about with her when she was out of doors?"

Mrs. Yeo wiped her eyes. Tears had been running down her face, but she spoke steadily, though her voice was husky. "Her used to do, sir. I'm telling the truth when I say her didn't come into village much of late. But I've been in with her many a time helping with a sick neighbour, at nights maybe. Her always brought that old hand-bag along with her, and her nursing bag, too. But her didn't use it Sundays. On Sundays her'd have the new bag Lady Ridding gave to her when we closed down the Red Cross room in Institute after peace day."

"Did you ever see inside this old bag when she was using it?"

"Not so as to really see. There was papers in it, old letters and that, and her money, and some little books, notebooks and that. 'Twas all full up, bulging like."

"Was it heavy? Did you ever pick it up?"

"I did once, and I mind I laughed at her, saying she'd been robbing bank, 'twas so heavy, and her said her'd got her keys in it. Her always carried they, seeing those young servant maids came from bad homes and 'twasn't wise to trust they." Mrs. Yeo broke off, and then said: "Was her robbed, sir? Did someone snatch her bag down there by the mill?"

"I think so, Mrs. Yeo. It was empty when it was found, but there's a very strong old-fashioned safety catch on it, and I don't think it would have come undone by itself."

2

"Why didn't you report that this bag of Miss Torrington's was missing, Hannah?"

Macdonald was sitting in the Warden's office at Gramarye. The bag lay on the desk in front of him, and it was the first thing Hannah Barrow set eyes on when she came into the room. She was as neat and clean as ever, if less severely starched, but her wrinkled pippin of a face seemed to have shrunk and puckered, and her eyes were frightened and sunken. She stared at the bag as though she couldn't take her eyes from it, and her fingers knotted themselves into contortions, with her knuckles showing white and shiny.

"Missing? That there? 'Tis an old thing. Sister was a-going to give that away. Her had a new one. Sergeant took it, with Sister's purse and note book and all. I showed it to he—a good new bag 'twas."

"Yes. I know that Sergeant Peel has the new bag," said Macdonald, "but Miss Torrington only used that one on Sundays. She always took this one with her whenever she went out, as you know quite well. But when the sergeant asked about her hand-bag, you told him about the new bag, but you didn't say anything about this one."

He spoke slowly and evenly, without any suggestion of sharpness in his voice, as patiently as a schoolmaster might talk to a dull pupil, and with the same expectant note of one who hopes for the right answer. Hannah's mental age, he had concluded, was about twelve, but on the whole a very unintelligent twelve.

"Him didn't ask me," she said, pulling at her fingers till the joints cracked.

"He asked you if anything was missing," Macdonald persisted. "You knew this bag was missing, but you didn't say so."

There was a long pause: then she answered as a dull child might answer: "If so be I had, sergeant'd have said I stole mun. I know he. Terr'ble sharp him be." She broke off and then added: "Us all knew Sister kept that bag by her. I said to cook, 'Sister's old bag's not nowhere' and Cook said, 'That be'n't our business. Us hasn't got t' old bag. Likely it fell in mill-race or maybe they've got it. But it be'n't our business.' And I said, 'that's right, that be. If I say Sister's old bag be'n't here, sergeant will say, "'Tis that old fool Hannah stole he'." Him went all around, opening everything with Sister's keys, counting this, counting that, spying and staring and jumping out on we with questions till us was fair dazed like."

Some part of Macdonald's mind was almost fascinated by the sing-song drone of Hannah's voice: there was a peculiar primitive rhythm to her sentences, and this, together with the liquid Devonshire vowels, gave the effect of some ancient ballad, akin to song rather than speech.

"What did she keep in this bag, Hannah?" asked Macdonald, sensing that he was more likely to get an answer by the method of assuming that Hannah knew all that there was to be known.

"Us never knew for sure, sir. If Sister sent for we, 'twasn't like you saying, 'Come right up to table' or, 'Sit down, Hannah.' Us stood by the door and took our orders without drawing near. And if so be, 'twas something to be fetched and paid for, Sister would put the money down on that table there, always just right, and make me count it out, but fares or stamps or register letter, and she'd say, 'Put that in your pocket, Hannah, to keep it safe.' But she'd never open her bag and take out her purse. 'Never put temptation in no one's way' Sister would say, meaning them young girls we had who knew no better," ended Hannah sanctimoniously.

"Did Sister carry the bag about with her when she was in the house?" asked Macdonald.

"No, sir. Only when her went out. Her locked it away in the house. I can't say for where. I never did see where she kept mun, and none other did, neither."

"But she kept her keys in the bag, Hannah," said Macdonald mildly, careful not to let his voice give away that he was getting more and more interested. She came right up to him, a withered elderly little body who put out a knobbly hand and touched Macdonald's arm with the confiding gesture of a child.

"Her had two lots of keys, her must have," said Hannah. "Her never did say so, and I never saw them together, but her must have had two lots."

"How do you know?" asked Macdonald, and she replied simply:

"Them had different key rings. One was brass, one was steel."

The phrase 'out of the mouths of babes and sucklings' flashed through Macdonald's mind: he had had previous experience of the fact that illiterates, and even partially defective persons, could be very observant of small details which pass unnoticed by the intelligent.

"I'm glad you told me about the key rings, Hannah," he said. "That may be very helpful. Now there's another thing you could do for me. I want to see the medicine cupboard again."

"You can and welcome, but I never touched he since you saw it afore."

"I don't expect you have, but I know now what a good memory you've got. You'll be able to tell me just what you did when the children had their medicine. I expect you know all the bottles and all the doses, too."

"Them has been the same so long I couldn't help but know they," she replied. "When the war come, they began to give 'em all cod liver oil, the dear lord knows why. Them did well enough without it. But mostly 'twas the same. Doctor he wasn't one to change. Him be a wise and good man, kind him is, kindest soul I do know. Him's the same to all, saint and sinner too. You ask in village, they'll tell you."

"Yes. They all say the same," agreed Macdonald. "They like Dr. Ferens, but they miss old Dr. Brown."

"He was homely like. Never frightened the childer," said Hannah.

"Look, Hannah: as we're going upstairs, you can show me just what happened when Dr. Brown came for his weekly visit. He came on Monday mornings, didn't he?"

"Iss. Mondays at eleven to the minute. I was always ready for he, to open door and take he up to dispensary, and the childer, they was ready and waiting, too."

"I'll go to the front door and you can let me in and pretend I'm doctor," said Macdonald, and she nodded, evidently quite proud to be asked to assist.

Hannah was nothing if not thorough. She had been drilled to the same actions for so many years that she performed them accurately. On opening the front door, she said: "Good morning, doctor" and waited.

Macdonald said: "Good morning, Hannah… My hat and gloves…" (He had neither.)

"And your stick," she said firmly, setting them on a chair in dumb show. "If you'll kindly step upstairs, Sister's quite ready."

She led the way up to the little room called the dispensary, knocked on the door and opened it. "Doctor, Sister."

There were two chairs, and Hannah indicated the more important for Macdonald. "Doctor'd mention the weather and maybe his rheumatiz," she went on. "Sister would answer very polite—her stood up by table, see—and doctor'd say, 'Anything to report?' and generally 'twas, 'All doing nicely, thank you, doctor,' and her would show him lists of the children's weights and that, and mention if we'd any in bed. And then him'd say: 'Well, have them in. I like to see them,' and then I'd go to door, so, them being all ready on landing, and them'd come in, walking round table so, while Sister said their names: girls first, then boys. And us taught them all to say, 'Good-morning, doctor. Thank you.' And times he'd stop one and say, 'Put out your tongue, now. Sister will give you a nice drop of summat to-night' though 'twas always that Gregory powder he meant, and a real poisonous taste that has: and then I'd see the childer go downstairs all quiet and respectful like and Cook'd be waiting with their milk and a bite o' summat. If so be we had any in bed, I'd show the way up and wait inside by bedroom door till Doctor and Sister had done, and then I'd bring they down in here again. And maybe doctor'd write an order if so be we wanted more medicine or plasters or such-like, and he'd give the paper to Sister and her would copy the order in her book, and doctor might say a word or two about they in the village—new babies and the old folks he called his dear old chronics, and then he'd always say: 'Mustn't stand gossiping. Hannah wants to get on with her work and I can't find the way downstairs unless her shows me,' and in winter maybe he'd say: 'Give me an arm, Hannah, my dear. My rheumatiz is playing up to-day, and you two women'll be the death of me with your polished floors,' and I'd take he downstairs and give mun his hat and his gloves and his stick and say, 'Good-mornin, doctor, and thank you.' 'Twas always the same."

"Thank you, Hannah," said Macdonald. "You've got a very good memory. Now when Doctor Brown wrote the orders for more medicine from the chemist, didn't he ever look in the medicine cupboard?"

Hannah's face puckered in disappointment. "I did forget to put that bit in," she said. "Doctor, he had many a good laugh at our medicine cupboard. 'None o' they new fangled notions here,' he'd say, 'Gregory powder and Epsom salts and Cascara, Bicarb, Chlorate o' Potash, Ammonia-quinine, Cod-liver oil and Castor oil: good old-fashioned remedies and you can'a beat they.'"

She went through her list complacently, and Macdonald told Reeves later that the list sent a reminiscent shiver down his own back. He had been dosed with all those remedies in his own childhood, and the one he had resented most was the Chlorate of Potash tablets, which had tasted repellent. He got up, took the keys from his pocket and unlocked the medicine cupboard. It was a tall built-in cupboard with double doors. In the right hand section were all the 'good old-fashioned remedies,' together with medicine glasses, thermometers still in their glass of disinfectant, methylated spirits, enamelled basins, rolls of bandages and cotton wool, boracic powder and carbolic ointment. All the bottles were clean and polished and not a drip or stain sullied the scrubbed shelves. The other half of the cupboard was latched top and bottom; when opened, it showed one of the shelves shut in by an extra door, labelled 'Poisons.' Macdonald unlocked it and surveyed the contents: there were several bottles of disinfectant, camphorated oil, chlorodyne—and a bottle of aspirin. Hannah pointed at the latter.

"Sister never did hold with they," she said. "The house-maids would make free with aspirin and such-like if so be they'd a headache or that, and Sister wouldn't have it noways. If so be we found they'd been a-buying they when them was out, Sister'd take 'em away. Her always went through their rooms reg'lar, and the place they'd hide things in you'd never believe." (When Macdonald repeated this to Reeves, the latter so far forgot himself as to say, "I can't think why the woman wasn't drowned years ago—poor brats of girls.") "Sister always kept this cupboard locked, and her gave out all the doses herself," added Hannah.

"When Miss Torrington had any medicine for herself, was it kept in this cupboard?" asked Macdonald.

"'Tis hard to say, sir. Her never had no medicine in her room, but if her kept any in here, 'twould be in that locked part, and her didn't often open that for me to see. And her wouldn't let me see her taking no medicine, because her was proud of never being sick."

Macdonald set both cupboard doors open wide, together with the 'poison cupboard.'

"When did the bottle of brandy disappear, Hannah?" he asked quietly.

She shook her head. "'Tis hard to say. I'd tell you and

welcome. I'd tell you anything, you been that homely and quiet with it. But her didn't often open that part o' cupboard so's I could have a good look, see. I know that be there. For years 'twas there, and Sister'd say, ''Tis of the evil one, Hannah, and if so be I didn't lock it away safe, maybe 'twould be putting temptation in the way o' poor weak souls.' That was there, sure enough, but when sergeant opened the cupboard, that'd gone. I don't know how long ago that went."

She picked up her apron and began pleating it in her fingers, her face puckered up like a troubled infant's. "Was it that…made Sister come over dizzy like, sir?"

"What made you think of that, Hannah?"

She went on screwing up her apron. "Her'd got queer like. Her was always hard, hard as a stone her heart was for all her loving talk, but these last months her's changed. 'Tis true. Something about she was fair frightening. I can't tell you for why—"

"But when did it come into your mind that she'd been drinking brandy? You say you didn't know the brandy bottle had gone until Sergeant Peel opened the cupboard."

"No. Not till sergeant opened it, like 'tis now. Then I saw 'twere gone."

"Did you think Sister had taken it when you saw the bottle wasn't there any longer?" Macdonald's voice was as even as ever, his tone pleasantly conversational. Hannah sidled up to him and put out her knobbly hand and twitched his coat, looking up at him in a way that was oddly childlike, but something about her eyes was different: their silly complacency had given way to a distraught look, half wild, half sly. "She's going to tell she murdered the woman," flashed through Macdonald's mind, but Hannah whispered:

"I smelt her breath when I went to pick her up." The

knotted fingers still twitched at Macdonald's coat, and her words came in a rush now. "'Twas so long ago since I smelled that. Years and years 'twas. But I knew it. My pa, he drank. In Bristol us lived, down by the docks, and us was poor...poor. Hungry and cold I was. Him was like a mad thing when him was drunk. He beat my ma, beat her like a dog. I mind the smell o's breath, all that time ago. I'd forgotten that; never give it a thought all these years, but I minded it when I picked Sister up." Her breath was coming fast and she was nearly sobbing, struggling to get her words out, her hand still pulling at Macdonald's sleeve. "I never thought o' that, not all these years. I put that behind me. I'd not smelled that since he hit ma over head with poker: him killed she, poor besom...and me there..."

Her laboured voice broke off in a clucking sound, and then she began to scream, and went on screaming with a shrill dreadful iteration, while her fingers still clawed at Macdonald's sleeve.

CHAPTER XV

1

Hannah's screams were dying away as Cook came pounding upstairs, her heavy tread slamming on the linoleum, shaking the staircase.

"Sakes alive, what be that?" she burst out as she flung the door open. "'Twas like a soul in torment. God ha' mercy, what be you done to her?"

Macdonald had got Hannah on to the chair and she sat crumpled up in it, her puckered face clay coloured now. Her eyes were shut, though tears still trickled down her cheeks, and her mouth was open. Macdonald found the pulse in the skinny wrist and realised that Hannah hadn't even fainted. She had screamed her nerve storm out and exhaustion had claimed her. Her head fell sideways grotesquely, and she sobbed jerkily, in the exhausted state that can come suddenly to children and the subnormal after a crisis of excitement.

"I haven't done anything to her. She started talking about her own mother's death and worked herself into a state of hysteria over it," said Macdonald. "I'd better carry her upstairs to her room and get the doctor to come and see to her."

"Sakes, her do look in a bad way," said Cook. "Had us better get her summat—brandy or somesuch?"

"Have you got any brandy?" asked Macdonald.

She flashed him a glance. "In this house? O' course not. But I could run across to Mr. Barracombe. Sister wouldn't have no liquor in this house."

Macdonald picked up the skinny little form. "Go on upstairs and open her bedroom door for me. It's not brandy she wants. It's something to get her quiet."

Cook thudded out of the room and on up the stairs, panting and muttering, and Macdonald followed and laid Hannah on a narrow bed in a room almost as bare as a prison cell.

"Cover her up with some blankets and then get a hot water bottle," he said, "but don't give her anything. I'll go and ring up the doctor."

"Her do look mortal bad," groaned Cook.

Macdonald ran downstairs to the office again and called Ferens' number on the telephone. "Is that Dr. Ferens? Macdonald here. Will you come over to Gramarye, at once, please."

"Gramarye? You want Dr. Brown."

"I don't. I want you. At once, please."

Ferens expostulated. "My God…what for…" as he hung up the receiver. But he was at the front door within two minutes, case in hand.

"It's Hannah Barrow," said Macdonald. "She got talking and worked herself up into a screaming fit and she's flat out. I carried her up to her bedroom. D'you know your way?"

"No. I've never been inside this house before. She's not my patient, you know."

"So you've told me. I called you because I judged you'd be better primed to cope with the occasion," said Macdonald, as he led the way upstairs. "Having studied the contents of the medicine cupboard here, I thought another opinion was indicated."

Ferens stopped dead. "You don't mean…"

"No, I don't," retorted Macdonald. "She screamed herself to exhaustion, that's all. Give her a bromide, or whatever suits the occasion and let the poor little cuss go to sleep. I'll tell you about it when you're through."

Hannah Barrow was now covered up in grey blankets, (good 'government surplus'), her cap was over one ear and her hands clawed feebly at the blankets as she sobbed and hiccoughed. Cook was standing beside the bed.

"I'd be glad if you'd take my notice. Me nerves won't stand any more of this," she said as she saw Macdonald.

"Have you filled those hot water bottles?" he snapped, as Ferens came into the room.

Cook gaped at him. "'Tis Dr. Brown should come to see to her," she proclaimed. "Her's registered with Dr. Brown."

"I'm doing locum for Dr. Brown this time," said Ferens cheerfully. "You go and do what the Chief Inspector tells you and fill some hot water bottles. He's got more sense than you have."

Cook sniffed noisily and followed Macdonald to the door.

"Us haven't got no hot water bottles. Sister didn't hold with they. A warm brick, now—"

"Then go across to Mrs. Ferens and borrow two hot water bottles," retorted the doctor, "and hurry up about it."

2

"Well, that's Hannah Barrow's life story," said Macdonald.

He and Raymond Ferens were sitting in the office at

Gramarye. The casement windows were open wide now, and the warmth and sensuous fragrance of midsummer floated in, merging with blue cigarette smoke to make the cold bare little room seem alive and lived in.

"Poor little wretch," said Ferens softly.

Macdonald nodded. "Yes. I shan't forget that story in a hurry. I wonder if it's possible that the memory of her mother's death was blotted out by the hideous shock of witnessing it. I believe it does happen in some cases. The memory is suppressed, clamped down, as though a scar grows over damaged tissue and hides it."

"Of course it happens," said Ferens. "It's that sort of memory, shut down in the subconscious, that can wreak havoc in people's lives. But I thought you weren't interested in psychology?"

"I didn't say I wasn't interested. I said I refused to be obsessed by it. I still do," said Macdonald, "but I did believe that when Hannah was telling me about it, her mind went back to that horror which some circumstance had routed out, and she was no longer Nurse Barrow of Gramarye, but a Bristol slum child. It was that word she used—in pity and horror. 'Poor besom.' It's an old word and an ugly one. It's certainly not a word the respectable Hannah Barrow would have used."

Ferens nodded. "You're probably right. It was the telling of it which broke her up. That uncontrolled weeping was quite characteristic of the whole case." He broke off and looked out of the window, and the silence which followed in the room was broken by a thrush, singing its heart out on the top of a beech tree.

"I suppose you realise you've got a complete explanation of the Warden's death?" asked Ferens abruptly.

Macdonald nodded. "Yes. The psychologist's explanation. That's what I meant when I said I refused to be obsessed by it. But if you would like to put forward your own idea of what may have happened, I shall give full consideration to it."

"It's the story of the missing brandy bottle which clinches it, to my mind," said Ferens slowly. "Let us trace the case history. A slum child in a dockland district, undernourished, ill-treated: the father drank, and eventually killed the mother with a poker. The child was taken to an orphanage. They probably looked after her, according to the lights of fifty years ago, and they would certainly not have let her talk that memory out of her system. It was, as you say, clamped down. I gather from what you say that the job she was put to was in what would pass for a respectable household. The mistress of it beat the girl and ill-treated her and half starved her, but I gather there was no mention of alcoholism. Orphanages may make mistakes in the characters of employers, but they're careful not to send into houses where drunkenness occurs."

"Perfectly true," said Macdonald. "The mistress of the house was a teetotaller."

"Very well. Hannah tripped up her tormentor on the stairs and the woman broke her neck. Result, a prison sentence. Then a period in an institution. Rehabilitation, as we say nowadays. Then Gramarye, and over twenty years of drudgery, and up-lift which brought contentment of a sort. Hannah was now respected. She was Nurse Barrow. Life went according to pattern. She was taught to do the same thing in the same way, day after day, year after year. She was educable to that point—she could do just those things the Warden had trained her to do, and I think she was probably happy doing them. Do you agree to all that?"

"Yes. To all of it," said Macdonald.

"Very well. Note that since the day the child had seen her drunken father kill her mother, she had never experienced drunken violence again—until she saw Sister Monica drunk. Saw it, smelled the cause of it—and it turned her brain. She remembered the last time. After that she wasn't responsible for her own actions any more. Her father hit her mother. Hannah repaid that hit."

Ferens broke off and lighted a cigarette. Then he went on: "As you know, I'm not a psychiatrist. It's quite probable that, despite your scepticism, you know more about the subject than I do. You get trained psychiatrists on to all crimes of violence. I know you won't be biased by anything I say, but I'd suggest you get a psychiatrist on to this job."

"That's inevitable," said Macdonald, "and I'll lay a bet the first thing Hannah will tell them is just how she killed Sister Monica. I thought she was going to tell me just before she began screaming, but she told me how her father killed her mother instead. So the confession is deferred until another occasion. How is she, by the way?"

"She's all right. Fast asleep. She'll sleep the clock round. I saw to that. She's as tough as they make them, physically."

"I noticed that her pulse went on ticking over quite strongly even after her *crise de nerfs*," said Macdonald. "She won't die of her brain storm."

Ferens sat very still. Then he said: "Do you think she did it?"

Macdonald replied: "Do I think that Hannah Barrow killed Monica Emily Torrington? I've been very careful not to ask you that question, Dr. Ferens. I asked you to state what you thought the possibilities were in the light of your own experience of psychological processes. You replied, very reasonably, with a statement which covered the case history. I agreed as to all that. You then made two assumptions which are, to my mind, unproven. It's my job to examine them. Until I've examined them, I am not going to answer your question, or put the same question to you."

Ferens still sat in his place, and the thrush still sang from the beech tree. Then Ferens said: "Two assumptions?"

"Yes. Two," replied Macdonald, and Ferens got up.

"I'll go and think it over. Do you want any help here? My wife would come and sleep here, or spend the night here—if you like."

"Thanks. That's a very kind offer. I'll let you know if we want assistance, but you think your patient will sleep through the night?"

"Lord, yes. She won't stir. Incidentally, you realise she'll probably have forgotten the whole incident when she wakes up. It happens, you know."

"Yes. I realise that," replied Macdonald.

3

After Ferens had gone, Macdonald went up to Hannah Barrow's bedroom. The latter was fast asleep, her wrinkled face framed now by two stiff little plaits of grey hair, her knobbly hands lying still and decorous on the grey blanket. Emma Higson was sitting beside her, snivelling miserably into a large handkerchief.

Macdonald stood at the door and spoke very quietly. "Come downstairs now, Mrs. Higson. Hannah will be all right. She's sleeping quite peacefully."

The stout body got up and tip-toed painfully across the room. "Is her going to die?"

"No. She'll be perfectly all right in the morning. It was

only that she got excited and upset. It's been a big strain for both of you, I know that. Come downstairs. I want to ask you one or two things."

He led the way to the office, but Emma Higson drew back. "Not in there. I couldn't abide that. Gives me the 'orrors."

"Very well. We'll sit in the kitchen. Make yourself a cup of tea, and give me one, too."

Emma looked at him in surprise, but her face brightened up. "So I will. Never knew a man that wasn't ready for a cup o' tea when things was troublesome. Are you sure her'll be all right up there?"

"Yes. I'll lock the front door and close those windows. You go and put your kettle on."

A few minutes later, Macdonald was sitting at the well-scrubbed kitchen table with a tea pot between himself and the cook. After she had had her cup of tea, he said:

"Cook, I'm not going to ask you anything that need worry you. It's nothing about Hannah. I want you to tell me exactly what happened when Miss Torrington slipped on the stairs."

"Her come over dizzy, poor soul," began Cook, inevitably.

"What time was it, and what day of the week?"

"Sunday, 'twas. The Sunday before her was took. Just after dinner, two o'clock, maybe. I'd just a-done scouring my pans."

"Then you were in here, in the kitchen?"

"In the scullery, there. Dot and Alice was just a-tidying of themselves after washing up. Sakes, the noise it made! I thought the roof had a-fallen in." Cook was getting into her stride now. "I ran out into hall. Right down her'd fallen, and her was sitting on bottom stair, and Hannah was there with her."

"Did Miss Torrington look ill?"

"Her looked queer like, not herself, and I don't wonder

at it. Her had fallen down the whole flight and them stairs is perishing steep. Doctor, him said time and again those stairs'd be the death of him. Didn't hold with all that polish."

"Was Miss Torrington very white in the face after her fall?"

"No, that she wasn't. Her face was red like. I know it came into me mind she'd had a seizure, but 'twasn't that. Her got up all right and her said: 'I'm not hurt, Cook, so do you go back to your work,' and her leant a bit on Hannah's shoulder and went into the office, and at tea-time her was all right again."

"That was the second time she fell, wasn't it? What about the first time?" asked Macdonald.

"That'd've been the Friday, two days before. 'Twas after breakfast: the children had been upstairs and Sister had given they their cod-liver oil and then they all went out into garden. Dot and Alice was a-sweeping of the dining-room and Hannah was doing the dispensary. Sister had been to wash her hands in the bathroom, and her fell down in the passage upstairs. Her said that time that 'twas summat on the floor—maybe the children had been throwing the soap about. I said: 'Better have doctor, Sister. That's a shock that is, and we're none of us so young as us once was,' but her wouldn't hear of it. Her sent Hannah for the ammonia stuff Sister keeps in her bag, Sal...whatever that be."

"Sal Volatile?"

"That be it. Very powerful that be. Sister gave that to me once when I caught my finger in mangle and come over queer, and it didn't half make I cough, but 'tis good, indeed. And Hannah did count it out in drops like Sister did say and that pulled her together. Though her did go and lie on her bed awhiles, and that's the first time I ever did know Sister to lie down. Her hadn't no patience with 'uman frailties."

"Dr. Brown tells me that Miss Torrington has always had

very good health, but he thought she had been failing of recent months. Did you notice any sign of illness in her apart from the two times she fell down? Was she ever uncertain in her movements, or confused in mind, or in her speech?"

"That her wasn't," declared Cook. "Between you and me, sir, Sister was a tartar in a manner of speech. Very noticing, her was, and as for speech, her were as clear as yourself, and a sight sharper with it if so be anything wasn't just so. And when her moved, her was neat as a cat, and as quiet. Very upright Sister was. Real old-fashioned, with a back like a ramrod." She paused a moment, cogitating deeply. "Her was never one to ask for sympathy, and if so be her wasn't feeling so good, her'd never say so. Maybe her had a bit of stomach trouble, because her cared less and less for her food. Her'd never been a big eater, but lately her did only peck at her food. Hannah marked that. 'Sister's not eating,' Hannah'd say, her being in dining-room for meals. Us had ours in kitchen, me and Dot, Bessie and Alice."

"Several people have told me that Miss Torrington seemed to have changed quite a lot this past year or so," said Macdonald and Cook nodded.

"Yes. Her changed. Sharper her was. I reckon her brooded like. I said all along her brooded over that Nancy Bilton. 'I ought to've saved her from herself,' Sister said. She took that hard. 'Twas a failure, if you sees what I means, and Sister took failure hard. And then some said in village as 'twas Sister's fault the girl went and drownded herself, and Sister's always been so well thought of in village. So maybe it was only to be expected she'd brood. But as for falling downstairs and getting dizzy like, that was her eyes, sir. Her wouldn't wear glasses save for reading and that, and often not then. You see, her fell after her'd been reading, and that without glasses."

"But you said it was just after meals that she fell down."

"And so 'twas. Sister did always read a chapter to the children after meals. She said 'twas good for them to sit quiet a bit. You could have heard a pin drop when Sister read a chapter to they. Her was a wonderful woman right enow."

4

Cook had filled the tea pot again from the kettle which sang peacefully on the old-fashioned range, and she poured out another cup for Macdonald and another for herself. The stout body had got over her upset, and was almost enjoying her prolonged gossip. Macdonald went on with his questions quite placidly, almost as though he also were enjoying a quiet talk.

"When the chemist sent medicine up here, were the bottles packed up in a parcel?" he asked.

"Of course they were. Sister was very particular over they. The parcels was sent up to dispensary, as her called it, and Sister unpacked they and put 'em away. Always kept the key o' the cupboard herself, Sister did."

"And what happened to the empty bottles?"

"Sent back to chemist, corks and all, after I'd washed they out particular."

"Have any bottles gone back within the last week or so?"

"No. Not for a long time. There's been no illness to speak of, and the children don't have to take their cod-liver oil summer time."

"Dr. Brown said he ordered some medicine for Miss Torrington recently. It's not in the medicine cupboard and you say no empty bottles have gone back."

"No. They haven't. Chemist'll tell you so. But if 'twas for Sister herself, that's different. She never liked no one to know nothing about she. I do mind doctor gave her cough mixture last winter. Hannah heard doctor say he'd send that up. But I never saw no bottles with Sister's name on. Her washed the labels off and swilled they bottles out herself. Queer her was that way. Very secret."

"When the bottles are ready to go back, where are they put?"

"In that box by back door. Always the same place. The chemist's boy, him knew. But there's none there now."

Macdonald dropped the subject, finished his tea, and then said equally placidly: "I was asking Hannah about that old black bag Miss Torrington used to carry about with her."

Cook looked round at him quickly. "Sister's old bag? Have you found mun? I know I reckon Sister never went outside o' this house without mun. 'Twas like part o' she."

"Why didn't you say at once that it was missing, especially as you knew Miss Torrington always carried it?"

"No one never axed and 'twasn't my place," she retorted sharply. Then she went on more slowly, as though she regretted her tartness. "'Twas like this here, sir. Sergeant Peel, he'd been on at us over Nancy Bilton when her died. Now I couldn't a-stand Nancy Bilton, her was a nasty pert baggage, and bad with it. Not that I never wished she any harm. But sergeant, he picked up every word us said and tried to twist it around. And I learnt one thing from he that time—never to say nothing beyond what's axed. And as for Sister's old bag, it do stand to reason that if her fell in mill stream, her bag'd fall in too, and if they wanted to find aught, them could drag for it. I said that to Hannah, when her came to me all in a flap. Don't you go out of your way a-telling sergeant things, I said. Him'll say us stole mun, iss, feggs, us that's been trusted here since him was nought but a gaping lad."

She began to put the tea things together, and then stood, arms akimbo, for a further effort of oratory.

"Don't you drive she too far, sir, our Hannah. Her's like a child some ways, for all her'll work till her do drop. There's no more wickedness in Hannah than there is in a little babby. But her do take things to heart; and if her's the next to be fished out of mill stream, that'll be plain wickedness, that will."

"I think we can make sure that doesn't happen," said Macdonald.

"I wouldn't be so sure. Why can't you be a-done, sir? Sister, her came over dizzy and her brooded like. That's good enough for I. All this here's not going to bring Sister back."

Macdonald would dearly have liked to ask, "Do you wish Sister *would* come back?" Perhaps some reflection of his impious thought reached Emma Higson's mind, for as she lifted the tea pot she said: "Not that it's for the likes of we to question the ways of Providence. And when you've done your lookings around in this house, sir, I'd take it kindly if you'd say so, and let me lock up proper like. Us don't want no more carryings on to-night."

CHAPTER XVI

1

When Macdonald left Emma Higson in the kitchen, he went back to the office, where Reeves was industriously writing a report. Reeves had been admitted to the house by Macdonald when the latter sent Cook into the kitchen to put the kettle on, Macdonald having undertaken to lock the front door and close the windows.

Macdonald said: "I'm leaving the house to you. I'll be back later—garden door around eleven o'clock. Hannah's safe in bed."

"I'll be there," murmured Reeves.

At that moment the telephone rang: before he answered it, Macdonald opened the door and called: "All right, Mrs. Higson. I'll answer it." He shut the door and lifted the receiver. It was Dr. Brown.

"What's this about Hannah Barrow being ill? If she is ill, why wasn't I called?"

"I called Dr. Ferens because he was nearer, sir. She seemed

in a bad way, but it's nothing to worry about. I was just coming down to see you."

"And who's looking after Hannah? I tell you I don't like it. The devil's let loose in this place."

"Mrs. Higson is here, sir. She's quite reliable."

"Reliable? How do you know who's reliable?" snapped the old man. "Everybody seems to be taking leave of their senses. Did you say you were coming down here?"

"Yes, sir. I'll be with you within five minutes."

The old man was still muttering to himself as Macdonald replaced the receiver.

Leaving the door of the office wide open, after a nod to Reeves, Macdonald went towards the kitchen, whence emerged a good savoury smell and splutter of frying bacon and eggs.

"Mrs. Higson," he called, and getting no reply he went into the kitchen and found Emma busy with her frying pan. "I'm just going, Mrs. Higson," he called across to her. "Would you like to come round the house with me and satisfy yourself there's nothing to worry about, or will you be quite happy in your mind if I go round myself?"

"Thanking you, sir, if you'll go around that's good enough for I. I'll have me bit of supper and then go upstairs to be near Hannah. And I tell you straight I'm not letting nobody in here after I've bolted door when you go out."

"Quite right. And you can bolt all the other doors, too. I'll give you a call when I've been round."

Conscientiously, Macdonald went through every room in the house. Reeves was there somewhere, but Macdonald didn't catch sight of him. Nobody was better at a cat and mouse act than Reeves. Hannah was snoring peacefully, still lying sedately on her back, but her wrinkled face was a normal colour and her scrubby hands were as red as nature meant them to be, relaxed on the grey blankets which Emma Higson had tucked in so neatly.

Macdonald went downstairs to the office, collected his attaché case and the sheets of Reeves's report, and then went to call Emma Higson, who saw him to the front door.

"It's been a fine old upset and all," she said, "but if so be us has got to have policemen all over house, us'd as soon have you as anybody, meaning no offence."

"Very kindly said," replied Macdonald. "You get up to bed and have a good sleep. Good-night to you."

He heard the bolts shoot into their old sockets with a purposeful rattle as he turned away into the fragrant witchery of the summer evening. Milham on the Moor looked lovely enough to catch at the heart, the evening sun glowing on rose and ochre of cob walls, on golden thatch and enchantment of carven stone, all embellished with roses and honeysuckle, scented, colourful and serene.

2

"Why couldn't you let Hannah alone?" demanded old Brown indignantly. "She's a borderline case, I know that, got the mind of a child, but she's a good old soul. D'you think you could put her in a witness box? Not if I know it. She hasn't got her full complement of wits, and I won't have her bullied."

"No one's going to bully her, sir. Certainly not myself," replied Macdonald patiently. "I realise as well as you do that her intelligence is limited. She couldn't be taught to read and write, but she could be taught to do routine tasks, and to do them well. Because her world is very limited, she remembers accurately all the small things she has been taught to do by rote. And she notices any deviation from the normal. I'm quite convinced she was telling the truth when she said she smelt alcohol in Miss Torrington's breath."

"I've no doubt she did," growled the old man. "And how much farther does that get you? You've got your analyst's report, and you've got the evidence I gave you about the bottle of brandy. You say it's gone. Well, where do you think it went to? Do you think Hannah Barrow drank it?"

"No. I don't," replied Macdonald.

"Then what more evidence do you want? If you put the facts you've got before a jury, do you suppose they wouldn't be satisfied?"

"It's not my job to satisfy a jury. It's my job to get all the available facts, not for a jury in the first case, but for my superior officers and for the Director of Public Prosecutions. And there are a number of facts for which I have not yet found explanations."

"D'you think Hannah Barrow can supply the explanations?"

"Not the explanations, no, though she has produced some interesting facts. I'm hoping that you can help me with some of the explanations."

"I've been doing my best," rejoined Dr. Brown. "What's your trouble now?"

"You told me that you prescribed for Miss Torrington recently—a sedative and an indigestion mixture."

"Quite right. I also told you that she probably poured the stuff down the sink."

"She didn't do that. Bismuth was found by the analyst—"

"I know that. Good God, are you going to tell me now the woman was poisoned?" snapped out old Brown.

"No, sir. She was drowned, after being rendered unconscious, or at any rate incapacitated, by a blow on the base of her skull. But since she had the medicine you prescribed, I can't understand why we haven't found the bottles, or any remains of the medicine. You may consider that fact so trivial as to be irrelevant. I do not. It's just an odd fact which ought to be explained."

"Well, I suppose you know your job," sighed the old man. "Admittedly I can't see what you're getting at, but I'll do my best to help. I ordered her physic a fortnight ago. The mixtures should have lasted a week. I repeated the order, without consulting Sister Monica about it, a week ago. The chemist will tell you that."

"Yes, sir. I have verified that. So it's to be assumed that there were several doses left of the second batch—a three days' supply. But there's no trace of the bottles, and Mrs. Higson, who always washes out the bottles before they are sent back to the chemist, knows nothing about them."

"All right, all right," growled Dr. Brown. "You're very thorough. I grant you that. You want all your T's crossed and your I's dotted. Very commendable. How long have you been on the job here?—tell me that."

"Since midday yesterday, sir."

"A day and a half, eh? And you reckon you've got things taped, including the aberrations and eccentricities of a woman like Sister Monica. I tell you that woman was about as complex as an ant-hill. She'd got her own peculiar pretensions. One of them was that good health is a matter of faith. She preached it to all and sundry: 'Keeping well is will power' she'd say. And to prescribe medicine for her was tantamount to insulting her. When I ordered her physic I didn't believe she'd take it, but you say she did take it. Very well, I'll accept your word for it, but I'll tell you this. She'd have seen to it that no one saw her take it, and that no one in that house knew she was taking it."

"I follow that quite clearly," put in Macdonald. "It's in character with what Hannah said about her."

"It is, is it? Well, you can take it from me that those bottles of physic you're so worried about are in the house somewhere. Not in the medicine cupboard. Dear me, no. Hannah Barrow may be an illiterate, but she knows the size and shape and colour and name of every bottle and box and tin in that cupboard. She's had twenty years to learn them in. Sister Monica wouldn't have put her own bottles of physic anywhere that Hannah could see 'em." He broke off and pointed a finger at Macdonald. "You're going to tell me you've searched the entire house, you and that young fellow you brought with you—"

"No, sir. I'm not going to tell you anything of the kind. I haven't had time to search the house. I've been too busy getting acquainted with the people who revolve around the case, what we call the contacts."

"Well, you're honest. I'll say that for you," said the old man. "I'm not belittling what you've done, Chief Inspector. You've routed out more than I'd have believed possible in the time you've been here, and pretty fools you've made some of us look, I admit it. But if, for your own reasons, you want to find those bottles of physic, you go and look for them. They're there somewhere, where she hid them. She loved hiding things. She'd put things away in the linen cupboards, in the clothes cupboards, in the sewing room, in the store cupboard, in any one of those elaborate hoards of impedimenta she delighted in. You'll have a job, I promise you, but you'll find the stuff if you go on looking long enough. If you're going to do it this evening, I wish you joy of it. They didn't wire the place properly when they put electricity in: took the Warden's advice and economised by not putting lights in the linen room and cupboards and so forth: penny wise, pound foolish—the very places you wanted artificial light, because there aren't any windows."

"I'll leave it till morning, when the sun's at its brightest," said Macdonald. "In any case, I don't want to go there again this evening and make any more disturbance. In my judgment, Mrs. Higson can look after Hannah all right."

"In your judgment," echoed the old man wearily. "I suppose we've got to trust your judgment. You've had precious little reason to trust ours. If you put the facts you've discovered down in black and white—damn it, there's a lot of black and not much white. I went up and saw Lady Ridding after you'd been on at her, and I gather there wasn't much left to admire in Sister Monica's character by the time you'd done with it. Yet that woman worked faithfully and well for best part of a lifetime. And Hannah—a gaol bird, eh? I tell you Hannah's worth her weight in gold. And what's the result of it all? Because Sister Monica took to the brandy bottle and fell into the river when she was tipsy, you suspect Hannah of God knows what, and I suspect Higson of planning to murder Hannah. I tell you it's enough to drive us all mad."

"I don't think there's the remotest likelihood of Mrs. Higson planning to murder Hannah," said Macdonald quietly.

"Why not? You're guessing your way along, aren't you? I'm sorry, Chief Inspector. I'm an old fool, but I'm so upset over the whole miserable business, I'm past talking sense. I'll get off to bed, and leave you to your job. But don't get it into your head that Hannah Barrow's the malefactor. I know you've little reason to respect our judgments. I admit you've uncovered enough human weaknesses in this place to make you pretty scornful of our mental processes. We couldn't see a thing sticking right out under our noses—the fact that the

Warden of Gramarye had taken to the brandy bottle. That's the operative factor in this case. Not the 'old unhappy far off things' you've been so successful in digging up. The fact that the woman had taken to alcohol and I didn't spot it is what upsets me. You say that even Hannah spotted it—and I didn't. No fool like an old fool." He gave a contemptuous snort. "I don't wonder you sent for Ferens when Hannah collapsed. You were quite right. But you couldn't have done anything which was more calculated to give me a knock. Didn't trust me to deal with a case of hysteria."

"I did what I thought best to do in the circumstances," rejoined Macdonald quietly. "And now, sir, I've got a report to think over. I'll bid you good-evening."

3

Macdonald walked back to the Mill House when he left Dr. Brown: the latter's house was a quarter of a mile beyond the village on the level ground of the river valley, whose lush green was glowing in the last rays of the westering sun. Turning in at the footpath between the Mill House and Moore's farm, Macdonald crossed the wooden bridge and walked up the steep path towards the Manor House. He was nearly at the top when he saw an elderly lady walking towards him, and he stood on the outer side of the path to let her pass. She stopped deliberately, saying: "Good-evening. Am I right in thinking you to be Chief Inspector Macdonald?"

"Yes, madam."

"My name is Braithwaite. I should be so glad if you could spare me a few minutes. I have been away from home for some days, and I was deeply shocked by the news of Sister Monica's death."

Macdonald liked the look of the resolute, sensible face, and the sound of her deep pleasant voice. He glanced round, and she said at once: "This is a most inconvenient spot for a conversation. I will walk back to the top with you, if I may. There is a seat by the Manor wall where we could talk in comfort."

"By all means," said Macdonald.

She turned resolutely up the hill again, walking sturdily, and said nothing more until they reached the top and she turned to the right, and led the way to a garden seat, placed to command the glorious view of hill and vale and distant moor. She was panting a little as she sat down.

"That has always been a steep hill, Chief Inspector. I find it gets steeper. One day I shall find it is too steep." She turned and looked full at him as he seated himself beside her, and went on: "I ought not to waste your time, but I have been to see Lady Ridding. She was so very incoherent that I am quite bewildered, and I should be so grateful if you could tell me the real facts. You see for years and years Sister Monica has been held up as a monument of all the virtues. Now she is dead, she has become a synonym for all the vices."

"Would you like to tell me your own estimate of the Warden's character, madam?"

"Well—it's a bit hard. I scruple to speak harshly of the dead. But I disliked her, very much indeed. She was one of those women who cover a selfish and assertive mind with a cloak of humility, and there was something abnormal about her, almost pathological. Also she was a malicious gossip, an eavesdropper and a raker-up of other people's secrets. I have known all that for a long time. But—do you really think she was murdered?"

"That is my opinion," replied Macdonald. "I have no absolute proof."

She sat silent for a while and then said: "When I left Lady Ridding, I came and sat here by myself and tried to think things out. I've never been a clever woman, but I've a certain amount of commonsense, and I have known this village and the people in it for a very long time. It's nearly two years since I tried to get the Committee to pension off Sister Monica. It wasn't only that I knew she was too old and too set in her ways to be left in charge of very young children, though all that was true. I felt she had changed: that her character had deteriorated in some way I couldn't quite define. Previously, I had disliked her: but more recently I found something almost frightening about her."

She broke off, and Macdonald said: "You are telling me the same thing that the village people have told me. The Warden had changed. It's obvious, too, that she was no longer trusted. Can you tell me when this change in attitude occurred?"

"In attitude—you mean when the village ceased to trust her? I expect you have guessed: it was after Nancy Bilton's death. But Sister Monica herself had changed before that."

"Will you answer this question, Miss Braithwaite, even though it's a hard one: do you believe that the Warden caused Nancy Bilton's death?"

"Yes. I'm afraid I do. I have no facts to give you, none whatever. It was just an unhappy feeling."

"And did the village people share your belief?"

"I can't answer that. I never asked, or discussed it with anybody at all at the time. But I believe the mistrust which developed was due to the fact that the village people were never sure she hadn't done it. Only they would never have admitted it. And indeed, there was no evidence, either way."

She sighed, and then went on: "You will be wondering why I am wasting your time. I asked you to stop and talk to me because

I had an idea as to what might have happened. Lady Ridding said that Sister Monica had been drinking. I can believe that. She may well have wanted to forget—quite a number of things. And she knew that the village had turned against her. Her power had gone. Granted the woman's character, her craze for domination, I can well believe that if she got drunk she would have been capable of boasting of what she had done. I'm probably putting this very badly, but do you follow what I mean?"

"Yes. You think she boasted to someone that she *had* killed Nancy Bilton, and that someone took the law into their own hands and meted out their own idea of justice?"

"Yes. It's the only reason I can think of which would have made anybody in this place commit a murder—that they felt it was the only way of arriving at justice."

"I'm very much interested in what you have said, Miss Braithwaite. A similar line of thought had occurred to me. But I think there are some additional complexities which I am not at liberty to tell you."

Miss Braithwaite stared out across the parkland: the sun had gone now, but the clarity of light remained; every tree, every branch and flower was still and clean cut in the lucent after-glow, not a breath stirring in the evening air. Then she said: "If such a confession—or boast—had been made to you, and you knew that you had no hope at all of bringing the woman to justice   you see, there *was* no evidence—might not you have meted out rough justice yourself?"

"I hope not," said Macdonald soberly.

4

She had left it at that, and Macdonald had let her go, and watched her sturdy figure in its sensible silk dress as she went down the path, keeping in carefully to the side away from the drop. When she had disappeared, Macdonald took out the pages of Reeves's report, and read them while the larks sung high in the faint blue vault of heaven, and the thrushes and blackbirds pealed out long phrases of liquid song. Reeves had his own manner of writing a report for Macdonald's eye. It was a sort of colloquial shorthand, and might have been obscure to one unaccustomed to Reeves's phraseology. To Macdonald it was entirely lucid.

Reeves had set out to discover 'who had been helpful;' who, in short, had broken into the shed and left Sister Monica's old black bag under the sacks. Starting from his assumption that this was a variation to replace the 'her was dizzy' theory, Reeves began his investigation by studying the footwear of his suspects, the latter being those who knew about the experiment which Ferens and Sanderson had conducted last night. By dint of playing experiments of his own connected with gauging the velocity of the stream, Reeves had attracted some of his suspects to the damp ground by the river, and had got impressions of their boots while they gave him advice and information. Three of these impressions were easily recognisable. Farmer Moore wore heavy nailed boots with horseshoe-shaped irons on the heels. Wilson, the electrician, had patterned rubbers on his heels. Venner had nailed boots, with two nails missing from the right heel. Taking measurements and diagrams, Reeves had set out for a 'preliminary reconnaissance' along the most probable route from the Mill to Greave's hut. This route lay beside the river for the first mile, along a footpath which did not dry out before the heat of August. Thereafter, when the path turned into the woods, it crossed two 'splashes'—subsidiary streams which joined the river.

By the river itself, and in the mud by the splashes, Reeves found traces of Venner's boots, going in the direction of the hut, but there was a variation. In these 'outgoing' prints only one nail was missing from the right heel. It was when Reeves spotted some "incoming" prints that he got hopeful: when Venner had returned home he had lost the second nail.

During the greater part of the time that Macdonald had been talking to Mrs. Yeo and Hannah, Reeves had been crawling about in the rough ground near the hut in the woods. He had remembered that part of the ground they had scrambled over was rocky—the rock cropped out on the rise where the hut was built—and rocks may loosen nails in a worn heel.

Reeves finished his report in laconic style. "I found the nail. I've known men hanged on less."

CHAPTER XVII

1

Macdonald sat on the seat where Miss Braithwaite had left him until the colour had drained out of sky and air. Nobody came up the path from the mill, no one descended it from the village. On that June evening it was as lovely a walk as any human being could wish, but the path was shunned now by all who had habitually used it. Sitting very still, listening intently, Macdonald heard all sounds from the village die away; the children had all been called home by their parents. Tired and thirsty hay-makers had left the meadows before moonrise, certain of another fine day on the morrow, tractors had ceased their clamour, and not a car ground up or down the steep village street. Everyone was safely within doors, gossiping without a doubt, but preferring to gossip with their own families.

As the bats cut erratic tangents across the pale sky, and white owls floated silently on the warm scented air, it occurred to Macdonald that Monica Emily Torrington had cast a shadow on the village: that her power was still felt, undercutting all the confidence and serenity which should be the normal complement of neighbourliness. "Peel was right," thought Macdonald. "Everybody here is involved in this thing one way or another. They started by refusing to admit what they knew to be true, and it's gone on and on, getting more fantastic with every effort of concealment. It's time it was stopped."

When the enveloping twilight had deepened so much that a man could only be seen at fairly close quarters, Macdonald got up and began to stroll silently round the containing wall of Manor, Dower House, Church, and Gramarye itself. Each was hedged around with impassable clipped hedges of yew or holly or thorn, in which gates were set, but they were all contained within the ancient stone wall, close up against the hedges in some places, in others the wall and hedges parting company. Gramarye was entirely in darkness, but the Manor and Dower House showed lights in the graceful mullions and oriels of the ground floor. The Manor House windows were curtained, but those of the Dower House were open, their lights shining gaily out across lawn and flower borders and hedge. John Sanderson's house showed lights in the lower windows, but the village street was dark now, candles all put out.

Just before eleven o'clock, Macdonald went through the park gates into the garden of Gramarye, keeping in the shadow of the ilex trees until he came to the garden door—a small side door which opened into a passage between Sister Monica's office and the parlour. He turned the handle of the door and found it yielded silently to his touch as a well-oiled door handle should, and the door opened with neither creak nor groan. Closing the door behind him, Macdonald stood still in the darkness, as he had stood so often in other buildings. Houses, barns, shops, flats, warehouses, all dark, as this passage was dark, but having in the darkness their own character because each had its own peculiar smell. Gramarye smelt of floor polish and carbolic and soap: something of the unwelcoming smell of an institution, but behind the overlay of modern cleanliness, the smell of the ancient house declared itself, of old mortar, of stone walls built without damp courses, of woodwork decaying under coats of paint, of panelling and floor boards which gave out their ancient breath as the coldness of the stone house triumphed over the warmth of the midsummer evening. It flashed through Macdonald's mind that he would remember the village of Milham on the Moor through the fragrance of midsummer, new-mown hay, roses and clove pinks and honeysuckle, the "unforgettable, unforgotten river smell"—and lime trees in flower: all these wafted on the warm air in sensuous delight. But he would remember Gramarye for its chill stone smell, coupled to the soap and polish and disinfectant which were so virtuous in intention and so comfortless in achievement.

He walked along the dark passage to the little square entrance hall, where he could see a rectangle of half light—the diamond-paned window beside the front door—and he stood and listened to the creepy rattle which told of mice scuttling or nibbling in the ancient beams. It was next to impossible to rid an ancient house of mice, unless you kept a company of cats. "She would have thought cats were unhygienic," thought Macdonald, who liked cats. He went slowly and silently upstairs to the first floor, and sat down on the top stair. He knew that all was well in the silent house. Reeves was here—somewhere—as good as a watch dog and an insurance policy in one. Reeves would have been all over the house, as silent as a shadow, prying and guarding both. He would have looked in at the two sleeping women, quite calm and unembarrassed. Reeves was a very domestic character.

There was nothing to do but to wait, so Macdonald settled himself comfortably on his top stair: "Waiting for somebody else 'to be helpful,'" as he told Reeves the next day.

2

It was midnight before anything happened. The church clock had just struck, with maddening deliberation, slower than Big Ben. Then Macdonald thought: "It's generally a cold draught. This time it's warm." Somebody had opened the garden door, quite silently. They must have left it open, wide, for the still air of the stone house was astonishingly animated by a breath of warmer air laden with the scent of hay and clove pinks. Incredibly the fragrance of the summer night was diffused into the institutional carbolic of Gramarye, and the song of nightingales became suddenly louder and closer.

Macdonald stood up on his top stair and moved a step to the left, waiting for a sound from below. It wasn't long in coming: the footstep was quiet enough, the faintest shuffle of list slippers, but the person who moved was heavy in body, and the old boards creaked and sprang...crack...crack...crack. "The Warden would have used that door when she came in from her midnight wanderings," thought Macdonald, and then, strangely, came a deep sigh from below: a sigh compounded of fear and physical weariness and mental stress, sounding preposterously loud in the enclosed space of the panelled passage. Then came a slight rattle and fumbling. "The office door...drawn a blank there," thought Macdonald. (Reeves had seen to that.) "The parlour? Well, it's not very helpful, sheeted and shrouded by the industrious Hannah, and not so much as a wall cupboard to conceal a promising clue. Kitchen quarters? I think not, and certainly not the schoolroom or chapel room. Most unsuitable. Coming up? I thought so."

Macdonald slipped like a shadow into a room immediately behind him, where drawn blinds kept out the faint luminosity of the starlit northern sky. He slipped behind the door, which was half open. It was one of the children's play rooms, and as such would be of little interest to the unknown 'helper.' Macdonald stood so that he could see through the crack of the door should a glimmer of torch-light be shown. "They'll have to use a light sometime. Even a cat would be defeated by this floor of the house," thought Macdonald. "Reeves again. He's pulled all the blinds down, thoughtful fellow. If ever a chap learnt by experience, it's Reeves."

The stairs creaked so loudly that Macdonald thought that even Emma Higson would wake up, though he had noticed she was a bit hard of hearing. Evidently the nocturnal visitor thought so too, for there was a full minute's cessation of movement. The only sound was laboured breathing, heavy, distressed, and quite unreasonably loud. Then the shuffling footsteps moved on, along the passage to the right, and a slender upright of light showed down the hinged edge of Macdonald's door: the torch had come into operation.

Macdonald moved out from behind the door and stood flat against the wall beside the door jamb, whence he could see through the doorway along the passage, without being seen if the visitor turned round. Against the faint glimmer of torch-light a dark figure showed for a moment in silhouette, and even Macdonald's well-disciplined nerves contracted in response to the totally unexpected. The dark figure was cloaked and veiled: against the uncertain torch-light was the silhouette of a tall form clad in the garments of an old-fashioned hospital nurse. "If Hannah were here to see that, she'd scream the place down," thought Macdonald. "Spirits and souls of the righteous...or angels and ministers of grace defend us. I never thought of that one."

The figure turned left at the end of the passage, and the blur of torch-light showed only the line of the old wall, a bulging, leaning line, where the wall of the ancient passage turned to form a recess which had once been a powder closet. The recess was now occupied by a built-in linen cupboard and a small matchboarded apartment called the sewing room. It held a sturdy table, an old-fashioned sewing machine with a box top and shelves on which sewing materials—cottons and tapes, and buttons and hooks, scraps of patching materials, and pins and needles—were arranged in appropriate boxes: a neat, efficient little apartment, but quite lacking in interest, or in any place of concealment for anybody or anything.

Macdonald came out of his dormitory and began to move down the passage towards the sewing room. He kept close to the wall, so that the tell-tale boards should not creak. At the far end of the passage, another bedroom door would give him cover and an opportunity to observe what was going on in the sewing room. Step by step he moved, putting to account all that years of training and experience had taught him about the matter of moving silently. Macdonald had listened so often to other people who were trying to do that most difficult thing—to move without giving warning of their movement to one who might be listening. He had emptied his pocket of coins and cigarette case and match box: he had taken off his wrist watch: he had not smoked for several hours. The omission of any one of those precautions had served as a signal to him when he was tracking others in the dark. Coins can clink unexpectedly: a match box can obtrude itself through the stuff of a pocket and scrape the angle of a wall. In profound silence even the tick of a watch can become audible. The rest was physical training and physical fitness: the ability to breathe silently, the balance to maintain immobility when another step would be a giveaway. Silently he moved on, aware of rustlings and fidgetings and clinkings from the sewing room, and of that laboured breathing which is the unconscious accompaniment of mental stress.

When he gained his doorway and turned towards the sewing room, the sight he saw in the dim torch-light was fantastic enough to have frightened the whole village into hysteria. The cloaked veiled figure had its back to Macdonald, and he knew it must be so exactly like that mythical figure—Sister Monica. Anyone knowing her might well have been convinced that the dead walked. Sergeant Peel had said: "They're a superstitious lot." Cash in on the superstition—a sound way of avoiding a challenge in a village where nerves were already on edge.

3

Macdonald stood and watched while the cloaked figure fumbled, the dark body, with the cloak stretched out by the elbows, obscuring the hands. Macdonald knew that he had only to take three sure and silent steps to be able to put his hand on the solid shoulder beneath the cloak. But he did not move because he knew what the reaction would be—a howl of fear, a crash of overturned furniture which would sound like bedlam let loose through the silent house. Upstairs Hannah Barrow lay sleeping, and Macdonald was a humane man. Whatever she had done in the bitter circumstances of a harsh life, he did not want to frighten her into gibbering insanity by breaking into her sleep with an uproar which a false move might cost now. In any case, what was the hurry? Reeves was in this house, and Reeves would know all about the intruder. He would wait until he got some signal from Macdonald, and then they would act together, silently and expeditiously.

Unable to see what the cloaked figure was doing, Macdonald guessed by the position of the figure and the sounds which emerged. Something was unlocked. There was only one object with a lock on it in the sewing room—the box cover of the ancient sewing machine. "Not a bad place to hide anything," thought Macdonald. "It's so much less obvious than a drawer or a box or a cupboard. You expect a sewing machine to be a sewing machine, not a receptacle—" His train of thought was cut short by a sound which made Macdonald's pulses jump. Dealing clumsily with the old-fashioned box cover, the intruder in the sewing room had let it slip, and it slammed down with a bang which sounded as startling as the trump of doom. "You silly fool…can't you do it quietly?" flashed incongruously through Macdonald's mind. But no reaction came from the silent house, and a moment later the small lock clicked again, amid the heavy breathing of the startled intruder. The shaking of tremulous hands told a story of fear, and the breath came in short gasps now. At last the cloaked figure turned away, along the passage, the way it had come. It was a second later that Macdonald heard a sound upstairs. Someone had woken up.

4

It was Emma Higson who woke up. "All in a sweat," as she said afterwards, she lay trembling in her bed for a while, and then, with considerable courage, she got up and crept to the top of the stairs. She had in her hand an electric torch, (necessary in a house with such niggardly wiring as Gramarye). It was a bicycle lamp with a new battery, and she turned it on just as the cloaked figure reached the stairs. The beam fell on the cloak and the bent veiled head, and Emma Higson's nerves gave out.

"'Tis Sister, dear God o' mercy, 'tis Sister..." she screamed.

The torch fell from her nerveless hands, jerked itself out, and Emma Higson's shrieks rent the air as another crash resounded through the darkness, and a heavy body went headlong down the polished stairs, right down the steep flight from top to bottom, with one final crash as the helpless body hurtled against the wall at the bottom.

Emma Higson screamed on. It was Reeves's homely voice which first penetrated her panic.

"It's not Sister, you silly old fool, it's just somebody playing the goat. I tell you it's not Sister."

Macdonald had got to her by that time, his own torch-light showing the familiar stairs, empty of the apparition which had appalled her.

"It's all right, Cook. It wasn't a ghost. Ghosts don't make a row like that falling downstairs. What about poor Hannah? She'll be frightened out of her life."

Emma Higson left off screaming and staggered to her feet with Macdonald's firm hand under her arm: she was still in a state of semi-hysteria, and between her sobs she clucked out, "Please to take me notice. I can't abide any more..."

"I'll take your notice, Cook, but better come and see if Hannah's all right," persisted Macdonald. They went in together to the narrow little room where Hannah lay on her back with moonbeams playing over her withered face. She hadn't moved since Macdonald last saw her, but the uproar in the house must have disturbed even her solid slumber, for suddenly she began to snore; turning over, she tucked a hand under her cheek and a diminutive grey plait slipped askew across her peaceful face.

"I'll light the candle for you," said Macdonald serenely, but Emma Higson had recovered herself.

"That you won't, and me in me night shift," she said tremulously.

"All right. I'll bring you up a cup of tea and put it outside the door," said Macdonald.

"I won't say no," she sniffed, and then uttered the remark which Macdonald always thought of as 'the curtain' to that particular act.

"Doctor always said them stairs'd be the death of someone. Him was right, seemingly."

5

Macdonald had been aware of sounds downstairs which were certainly not due to Reeves's activities, though doubtless Reeves was fully occupied. When the Chief Inspector went downstairs, he found that the lights were on in the hall, and another man had appeared on the scene. It was Raymond Ferens, who was bending over the body of the man who had fallen downstairs. The cape and the veil had been loosened and thrown to one side and lay, a negligible huddle of dark material, looking oddly inadequate for the result they had achieved. Ferens stood up saying, "He's alive…just. I think his neck is dislocated, apart from the head injuries. I suppose we've got to get an ambulance."

His voice was irresolute, but Reeves said, "I'll ring through to Milham Prior."

He produced the key of the office and went in, and Ferens said to Macdonald: "I was out in the garden and I heard someone screaming, so I came over at the double and your chap let me in."

Macdonald nodded, looking down at the grey face on the floor. "How much did you know about this, Ferens?"

"I didn't *know* anything at all," said Ferens, and he looked Macdonald straight in the face. "Neither was it my business to guess. I've told no lies at all, and it wasn't up to me to hazard possibilities. It was your job, first and last. I said from the start that Gramarye was no business of mine."

"Yes. I noticed you were adamant on that point," said Macdonald. "And how many people in the village knew—or guessed?"

"I don't think anybody knew, if by knowing you mean having any evidence," said Ferens slowly, "but villages like this one have their own sort of awareness. I can't define what it is. It isn't detection, in your sense of the word. It isn't intuition. Awareness is the only word I can use."

"Awareness of human nature," said Macdonald quietly, "and much greater powers of observation than townspeople ever realise. Country folk study human nature as they study the weather, and they're more often right than either the psychologists or the meteorologists. They did their best for him. Some of them risked a criminal charge to try to get him out of the mess."

"Because they were fond of him. Good man or bad, he'd doctored them for half a lifetime. He was part of their village."

Macdonald nodded, looking down at old Dr. Brown's face, so still and grey, as he lay on the floor.

"Can't you understand..." broke out Ferens.

"Oh, I understand—but it's no good," said Macdonald.

"And you know it's no good," he concluded. "The thing he did was worse than the thing he tried to escape from. There's no all clear via murder."

CHAPTER XVIII

1

"I tell you I didn't know," persisted Raymond Ferens stubbornly.

"All right. Have it your own way," replied Macdonald placidly. The four of them—Raymond, Anne, Macdonald, and Reeves—were sitting on the lawn of the Dower House. Reeves was lying prone, his hands busy with the making of a daisy chain, and Anne Ferens watched him with amused eyes. It was she who took up the argument:

"What *is* knowledge? It's as elusive as wisdom. If you put me in the witness box and I said, 'I know she was wicked,' you would demand proof, chapter and verse. If I said, 'I have an extra sense, and it tells me when a person is wicked—by the pricking of my thumbs,' wouldn't the judge rebuke me for levity and say that feelings are not evidence?"

"Probably," replied Macdonald, and Reeves put in, sotto voce:

"Depends on the judge. He wouldn't admit your feelings as evidence, but he'd make a mental note. Some of them are both sensible and sensitive. Sorry. Don't mind me."

Macdonald took up his tale. "When I first called on you, Dr. Ferens, I expected you to say quite a lot about Dr. Brown: to quote his opinion, refer me to him for evidence, give the usual unsolicited testimonial by which medical men uphold their mutual probity. But during the whole of that conversation you did not mention Dr. Brown once. And about Gramarye you would only say, 'It was not my business. I made it clear from the outset that I took no interest in Gramarye.' It seemed plain to me that you did not want to talk about Dr. Brown. And as for your insistence that from the first you took no interest in Gramarye—well, shall I adopt Mrs. Ferens' useful allusion, and say I wondered if your thumbs had pricked when you first made the acquaintance of that ancient charity, its Warden, and its Medical Officer?"

"Of course, you're perfectly right, Chief Inspector," said Anne Ferens. "Raymond is constitutionally honest and not at all unobservant, and the two qualities often cause him mental indigestion. He felt at once that there was something phoney about 'that ancient charity etc.' I know he did. If he were one of those chatty husbands who tell their wives all, he'd have said to me: 'That damned old fool must have got in a mess with that ghastly female at some stage in their lives, and she's got a hold over him.' But he didn't say so. Not even to me. Although I knew he thought it."

"How did you know?" demanded Raymond indignantly.

"Because of the way you ticked me off when I said Sister Monica was wicked. You were horrified. Therefore you insisted on an extra degree of punctilio from me. It was to be hands off Sister Monica. So I was sure there was something."

Reeves sat up here. "This isn't evidence, but it's a darned sight more interesting than most evidence is. What people think is far more relevant than our police methods allow for."

"That's enough from you," said Macdonald firmly. "And Mrs. Ferens has produced evidence of a negative sort. What people avoid saying is just as informative as what they do say. And, finally, Dr. Ferens was all in favour of a verdict of accident. So now, having cleared the decks of all that, let's get down to evidence which could be entered in an official report. We'll take the findings at the autopsy first."

"The most relevant being a bruise on the occiput, some alcoholic content in the cadaver, and the state of being *non virgo intacta*," said Ferens.

Macdonald nodded. "And then there was the additional fact of deceased's capital investments. All these facts were equally important. The bruise on the back of the head could most easily have been caused by the swinging of a heavy stick; a strong walking stick with a heavy crook or knob would have served, because if you swing a walking stick grasping the ferrule end, its velocity makes up for lack of weight. Neither Reeves nor I believed the bruise could have been caused by the head hitting the hand rail of the bridge."

"I'm still hoping you'll offer to come and do another experiment on that bridge, sir," said Reeves to Ferens. "You just try to hit the back of your head on that hand rail. It's almost impossible for a tall person to do it."

"I was of that opinion the whole time," said Ferens, "but I maintain that my opinions are not evidence."

"Well, we won't get bogged down in controversy at the moment," said Macdonald. "I have dealt with the first fact— the bruise on the back of the head. Next, the traces of alcohol. I did not suggest at any time or to any person that the analyst's report stated that deceased was either an alcoholic addict, or was inebriated when death occurred. In my own mind I was quite sure that she was nothing of the kind. The path from

Gramarye to the mill is both steep and dangerous, unless you watch your step. If deceased had been drunk when she walked down that path, the probability is that she would have slipped, and if she had slipped, she would have rolled over and over down the green bank until she reached the bottom. Anybody who did that would be badly bruised, all over. She was not bruised all over. It was while I was thinking this out that it occurred to me that her famous dizziness seemed reserved for rather odd occasions. It overcame her on a flight of stairs in her own home, and on a bridge with a perfectly good hand rail, but not on a rather hazardous path."

"So you dismissed the dizziness as irrelevant?" enquired Anne.

"Oh, no, I didn't," said Macdonald. "The dizziness was very well attested. Deceased had fallen right downstairs. I thought that was extremely relevant. Far from dismissing it, I considered it with care, and connected it with the alcohol. I argued that if a woman who was known to be a teetotaller was given a small dose of high alcoholic content it was quite likely she would 'come over dizzy.' Being totally unused to alcohol, she would be very susceptible to it. And one way of giving her such a dose would be to prescribe an indigestion mixture strongly flavoured with peppermint to mask the flavour of the alcohol."

"But wouldn't she have smelt the brandy?" put in Anne.

"I didn't say anything about brandy, Mrs. Ferens. I said alcohol. Absolute alcohol does not smell of brandy, although it does smell spirituous. And a very little absolute alcohol is very potent. Moreover it is used by field naturalists and botanists for preserving specimens."

"Algae," murmured Reeves. "Spirogyra, likewise Zygnema and Staurastrum. I learn some very high-hat terminology in our job."

"Well, I'm damned," said Raymond. "I might have thought of that one. I'd seen the Algae in absolute alc in the old boy's test tubes, but I didn't connect it up."

2

"Well, there was a theory to account for the famous dizziness," said Macdonald. "It was only a theory, but it was attractive. If dizziness could be induced beforehand, it provided the perfect explanation. 'Terrible dizzy Sister was.' And if the thing wasn't accepted as accident, and analysts and pathologists got busy, the disappearance of the brandy bottle explained all. It was good pre-war brandy, whose alcoholic content would have been high. But again, all this was hypothetical. Having considered it, I turned to other factors, especially the cash one—the nest egg in the building societies, paid in in cash by 'register letter' posted by the illiterate Hannah."

"Blackmail," said Raymond Ferens softly.

"I thought it the most probable explanation," said Macdonald, "so I looked around to see which persons in the locality might have been susceptible to blackmail to the tune of some £200 yearly over a period of ten years. And I considered that the amount of the sum paid eliminated the village folk at once. The Venners, Mrs. Yeo, Wilson, Doone—would they have paid out nearly £4 weekly for ten years? Of course they wouldn't. The idea was ludicrous. It represented over three quarters of what any of them earned. Not the villagers, and certainly not Sanderson—he'd only been here two and a half years. Not Dr. Ferens. He was a newcomer. Obviously one's mind went to the most wealthy—Sir James and Lady Ridding. I eliminated Sir James after some consideration. If there had been any cause or fact which would have resulted in Miss Torrington being able to blackmail Sir James, Lady Ridding herself would not have upheld the Warden through thick and thin. In other words, if Sir James Ridding had had an affair with the Warden in time past, Lady Ridding would have sacked the Warden out of hand. Not for one moment would Lady Ridding have countenanced such an outrage to her own dignity."

"But if Lady Ridding hadn't known," put in Anne.

"She would have known," put in Macdonald. "You make a great mistake if you think she is stupid. She isn't anything of the kind. Lady Ridding has the brains which make a profit out of pedigree cattle, dairying and mixed farming as well as market gardening. She is extremely astute. And the rumours which have been going round about her making vast sums out of black market butter seemed to me utterly silly. To make a success out of farming, which she certainly does, makes her very cognisant of regulations and penalties. It simply wouldn't be worth her while to take the risk of black marketing. And to do her justice, I think she has the commercial honesty which was characteristic of her generation. She'd drive a hard bargain, but she's too much commonsense to risk her dignity and good name for the profits on butter at 10/- a pound. And anybody who knows anything about dairy farming can tell you there isn't so very much profit in selling butter at 10/- a pound."

"Perfectly true," said Anne, "and I think you're quite right about her being astute. We tend to laugh at her because of the *grande manière* cult. *But,* Mr. Chief Inspector, since she is astute, wouldn't she have been aware of the goings-on which you postulated in a different quarter altogether, outside her own home?"

It was Reeves who answered this. "She *was* aware of it," he said bluntly. "I've no evidence for saying so. It's just that

I knew when I heard her talking, like Mrs. Ferens knew the Warden was wicked. And being a perfect lady brought up in the early nineteen hundreds, Lady R. knew when to look the other way, as a lady should. After all, the irregularity wasn't in her own household, and both Dr. Brown and the Warden were very useful to her."

Anne Ferens looked at him thoughtfully. "You're a bit shattering, aren't you...sitting there making daisy chains."

3

"I think it's time we got back to facts," said Macdonald. "At the moment Reeves is off duty: he can say what he likes. He has no basis in fact to support his statement that Lady Ridding *knew* that her medical practitioner and her Warden had misconducted themselves in years gone by, but I agree with him that Lady Ridding is past mistress of the art of looking the other way when self-interest prompts her to do so. I also think I'm on firm ground when I maintain that 'her ladyship' would not have tolerated irregularities in her own household. The fact that Lady Ridding supported the Warden was an indication to me that Sir James was not involved. I used the same argument about the Vicar and his wife. They both said Miss Torrington was wonderful: ergo, they did not pay her blackmail. All these arguments were hypothetical, so I turned to further facts. Dr. Ferens and the bailiff gave an excellent demonstration that it was highly improbable that deceased collapsed on the bridge. The fact that Sanderson assisted so vigorously in the experiment made it more than ever improbable that he was responsible for the murder. But after I had walked up and down that hill once or twice I pondered over another argument. Reeves and I postulated that deceased had gone to meet somebody near the mill, having met the same person there before. But why at the mill? It seemed to me that the garden at Gramarye, or that seat where I sat and talked to Miss Braithwaite, were much more convenient places to meet. What was there against them? The answer was the steep hill. If a person were aged and infirm that hill would be a tough proposition for them. Dr. Brown was one of the few people concerned whose age and frailty made it very hard for him to walk up that hill, and his car was so old and noisy that everybody in the village knew the sound of it. Again, there was nothing conclusive in that, but it fitted in with other possibilities."

"You give me the creeps," said Anne. "I knew you would be very expert fact finders, but I didn't think you'd argue out all the personal qualities, or that you'd notice so much about people's general behaviour. What on earth did you think about me—and Raymond?"

"I thought that you looked one of the happiest people I'd ever seen, Mrs. Ferens," replied Macdonald, "and you reminded me of a Gauguin colour scheme. I argued that since you looked so happy, the probability was that your husband was a very contented—and fortunate—man."

Raymond gave a shout of laughter. "Good for you. I am—and likewise, I am."

Reeves sat up again. "Climate," he observed. "It's all the thing these days—climate. Your climate seems based on a permanent anticyclone. Nothing in it for C.I.D. chaps. What the G.P.s call an uninteresting case."

4

"Let's try again," said Macdonald. "Facts and the elucidation thereof. It was a fact, bitterly resented by Sergeant Peel, that the village folk were quite unhelpful, and they stuck to it that Sister was wonderful. I managed to get that one unstuck a bit, and they admitted 'Sister had changed,' but they still stuck to the explanation of accidental death. Not one of them was willing to divulge a single fact which could assist the investigation. In short, they didn't want the investigation to succeed. When Ferens and Sanderson exploded the theory that deceased collapsed on the bridge, Venner was furious with them. I argued that the village had a pretty good idea, as villages generally have, as to what had happened, and the village was doing its best to protect somebody whom they held in high regard. And when somebody planted a very nice little piece of evidence in Greave's shack, I realised that the feeling of the village was very deeply moved."

"Tramps," put in Reeves disgustedly. "Never try that one on. Silly jugginses, they don't give the County police any credit for earning their wages. Tramps aren't invisible. One of the routine jobs the County men are good at is locating tramps. They can pull the whole lot in any day if they want to, and check up on their itineraries, real or imagined. I don't mind the village thinking the C.I.D. are mutts. After all, we're strangers, foreigners. But they might give their own chaps credit for a little gumption."

"All quite true," agreed Macdonald, "and Venner landed himself within distance of a capital charge by playing fool tricks with that bag which he'd found empty in the river."

"Nothing like feelings for making sensible chaps go haywire," said Reeves.

5

"Let's get on to Hannah. Hannah's a wonderful character," said Macdonald. "They found her uneducable at school, probably owing to the shock she'd suffered in childhood, but she's capable of arguing things out for herself which most educated people would miss. She noticed the smell of spirits in Sister's breath. After Peel had been to Gramarye, 'poking around in what didn't belong to him,' Hannah had a look round on her own. She found two bottles of medicine tucked away on a shelf she herself never used because it was right high up out of her reach, and the shelf was in her own housemaid's cupboard. Hannah did not know what the medicine was or why it was there, and she couldn't read the labels, but she sensed there was something odd about it. Unfortunately Peel had spoken sharply to her and frightened her, and in her half-childish, half-shrewd mind she decided that it would be better to throw the bottles away. Maybe they were poison, and if anyone had poisoned Sister, Hannah didn't want any bottles found in her housemaid's cupboard. So she buried them in the garden at the first opportunity, thereby throwing a spanner in the works without knowing it."

"The medicine being laced with absolute alcohol?" queried Raymond.

"Nothing of the kind," said Macdonald. "The medicine was exactly what it ought to have been. And to avoid confusing you further, I'm going to start in on a straight narrative. Some of it you know already, some of it you may have surmised, as I did, and some of it was told me by Dr. Brown before he died. Here is the story. Brown's wife went out of her mind, years ago. In the distress induced by this tragedy, he turned to Miss Torrington for sympathy and eventually she became his mistress. That is a not uncommon occurrence when a middle-aged man becomes very unhappy, and if the woman in the case had been an ordinary woman, the affair might have gone its course and been forgotten, as many such affairs doubtless are. But Miss Torrington wasn't an ordinary woman. She was avaricious and dominating beneath her habit of meekness. She eventually demanded money, and got it. Having got it, she hoarded it senselessly, as a miser does hoard. In short, Sister Monica became a miser. This went on for years, and the climax was reached when Brown, having retired from his general practice here, determined to leave Milham on the Moor and go to live in Wiltshire. It was then that Miss Torrington overreached herself. She demanded that Brown marry her. Brown refused. Miss Torrington then told him, in the authentic accent of Victorian melodrama, that she would follow him wherever he went and denounce him for what he was. Now Brown was old and tired. He wanted to get away from Milham in the Moor and the domination of Miss Torrington, and the thought of her pursuing him was a nightmare to him. He had realised what she was really like, and also what she was capable of."

"Is this where the ghost of Nancy Bilton comes in?" asked Ferens.

"Yes—as a ghost to haunt Dr. Brown. He had known all the time that Miss Torrington had come down to the river to meet him the night that Nancy Bilton was drowned. He used to meet the Warden behind the saw mill, because he would not have her come to his house to collect the money he gave her, and his heart was so feeble that he could no longer walk up the hill without exhausting himself. The longer he thought about it, the more certain he was that Monica Emily Torrington caught Nancy Bilton spying on them and threw her bodily in the river. Whether it was true we shall never know, but because Brown believed it was true, he persuaded himself that he was justified in finishing Monica Emily as she had finished Nancy Bilton."

"I follow all that," said Ferens. "The way she got her tentacles on to him and wouldn't let him go seems to me to be in character, but why on earth didn't he give her her money when he was at Gramarye? He went there every week."

"Hannah supplied the answer to that one," replied Macdonald. "Years ago, the Warden had arranged the etiquette for the doctor's visit. It was highly ceremonious. Hannah admitted him and marched him upstairs to the Warden in the dispensary. Hannah, in her capacity as nurse, stood at attention all the time while doctor saw the children. If any were in bed, Hannah accompanied doctor and Warden to the dormitories, in the correct hospital tradition. Hannah's eyes were likely to be on them all the time—or almost all the time—and Hannah saw doctor to the front door."

"Wait a minute," said Ferens. "About that medicine which you surmised was laced—"

"It was laced. Brown told me so," said Macdonald. "I was right there."

"Then he dispensed it himself?"

"No, he didn't. He was much too crafty. It came up from the chemists."

"Then how in Hades did he get the alcohol into it? You say Hannah was watching him all the time."

Macdonald took a script from his pocket. "This is an accurate account of Hannah's evidence. See if you can spot the loophole," he said.

Ferens read it carefully. "I don't see how he could have done it. One can argue she may have kept the medicine in the closed half of the cupboard so that Hannah didn't see it, but how could he have got at it?"

"When Hannah watched the children go downstairs,

all respectful like, and when the Warden was copying the chemist's list in her private note book," said Macdonald. "If Hannah had seen him fiddling in the medicine cupboard, it would have seemed quite natural. 'Him had many a good laugh over our medicine cupboard.' With Hannah out of the room for a couple of minutes, and the Warden busy writing, Brown took his chance and laced the indigestion mixture. To save you further worrying, I may as well tell you that he did come up that hill after he had thrown Monica Emily's senseless body in the mill stream, and emptied her bag of its contents, so that these could be destroyed. With the keys he had taken from her bag he let himself in by the garden door, went up to the dispensary and emptied out the doped medicine, replacing it by a harmless mixture. Then, because he knew Miss Torrington's mania for hiding things in odd places, he put the innocent mixtures in Hannah's cupboard, confidently expecting she'd hand them over to the appropriate authorities. He also removed the bottle of brandy. It sounds complicated, but it was a very logical ingenious plan. It was Hannah throwing the medicine away that scuppered it."

"I still don't see why that mattered," said Anne.

"You've an innocent mind, Mrs. Ferens. Brown was wise enough to tell me he had prescribed medicine for the Warden. It was on the chemist's list. And it was an essential part of his plan that the innocent bottles should be found by us, so that no suspicion should arise in that quarter. I told him that I couldn't find the bottles. He then began to panic, and determined that something had gone amiss. He guessed by this time that Hannah had disposed of the bottles in her cupboard. So he toiled up the hill, arrayed ghostlike in the Warden's best cloak which he had taken away with him the earlier night he was in the house, and proceeded to hide appropriate mixtures for me to find. His main argument was sound enough. There was no direct evidence. No one had seen him knock the Warden over the head and roll her body into the mill stream. If anybody in the village knew the truth about his one-time relations with the Warden and guessed at his possible guilt, they were obviously going to keep quiet over it. And the explanation of death being due to falling in the mill stream while under the influence of alcohol was just the sort of explanation a jury would accept."

"But why couldn't he leave it alone?" said Ferens.

"Because I was being tiresome over the medicine bottles," said Macdonald. "Brown wasn't stupid. He knew I should ask all about deceased's previous falls—her famous dizziness. Each occurred shortly after a meal. 'To be taken three times a day. After meals.' *'Ter die,'* as the prescriptions have it. He'd have noticed that himself, and thought I might notice it, too. So it was essential that the medicine must be found, in some improbable place, before I really set-to on a full dress search. If he could only prove the medicine had been harmless, he felt there wasn't any concrete evidence against him."

"And provided the village kept mum, he was quite right," said Reeves. "The way he handed over the money—a few pounds at a time in pound notes—was almost foolproof. You can't *prove* what a man's spent or not spent in ready money. It's only cheques, or large withdrawals of cash, which can be proved. It's anybody's money, so to speak. And as to motive—anybody in the village could have been credited with a motive."

Ferens suddenly laughed. "But only a medical man could induce dizziness three times a day, after meals. Well, I congratulate you both. I do admire other people's brains."

Anne turned to Macdonald: "Did anybody talk to you about Dr. Brown—any of your chief witnesses?"

"No. They all avoided mentioning him, or bringing him into their statements as one might have expected them to do."

"I must remember that," she said thoughtfully.

Reeves suddenly sat up. "Forget it," he said, and threw his daisy chain round Anne's neck. "It's not your line of country. You go and persuade her ladyship to let Gramarye to some nice young couple from away, who'll only think of the Warden as a bad joke and who'll take an interest in vegetable marrows. It suits you," he concluded, regarding the daisy chain with admiration.

"Forget it," murmured Anne. "That's good advice. I will. But I shan't forget you, either of you."

"That's very kindly said," replied Macdonald.

THE END